Status
Zero

Also by Roger Granelli

Crystal Spirit
Out of Nowhere
Dark Edge

Status
Zero

Roger Granelli

seren

seren
is the book imprint of
Poetry Wales Press Ltd
2 Wyndham Street, Bridgend,
Wales CF31 1EF

© Roger Granelli, 1999
The right of Roger Granelli to be identified as the Author
of this Work has been asserted in accordance with the Copyright,
Designs and Patents Act 1988

ISBN 1-85411-255-4

A CIP record for this title is available from
the British Library

*The publisher works with the financial assistance of the
Arts Council of Wales*

Printed in Plantin by CPD Wales, Ebbw Vale

1991

ONE

Mark hadn't expected the alarm. It must have been hidden some-where. He had checked the outside of the house. He always did. If this had been one of his early jobs he might have dropped the video and run but now he walked out calmly through the patio doors into the garden. Lights were coming on next door. Yellow lanced the lawn and voices inquired. There was no threat in them. They were flustered by the insistent bell, and glad it was not their place.

He stopped to spit in the fishpond, hitting a carp that was flop-ping near the surface, then put one hand on a post and hauled himself over a wooden fence. Lithe like a cat. The video cradled between his chest and other arm. He looked back to see a bald man in a red dressing gown peer into the darkness, but not enter it. His face round and pink and old. Wanker. Mark grinned, and thought of shouting the word out, letting them know he was slip-ping away like a ghost. But he was fifteen now, and a pro. He eased himself into the bushes that surrounded the houses, whistling to himself between his twisted teeth.

A few hundred yards from the house he sat down to watch the blue light of the pigs coming up from the valley road. Hoping to catch a sight of him. Some fucking chance. There was something about the light that always fascinated him. It was caused by him. It came for him. Was his. A pretty blue trickle he made happen on the hillside, winking on and off.

Before the blue reached the house Mark made off, cutting across the hillside he knew well. On the opposite hill the estate loomed, mooncast and beckoning in the clear night. In ten min-utes he would have the video weather-proofed and stashed. He felt good, knowing he could saunter home without worry then. Knowing that fifty bucks would be in his pocket by Saturday. It was easy.

Mark stretched up a leg and made a chink in the curtain with his foot. He was in bed, lying with hands behind his head, wonder-ing whether to get up. He usually did about twelve, his empty stomach bugging him to do something about it. It was dull wet grey outside and he couldn't see the houses higher up, which meant fog. Which meant winter was about to fall on the estate. The fog always came in October, after a night's rain when it was still a bit warm. He sank back into the bed, pulled the covers around him and strained to hear if his mother was downstairs.

There was no sound, and the only time there was nothing playing was when she was out. He remembered it was giro day. She'd be down the valley. Cashing it. Spending it. Back by two, ready to start on about school again.

Mark smiled and sighed at the same time before his face settled into a blankness. It was a standard face for his age, his breed, this place. Old-young, hair cropped so close his scalp competed with it, thin featured, an almost non-existent upper lip which made the lower seem pendulous and fleshy. A small scar under the left eye, a nick from a ten year old's penknife. The only remarkable thing about Mark was his eyes. They were grey green and when he lost it they bulged. He was known for it on the estate. Psycho Eyes. Normally they were hardly visible. He liked to look through slits, tilting his head upwards as if tasting the wind. He thought it made him look tough but boys took the piss behind his back. The older ones to his face.

He'd been awake long enough to be bored. With his foot he punched the on-button of his all-in-one hi-fi. The Sex Pistols carried on where they had left off the night before. He eased up the rotary volume control with his big toe until Johnny and Sid pounded the bedroom. Next door would start screaming but he would not hear her. A flake of emulsion escaped from a ceiling faded and mottled with nicotine stain. He reached for his fags and lit one, inhaling deeply then sending up a stream of smoke. When it reached the ceiling it swirled around. Blue snakes looking for a way out.

Hunger got him up. He yanked open the curtains, detaching the right one from its rail. It had jumped off the rail for years. He wiped clear a circle on the window, adding to the condensation on the sill, and squinted out at the lightening day. The fog was clearing. Along the street men were digging, hunched figures made bulky by orange waterproofs. Soaked by the drizzle of the morning, worked into every crevice by the hillside wind. Trying to avoid the wet streaks on the sill with his elbows Mark propped up his face and watched the diggers for a few minutes. He loved to watch men work.

Houses opposite were clearly visible now and higher up a line of them began to appear, as if just painted into the landscape. Slanting roofs pointing to a slate sky. Each one rising above the other as if they wanted out. The lower ones were boarded up. FUK OFF came out of the murk on one board, and PEACE TO

ALL PEOPLE on another. That one made him smile. Daniels and a few other cretins had painted it on, after that programme on the telly had said things were improving on the estate. They felt famous for a few days. The paint was the colour of blood, and it had dripped away from the words, so that they seemed to be permanently shaking.

Most people up here could not stand the fog. It made the estate like a prison, they said. Houses perched on the top of nowhere. Like stone pimples. Like a rash. Smack dab in the middle of the worst shit the weather could deal out. It had to be a joke, right? The estate from hell. But Mark didn't mind the fog. It was good for nicking. He didn't mind the estate either. The more busted up it got, the more he felt at home. It was home.

Mark managed to get up at the third attempt. The desire to get back under the covers was great. Nothing happened there he could not control. He went downstairs to the kitchen, eyes barely open, in T-shirt and shorts. On the shirt was a transfer of a fist with one finger sticking out. Inviting everyone to fuck off. He made himself a cup of tea and squeezed the last few drops of milk into it. And added three sugars. Standing at the front window he watched Julie walk up from the bus stop. Two supermarket bags heavy in one hand. A smaller bag in the other. That would be fags and cans. Most of the giro would be gone. There was a keen wind now, and the sky had a hint of sun about it. Like a lemon sweet. It caught in Julie's red hair - this month's colour - and made it shine. Her shell suit was a gaudy turquoise. Sometimes he hated the way she dressed. Sick colours and skirts up her arse. On other days he was a bit proud, that she hadn't fallen into the shapeless fat mass that was most mothers on the estate.

The old bat from next door came out. Grabbed at Julie's arm. Swamped her with whining, angry words. He could see her jaw working overtime, as if it was chewing something. Julie shrugged and pushed past her. He went to the front door and opened it, slouching against the doorframe. When Bat looked at him he scratched his chest and grinned. That got rid of her, but she left her usual slipstream of words.

'Wants locking up, he do. Well, I'm not having it.'

But she would. She had. Since he bought the hi-fi.

Julie struggled past him.

'Can't you see these bags are heavy? You been playing those records again? Christ, you're gonna get us chucked out of here.'

'Leave it out, Mam. No-one gets kicked out of here. They get kicked onto this place.'

'Always got some clever answer. Why can't you be clever in school? When you bloody go, that is.'

Mark took the two bags from her and walked with them six feet to the kitchen table.

'What you get from the shops?' he asked, grabbing the shapes inside the plastic. One bag had began to split. He helped a bag of crisps out of it.

'Ta.'

Julie sat down, breathless.

'You could come down with me sometimes. That hill bloody kills me. I waited ages for a bus, and it was wet when I went out. Don't 'spose you'd know that though.'

'Saw the fog.'

Julie noticed the discarded teabag.

'Good God, made yourself tea. That must have tired you out.'

Mark put a hand into the pocket of his shorts and pulled out a ten pound note.

'Here. Bingo money.'

Julie's face showed pleasure and concern. Her hand snaked out for the money and it was in her purse before Mark could change his mind. Whenever he sold a video he always gave her a tenner. It kept her sweet, or at least it was a good way to cut short her nagging. Julie no longer asked where the money came from. She knew. He liked to give his mother money. No other kid on the estate did anything like that. It made him feel good.

Julie Richards looked old for her age. She was well-lined about the eyes and as thin faced as her son. But she did not have his eyes. Hers were grey. She kept her hair short and changed its colour often. But Julie had hung onto her figure, which meant she never lacked for attention down the club, even if Psycho Eyes was her son.

Julie had hardly known Mark's father. He was one of a cluster of boys in her teens. She had been glad to move to the estate when Mark was two. Away from the persistent carping of her parents. It had seemed a good idea. Up on a mountain in the fresh air. Everything was new then. They were the first tenants in her two-bedroomed house. And lots of women were in the same boat as her. That was a million years ago. Julie opened a pack of cigarettes and let Mark take one. Since he had turned fifteen she had

10

given up trying to stop him. Trying to stop him doing anything was a waste of time. Stubbornness was Mark's middle name, and at least it had not stopped him growing. He was lanky now, pushing up to six foot. Mark devoured cigarettes, his eyes shutting as he sucked it all in. Already there was a yellow stain on one of his fingers.

Julie made some more tea and they sat at the formica kitchen table. On plastic chairs. They did not talk much. Mark was a loner and whatever thoughts he had hidden inside him. He exploded sometimes. Wild-eyed with temper over nothing, but he had not brought any trouble to the house, and was not violent with anything other than his tongue. Other mothers on the estate had it a lot worse. In the last year she had lost count of the nights he had disappeared, but he was always there in his bed in the morning. And the extra money came in very handy. Julie pushed back a few stray strands of hair and broke open a bag of frozen chips.

'I didn't hear you come home last night,' she murmured.

Mark finished his cigarette and squinted his squint. He looked through the glass of the back door at their ramshackle square of garden. Tired, uneven turf and a rotary clothesline. A listing, rusting sculpture. An assortment of his rubbish strewn around mixed with whatever the wind sent. A pair of crows squabbled over something in the bin. The dead sheen of their eyes caught Mark's own.

'Scavengers,' he murmured, 'like me.'

'What?'

'Look at the size of them birds. They don't go short.'

Julie knocked on the window pane and the birds flapped off.

'They give me the creeps,' she muttered.

Mark made a noise of contempt in his throat.

'You were out nicking again,' Julie said. 'You're gonna get yourself caught soon. Where will that leave us?'

'Leave it out, Mam. I never get caught. Haven't you realised that yet?'

'I've had a letter from the education lot. They're on about taking me to court.'

'That's a piece of piss. They're not that stupid. No point in it, is there.'

'You're going tomorrow, please, Mark. It's Friday, then it's half term.'

'Okay.'

She was surprised at his easy agreement and thought he must have deals to do in the schoolyard. But he was right. It was no point in trying to get him to go to school now. It was too late. And deep down she could not blame him. She had hated the place herself. Ape teachers selling stuff no-one was interested in buying.

Julie cooked chips, beans and burgers, Marks's favourite. The windows soon steamed up and dripped. The whole estate was awash with damp but she was used to it. Used to just about everything now. Julie felt quite good. Always did giro day. A sliver of hope raised itself in her. It was the feel of the notes in her purse that did it, even if they were gone so quickly. She had learnt that worry could only be taken so far if you wanted to survive. She was only thirty four. Plenty of time for things to get better. Pushing back a few stray strands of hair Julie smiled as she watched Mark wolf down his food. She'd go to bingo tonight, and the club on Friday. Wayne Humphries would be there, hanging around her with his tongue out. Perhaps she should give him a crack. At least he didn't have an ex-wife and a pack of kids around.

On giro day Mark did not seem so bad. His future not so hopeless. If he stopped scowling and squinting he would be good looking. And he wasn't thick. They had said that in all the schools. Infants, juniors and down the Comp. They kept on saying it until they grew tired of him, and his silent ways. Mark had that from his father, had the squint from him too. He had been a twelve week thing, a timescale she seemed to specialise in back then, and he had pissed off when Mark was a baby. The army took him in. Hid him. He was one of a long line of wasters who had come her way. Before she knew better she had dreamt up a stronger character for each of them. And each useless sod proved her wrong. She had never been able to help herself. Once she knew they were attracted to her any judgement she had slipped away. Then they were in control. A few fucks and off. And the word got around. Good looking and easy. It came with her to the estate. She was spoilt for choice down the club, but a choice of wasters and losers. People like herself.

'Think you'll get dressed today?' Julie said.

'In a minute. Don't start now. I give you a tenner.'

'Aye.' She reached out a hand to stroke what was left of Mark's hair. Mark recoiled and Julie stayed her hand. He did not like to be touched.

'What you looking at? If you can see anything, that is. Talk about squint.'

'Them crows. Big black bastards. They always come back.'

'Don't swear.'

Mark reached for another cigarette but Julie snatched up the packet.

'Get lost. They've got to last me through bingo.'

'Gonna win the jackpot tonight, then? Again.'

'You're getting a right sarky bugger, you are. I might win. Someone's got to.'

'Get real, Mam.'

'Hard sod.'

'I have to be, don' I? To look after you.'

'I'm going over to Mandy's. Get some clothes on, for God's sake. And if the gas comes, don't answer.'

Mark grunted an acknowledgement. In the garden the crows were disturbed by Bat next door. Bat-crows. Mark smiled. The birds wheeled away in a black flurry. He went to the window and flashed his shorts at Bat. She offered him her best glare. Eyes piercing, mouth sucked in where her teeth should have been, frizzy rats' tails hair. Bat out of hell. Mark's smile turned into a grin. He went back upstairs and turned the Pistols' tape over. And the volume up. Old music from before his time, but he liked its raw edge, the way it pumped something violent and dangerous through him.

'So you coming out or what?' Daniels asked.

Daniels came round after Julie went out. He was in the front room with Mark, sharing the leatherette settee. Daniels was a small, ferret-like boy, a few months older than Mark. Rake-thin, ribby, spindly legs. A runt who was an easy target on the estate. Hair cropped the same way as Mark's. Daniels liked to copy and Mark was his role model. His idol. He wanted to be anyone other than himself, and he was in awe of Mark's thieving skills.

'Nah, not tonight,' Mark answered.

'Come up the club. They got a disco on. Debbie and Emma'll be there.'

'They get on my nerves. Slags.'

'You going a bit fucking strange, or what? We had a good time with them in the summer.'

'That was then. I got better things to do now.'

'Oh aye. Brain surgery, like. Take me nicking again.'

'I work alone. I told you. Don't ask me again.'

'The Lone fucking Ranger, or what? You'll get done soon.'

'No way.'

'Psycho Eyes rules. Get me a can, then.'

Mark went to the fridge and broke off two cans from a pack. Daniels bugged him but he sometimes liked him around. He liked being looked up to. Daniels had a face full of zits and would not grow any taller than the girls he ran after but he was useful when Mark felt down. When a black bottomless pit opened up and he wanted to smash everything. Every useless fucker in the world. In Daniels he always had someone worse off than himself.

He had taken Daniels on a job once, when they were fourteen. The same house he had done last night. Someone had driven into the drive, headlights shooting through the windows. Daniels had almost crapped himself. He stood like a rabbit in the lights, zits shining like yellow pins, muttering 'Jesus' and looking at Mark for help. He'd had to drag the sod out the back and they left empty handed. Daniels had been sick on the way home, then he had bawled. From shame as much as fear.

'Here, drink this,' Mark said, 'then you can piss off.'

'Come up the club, mun. We can fuck 'em easy.'

'Aye, and half the estate, too. No thanks, I don't want to catch a dose. Or this Aids stuff they're on about.'

'Only ponces can get that. Arse-hole bandits.'

Daniels picked at a spot. A king zit. Translucent red and yellow, like a sweet stuck on his face. It was about to pop.

'I'm sixteen in a few weeks,' Daniels said. 'Can fuck off from school proper then.'

The zit popped and Daniels face was ragged bliss. He slurped his lager from the can as if his mouth was a straw. Mark wondered if it was still worthwhile having him around. The kid was nowhere.

'You got another year left,' Daniels said, with some pleasure.

'Nine months. What you gonna do, Daniels? You're fit for fuck all.'

'I dunno, do I? The old girl keeps going on that they'll stop her allowance money. That's what she uses for fags.'

Daniels cupped his thin hands around the can. 'MAM' was tattooed on three fingers, a letter on each. Mark had the same tattoo, done on his fifteenth birthday. They had told the man they were eighteen. He didn't believe them but did the job anyway. They'd been pissed. It was strange when Julie saw it. When he sobered up and saw the bold blue letters he had expected her to go ape but she just started bawling.

'Why'd you go and do something like that,' she said. He remembered the way she touched the tattoo, hesitant, as if it would jump off the fingers at her and stick on her forehead or something.

'It'll be there forever,' she murmured.

Since then he had teased her with it. Wiggling the fingers under her nose. Stuff like that. He knew it pleased her, somehow.

Mark let Daniels out, his bony figure trudging up the hill to the club. The estate's version of a youth club someone from outside had started. The fog was back. Daniels faded into it like he was nothing. Mark was torn. Despite what he'd said to Daniels he still quite fancied Emma. She was always there. No work was involved. She had the best figure on the estate and had been interested in him since he had given her half the money from a video in the summer. And she had flawless teeth. Something which had always attracted him. Julie's were the colour of her fags and his own went everywhere.

Julie managed to get him to see a dentist when he was fourteen. A git with beady eyes whose breath smelt like shit. He let the guy drill and fill but would not stand for having that metal thing on his teeth. It was bad enough being called Psycho Eyes without having a fence in his mouth, and talking like a baby. So his teeth remained independent, the bottom ones twisting over each other, like they were holding hands.

Mark stood outside the club, catching the muffled end of the DJ's last disc. The heavy thump of the rhythm vibrated the wall he leant against. It was tosser's soul music. Stuff to give the nerds one last chance to grab a piece of skirt. He didn't like discos and the nonsense you were expected to do in them. And the ones for his age in the club were dry. All the boys got pissed or glued up before they went in. The girls preferred pills. They did not mind who they went with then. He preferred to stay outside, on the edge of things.

Drizzle was drifting through the fog. Fog-drizzle, drizzle-fog, until the ball-freezing shit came. Mark did not understand how something so soft and noiseless could get right into him. It fell without hiss or stomp, yet it soaked him just the same. He turned up the collar of his denim jacket and moved back farther against the wall.

Within minutes kids began to fall out of the main doors. Boys shouting, threatening, strutting, girls pretending to ignore them. A noisy mass which would trail into the maze of streets, the babble dying to isolated shouts as people found their houses. Daniels appeared with Debbie and Emma. He had an arm around each of them and was spouting his usual nonsense.

'Oi!' Mark called, without moving out of the shadows, 'Daniels, you wanker.'

'Whosat?' Daniels slurred. 'Eh, it's Markie. Hiya, butt.'

He dragged himself and the girls towards Mark, who noticed that Emma did not seem to have a skirt on. There was something, but it protruded only a few inches below her bomber jacket. Her arse jutted out proud, as if carved in stone.

'Gerroff me,' Emma said, pushing Daniels' hand away now that she saw Mark.

'Alright,' Mark said. He took care with his pronunciation around girls. They thought he was different and he wanted to encourage it.

'Don' think I'm going with you, Richards,' Emma said. 'Standing in the dark like a weirdo.'

'We can go back to Debbie's place,' Daniels said, proud that his hero-friend had showed. 'Her old girl won't be back tonight.'

'You go,' Emma said. 'I'm going home.'

'Don' be like tha', mun,' Daniels said. 'Mark's been busy, 'an you Mark?'

Mark shrugged. Mystery was best. It hooked them every time. The less he told, the more they wanted to know.

'You two go on,' he said, offering cigarettes around. He detached Emma from the others and Daniels left with Debbie, his eager arm clamped around her like a lobster's claw.

'You gotta fucking cheek,' Emma said. But she stayed.

'Anyone in your place?' Mark asked.

'You're not coming home with me.'

'Let's go for a walk then.'

He put his arm around Emma, and propelled her along. Her high heels tried to resist, but not for long. He had learnt to ignore all her protests. They were just something she did. They didn't

16

mean anything.

'It's dry up by here,' Mark said, leading her to an alley at the side of the few shops the estate had. Shuttered-up concrete fortresses designed to repel all comers. An orange street light lit up Emma's face for a moment. Mark saw untidy makeup failing to mask freckles, an upturned nose and the white perfection of those teeth.

'I brought a few cans,' Mark said.

'Christ, you're a strange sod. This is your idea of a date, is it?'

He opened the cans. Emma was almost drunk already, by the look of her.

'I've got to get home,' Emma said. 'The old man's back again – bastard. Mam'll do anything to keep him home. Won't be long before he beats the crap out of her again.'

'Tell me about it.'

Mark took a long draught from his can, its opening cold on his lips. He pressed himself against Emma, forcing her against the wall, and ran one hand up her legs. Putting his can on the wall he let the other join it. She began to complain and moan at the same time. He pushed her as far into the dark as he could, where it was dry and stinking, and crowded her face with his own.

'You're a sod, you are,' Emma gasped. He ignored her and worked a hand between her legs. He was inside her in minutes, the condom fumble-handed, his jeans round his ankles in the pissy dirt, holding up her legs and pumping feverishly with his own thin white stalks. Hand over Emma's mouth so that she did-n't rouse the whole bloody estate with her screams. This is how he liked it. Quick, with no nonsense beforehand.

'The old man will kill me,' Emma murmured, as Mark walked her home.

'Tell the fucker you were talking outside the club.'

He felt her hold on to him tightly and try to put her head on his shoulder. He sucked on his cigarette and made out he didn't notice.

'I better not come any further,' Mark said. Emma's old man was handy. 'See you, then.'

He disappeared smartly, letting the fog take him before Emma could start. Vaguely he heard her call something out to him but her words were lost in the wind.

Mark walked home slowly. He had nothing to fear on the estate, and he enjoyed the orange lights soaking into the fog, making patches of colour, glimmering pools beneath each light. And no-one was about. That was best of all.

Julie was slumped on the kitchen table when he got back. She always stopped off at the pub with the bingo girls. Drinking to salute their weekly dreams. He thought of going up to bed without waking her but she would wake up in the middle of the night cold and hungry, and wake him by staggering around the kitchen. And be a whining pain all the next day. He shook his mother by the shoulder, feeling much older than her, much wiser.

'Wassat?' Julie said. 'Oh, it's you. Been out, have you?'

'Up the club. With Daniels.'

Julie screwed up her eyes a few times, until they could focus.

'Don't know why you bother with that pimply little git. Gives me the creeps. His mother's the same. Jesus, I haven't drunk snowballs for years. They went out with flares. The buggers creep up on you. Make us a cuppa, love.'

'What did your last slave die of?'

But Mark made the tea, and joined Julie at the table.

She stirred two sugars into her cup, and seemed mystified with the miniature eddies she created.

'Girl won three thousand quid tonight,' she murmured. 'Three fucking thou. What I could do with that.'

Mark reached for the sugar, his hand passing close to Julie's face. Her nose wrinkled, making her face look even more petite. As if someone had carved it out of a potato. Some of her blue eye makeup had smudged.

'What's that smell. Rubber? I know what you've been doing, you randy little bugger.'

Mark grinned.

'Don't tell me, it's that Emma, isn't it? Dirty little slut. You know it's not legal, don't you?' Julie took a slurp of tea. 'Well, at least you're careful,' she said. 'You always are. My careful son.'

Julie reached out a hand to Mark but he avoided it. She was nodding off again. He took the cigarette from her fingers and finished it himself. Then he pulled Julie up from her chair, put her arm over his shoulder, where it stayed on the third attempt, and helped her up to bed. As he had grown bigger it had become easier. And he had been doing it for two years now. He lay her down on her bed in the front bedroom, on the old pink bedspread which matched the old pink walls. As if Julie had decorated the room with her shell suits. There was a patch of mould in one corner, creeping slowly up the wall. The Council couldn't prevent it. It was the new windows, they said. Try opening them some time. Clever, useless bastards.

Mark kept his bedroom unheated. And he still had condensation. The whole house seemed to piss itself in the winter. But he liked his room, and the view from the back window. The way the hills swept down the valley. Grassy and not many trees, and not many people on them. He always took this in before he went nicking. It steadied him. None of the boys he knew bothered with the hillsides. They never strayed far from the streets and the pubs. Fiddling with knackered cars and bikes, and unable to leave their videos for long. Mark had stolen at least fifty videos but he had never wanted one. Time enough for that when he was old and wasted.

Julie began to snore, a quick rattle that made her flat nose twitch. When he was younger Mark had hated seeing her like this. He had felt shut out. Part of the furniture. But now he did not mind. She needed a drink now and then. And he felt in control, like he did when he handed over tenners. It had been nearly a year since there had been a man in her life. Their best year. Before there had been a string of geezers. A supply of daddies that changed often, and he had hated every one of them with a vengeance. And it had been the same for them. They followed a pattern. Acting bastards at first, so that they could shag his mother, then they got their feet under the table, and he became furniture again. Sometimes worse. Daniels' uncle had been violent. Violent with him. A number had been violent with Julie. It was one of his earliest memories of the house. Her screams, and vague pounding noises of things moving about. But Daniels' uncle was the first he had seen do it. He had run at him head down when he was eight, and winded him. 'Daddy' had slapped him shitless. He still heard the shrillness of his mother's despair that night, cutting like a razor through the house. And Bat running out into her garden, her face alight with pleasure. The pigs had come that time, but Julie got rid of them. Kept the slapper. He had been killed a few months later, crashing his bent motor into the central barrier of a motorway. Mark's heart could still remember the joy it had felt when his tearful Mam told him the news.

Mark took off Julie's red stilettos and pulled the sheets over her. He was more gentle now that she was asleep. She was right about his hands, they smelt like a tyre but he liked that, and would not

19

wash them until morning. In the back room he went instinctively to the hi-fi and The Pistols but stopped himself playing it as Julie's snores came to him across the small square of landing. It was like living in a doll's house and it seemed smaller to him all the time.

He sat by the rear window smoking for a time. Their terrace was at one end of the estate, the last houses. When there was no fog he was able to look right down the valley, marked at night by the orange line of the main road. He had done a lot of houses along that road. Tonight he could barely see to the end of the garden, where the busted bin loomed out of the dark.

Mark switched on a small table lamp. He pulled back a piece of loose carpet and prised up a broken piece of board with a knife he kept on the window sill. He took out the tin from under the board. This was his safe and bank all in one. Here lay all his illicit money. When The Man came up from Cardiff to take the videos the money went straight into the tin. And not much of it came back out.

He opened it and spread the notes out on the bed. He loved to count them. Six hundred and forty quid in twenties, two hundred in tenners, which made him the richest young guy on the estate. Only the older ones that dealt in dope had more, and they blew it on their own shit. Feeling the money, counting it, gave him a warm glow inside. It told him he was getting somewhere. He spent a little of his cut on fags and cans, sometimes clothes, but nothing to bring attention to himself. He had seen boys make good dosh from a motor only to flash it around like magpies and be picked up by the pigs. He had more to him than that. The tin was almost full, but there was room under the board for another. That would also be full by the time he left school. It was all from videos. No cars. No dope. No violence. Nothing else. He was a specialist.

Mark replaced the tin. The estate was still. For a place full of noisy bastards it surprised him by how quiet it could get. When the fog came it swamped everyone. They slid back to their concrete holes and crouched around their tellies. That wasn't living, for Mark. The tin was his future.

Mark would meet the Man on Saturday. The one who fenced all the videos. He came up from Cardiff once a month, Sunday night at ten. He'd found Mark through the grapevine, which linked illicit brotherhoods by lines of gossip, spite, greed, and double crosses. The Man was the only black guy Mark had ever met. They were few and far between in the valleys. The valleys would not stand for them. Pakis did not count. They were tolerated, more or less, for their food and generous opening hours. But blacks, no way. Yet Mark did not mind taking money from them. He worked to order. Nothing more than two years old, no rubbish, the more each model could dance the better. He got £30 - £50 for each video, and knew they cost ten times that in the shop but he was satisfied. So was the Man. 'Dealing with you, kid, is like going to Comet,' he liked to say.

The Man was not that old. Pushing thirty maybe, with a hard-as-granite, crater-filled, night-black face, and shoulders like a council shithouse. He drove a BMW and had a phone slung on his belt. It was always dark when they met up. Mark standing in the shadows of the lay-by with his plastic bag of videos, The Man's face merging with the inside of his car. The gleam of the whites of his eyes and the stink of his fine perfume. Mark never knew his name and would not have used it if he had. Names were not part of the deal. The Man was gone in minutes, his rich motor gliding away into the night. Mark hurrying home, anxious to be rid of the money burning a glorious hole in his pocket.

Mark left the house at ten past eight the next morning. Julie was still in bed. He looked in on her, saw a tiny figure swamped by the bedclothes. He was glad he would not be around to share her hangover. This was his token one-day-a-fortnight attendance at school. Enough to show his face and check out the action. Another day nearer his leaving. He never thought he'd envy Daniels anything but the little twat would be away sooner.

Daniels walked with him to the bus. A fresh crop of spots was sprouting on his face, pearls shining in the rare morning sunshine.

'Great last night, wan' it?' Daniels said. 'I stayed up Debbie's 'til gone one.'

Daniels jostled Mark as they sauntered along. Trying to stoke up a semblance of camaraderie in the wake of his triumph.

'Did you gerroff with Emma?' he asked.

'Might have.'

Mark hated talking in the morning. He hated mornings full stop. He frowned as he saw the girls at the bus stop, part of a milling crowd that was already bored.

'Let's go down here a minute,' Mark said, pulling Daniels into an alley.

21

'We'll miss the bus,' Daniels said.

'What do you care?'

Mark did not want to see Emma. To see the expectant look on her face that said he was hers. He could not be bothered with that. Not in the morning. Not anytime.

Daniels' meagre brain cells churned.

'I get it,' he said, 'you don' wanna see 'em. Then you must have shagged it last night.'

'Shut up, pizza face.'

Daniels grinned and put a touch of swagger into his step. Any notice pleased him. To survive, he had learnt to turn insults into praise. It might be all that came his way. They shared a fag and caught the next bus.

The school was squares of glass and concrete lumped together, and acres of flat roof. All in terminal decay. Dripping, leaking, rotting, broken. And windswept and exposed, like the estate. Kids had to trudge back and forth between two buildings.

'Jesus fuck,' Mark murmured, 'I hate this place.'

'An' me,' Daniels said. Already Daniels' clothes had rearranged themselves. His school tie had shrunk to a pitiful knot around his scrawny throat and one side of his shirt collar turned up. The streets' crap stuck to his shoes, like it was always meant to be there.

Mark also wore a uniform. Part of the new rules and too much hassle to flout. The school wanted to pretend its charges were just like other kids, in other areas.

Daniels wanted to go in by a side entrance but Mark directed him past the head's office, making sure they strolled in front of the large glass window. But there was no-one there. By the time they reached the classroom Mark was in full 'school mode'. Slouching insolence, aggressive disinterest, hands in pockets to give the impression they could come out fighting. At anytime. It was a role he had adopted but it had not always been his way. He could remember a time when school was not so hard to bear. A few of the teachers had even treated him like he was someone. But he could never see the point in what they taught. It was outside his world, a million miles outside it. He couldn't think of one boy from the estate who had done anything at school. They had no chance. If word got round that someone was actually trying he would be shat on. Stuff like that made people angry. No-one had got off the estate because of school. No-one had got happy because of school. He had learnt to read and write but Daniels could barely do that. And he could count his money expertly. Give him numbers and he could add them instantly. Julie used to delight in him doing this when he was a kid. He did not know where it came from. This was enough education for him.

The day passed like a snail. He sat at the back of a few classes, and missed others. The teachers left him alone. It was a tacit agreement. He did not take any part in proceedings but caused no trouble. The only relief from this tedium was to focus his mind on his next job. His preparation was thorough. He picked out a house weeks beforehand, from the many large old houses in the valley or one from the small clusters of private estates that were springing up. His patch had a radius of five miles, with the estate its centre. Whenever he carried out a job he always put the place down for a repeat visit. Usually in three months time, when they had sorted out the insurance and got another video. Once bitten, these houses were often alarmed, but that did not bother him, unless it was a fancy rig. He could climb anything and boxes on the sides of houses were a challenge. And they could be disabled in seconds, if you had the knowledge. Mark reckoned he had been born with it. His one real concern was to be certain his targets were empty. Early on he had entered a house where someone had been upstairs. Now he researched his victims' movements, and a sixth sense had built up within him. He could smell if a place was empty, able to sniff out people just by prowling around outside.

Daniels pushed Mark's elbow.

'Come on, butt, the bell's gone. You're miles away.'

Mark opened his eyes and caught a sliver of hillside behind Daniels' head. A few squares of field sandwiched between conifers. He loved the dark spaces of the forestry and wished he could fly up there in minutes, like the crows that came to his garden. Away from all the other kids. Away from everyone.

'Pizza-face,' he muttered, but Daniels was already out the door.

There was no dodging Emma at the bus stop.

Mark approached her with Daniels in tow, and a few other lads who saw Mark as someone to follow.

'You been avoiding me all day,' Emma said, 'bastard.'

She looked better without her paint-box face. Mark shrugged. Emma must have thought he was in school because of last night.

23

But it was just coincidence. He slitted his eyes, but let Emma pull him away from the others, from their grinning, smirking murmurs.

'We going out together or what?' Emma said.

'Might be.'

She dug at his ribs but he blocked her hand.

'Think you're so clever – Mark Psycho Eyes.'

His eyes almost responded to her challenge but he kept them down.

'I'm not a fucking slag,' Emma said.

Mark wondered what she thought she was.

'I was pissed last night. You knew that. Well, it's the last fucking time, unless we're going out proper.'

'Okay.'

'Okay what?'

'We're going out proper.'

He made an instant decision. Something prompted him out of the blue.

'Don't bullshit me, 'cos I'm not having it.'

'I'm not.'

Emma's temper evaporated and his twisted face softened. She put an arm through his and turned around triumphantly to face the girls at the bus stop.

'Take me out tonight then,' Emma said.

'Can't tonight.' Her fingers dug into his arm.

'I got work to do,' Mark said. 'I'll see you Saturday. Go down Ponty if you like.'

'I wanna go down Cardiff.'

'Right.'

Emma was uncertain of him, but determined.

'What you doing tonight, then?' she asked.

'Don't ask me stuff like that. Just work.'

'Oh aye, the whole estate knows about you.'

'That's what they think.'

They sat side by side on the bus, Emma's confidence growing visibly. She looked around for the approval and envy of other girls, and got it. Daniels sat behind them, his shining face leaning forwards as he talked to Mark. The double decker was usually wild on the way home. On a Friday, and with a week's holiday looming, it rocked. Mark sat at the back and enjoyed the antics whilst being too cool to join in. The air was busy with traffic:

24

books, pens, rulers, paper thrown about; nerds' bags emptied and their contents scattered. At stops a group of boys spat down on pedestrians, raising a cheer when irate faces glared up and fists clenched. Mark liked the double decker because, like him, it did not belong. It was old and cumbersome and farted out a fine black gunge as it ground its way up valley gradients to the estate.

Daniels tried to attach himself to Debbie as they left the bus but she pushed him away. She did not like to be seen with him in daylight, or when she wasn't drunk. Daniels was not over-concerned. He left Mark with a wave and a promise to see him on the weekend.

'I dunno why you let him hang round you,' Emma said. 'I couldn't let him touch me.'

She lingered by Mark's house as he went in.

'What time will I see you tomorrow?'

'Bout twelve,' Mark said, without looking back. She was out of his mind as soon as he shut the front door.

Julie was still in her dressing gown, sat at the kitchen table. Fag on, staring at the bottom of her coffee cup, as if it might contain answers.

'I can see you've had a good day,' Mark said. He swirled around the table, flapping his jacket. 'See, school uniform. And I've been all day too.'

Julie smiled up at him, creasing the yellow tiredness in her face.

'A miracle,' she murmured. 'Look, don't take the piss, love, not today. I got a head like a bucket. Can't get rid of it.'

'Have you took tablets?'

'Aye, just now. And I'm going up the club tonight too. Maybe I'm getting too old for it.'

'What, at thirty four? The teachers down the school haven't even had kids at that age. I'll get some tea on.'

Mark changed when Julie was ailing. The bond between them became less diffident, his spikiness blunted by his mother's need.

Julie watched him fuss around the tiny kitchen. The uniform made him look younger, and she could almost imagine him innocent. But his face did not match. That had never seemed to be young. It had always had a kind of hard knowing to it, but she was glad Mark was so streetwise. It was the only way to be in this place. His childhood had been short.

By the time Mark served up egg and chips Julie's head had cleared. He fried eggs perfectly. She was more haphazard, liable to puncture or overcook. Mark was precise. Careful. Part of that secret world of his, part of his holding back. Until one of his black rages came. Then his eyes bulged, arms spun out of control and he wanted to smash and throw. He frightened her then, though she had only received tongue lashings.

What Mark's future held Julie did not like to think. Once his thin frame took on weight he would be a very big man. There were not many on the estate. Most were runtish, older versions of Daniels. Weasels, she liked to call them, always looking to raid someone's nest.

After the meal they shared the last cigarette Julie had. Mark had the second half, and smoked it down until the tip sparked.

'You must have asbestos bloody lips,' Julie said.

'Hard, an' I?' Mark said as he tapped out the smouldering tip in an ashtray.

'When are you going out?' Julie asked.

'After you.'

'Don' s'pose I'll see you 'til morning.'

'Right.'

'Jesus, you'd give most mothers kittens.'

'Leave it out. Has anything ever happened to me?'

'No. Not yet.'

Julie dropped the subject.

'They're having a '70's night up the club tonight,' she said.

'Anytime but now,' Mark muttered.

'People don't want to know about now. It's nowhere. Humphries will be there I s'pose.'

'Aw, Jesus Christ, Mam, you're not gonna bother with him? Scumbag toe-rag.'

'Don't be like that. I got to have some company. Wayne's better than a lot.'

'That's not saying nothing.'

'Well, he haven't been married or had any kids.'

Mark glared at his plate and checked the cigarette packet to see if one had been overlooked. Julie reached out a tentative hand to touch his and he did not snatch it away.

'Thanks for doing the tea. Look love, I'm only thirty four, you just said. I get lonely. Don't worry, I won't do nothing daft.'

'Like you never have before.'

'You were little when the others were about. You're a man now.' She knew this pleased him. 'And unattached fellas don't grow on trees round here. Anyway, I'll see how I feel.' Julie rubbed at her eyes and massaged her forehead. 'Haven't had a boyfriend for over a year,' she murmured.

Talk of Humphries soured Mark's mood. He went up to his room and put The Pistols on. Sid Vicious fucking up 'My Way'. Mark's anthem. It had balls.

The clocks were going back on the weekend. This suited him. The earlier it got dark the more time he had for scouting. Tonight the job was two miles down the valley, where villa style houses dotted the hillside. He had noticed a few weeks ago that a house he had done before still didn't have an alarm. They must have known it would be no use against the likes of him. A youngish couple lived at the house, the guy a suit and tie job. No kids, which was good. They would be out on a Friday night.

When Julie left the house at half seven Mark had relaxed. His night's plan secure in his head. He liked to frame images of his work. How he would gain entry. Each job was another reel in his personal action film. It made him feel important. A star.

Mark stood in the front doorway as Julie left. She had a new skirt from the catalogue. Black plastic pretending to be leather, red stilettos that made her walk like a bird, and a short coat.

'Don't bend down in that lot,' Mark said. 'The boys'll have a fit.'

'Saucy sod.'

'Here's another tenner,' Mark said. He had never given her two in one week before.

'Thanks, love.' She stepped towards him to peck his cheek, swamping him with perfume. Mark allowed it, then stepped back before she could add to it.

'Don't get too pissed,' he said.

'Okay.'

Mark drank a few cans, lying on his bed in the unlit bedroom. Through the window the valley lights below stood out sharply. It was a cold, clear night, with no moon. Ideal nicking weather. At nine he left the house the back way, dressed in his standard working outfit. Black boots, jeans, donkey jacket with deep pockets. In one of these he had his plastic bags and a balaclava Daniels had nicked from a camping shop. That was black too.

Mark walked everywhere. It would take him an hour across the

27

hillside, working his way steadily down to his target. He knew his world to its very core. Whilst others lounged around the estate he had made it his business to check out every field and lane, the forestry and the common ground that made up the hillsides. Farmers knew his figure but did not bother him; he did not bother them. He knew what the terrain could offer him and what it could not.

He was in position by half past ten. It looked good. There was no car in the drive and just a passage light on. A dead give-away. There was an iron gate at the back, the only way through a tall privet hedge. He put on the balaclava and felt a surge of power Now he was all black, part of the night, and could glide past anyone. Softly he pushed open the gate. He prided himself that he was able to deny even the most knackered piece of metal a squeak. It was a matter of touch. This one was new and well oiled. He was at the back door in seconds.

The defences of the house were laughable. No deadlock and the top half of the back door was glass. He outlined a square near the lock with his glass cutter, and tapped out the glass with his wooden mallet. Muffled with an old sock. It came away cleanly, stopped from falling by the string. Reaching through a hand he found the key in the lock, as he knew it would be. These people must love to get done. The door opened smoothly and Mark stood in the doorway, ears straining until he was doubly sure the house was empty. Confrontation was always to be avoided, for the job might become messy then.

Mark didn't feel anything about his victims. They had something he wanted and that was it. He knew other lads trashed the houses, venting their envy of wealth by slashing, pissing, shitting. That was a waste of time.

He found the room with the video and detached it from the rest of the system. A black plastic bag was taped around it tightly, then it was put inside a larger sack. I'm Father Christmas in bloody reverse, Mark thought. He checked the front from behind a curtain. All was quiet. On a whim he went upstairs, something he rarely did. There was another video in the bedroom but it was part of the portable TV and too heavy to carry. Two chests of drawers gleamed out their dark, expensive wood at him. They had gold handles. Putting on his rubber gloves he opened the drawers from bottom to top, until he found a jewellery box. He had not taken anything like this before but a day at school told him that he must branch out. The Man would take stuff like this. He opened the box and ran a hand over its contents. A necklace caught the orange street light and winked it back. He thought of giving Julie something, if he could find anything cheap enough to blend in with her. It was her birthday soon.

He put the box in the sack and downstairs. He felt different tonight. Cocky. He sat down in the kitchen, at a table that seemed bigger than the downstairs of his own house. A cigarette packet had been left there. He took one out and lit up, pushing the smoke around the room. Let them smell his presence. The fridge caught his eye. Almost as tall as him and gleaming white. Inside it tried to be a supermarket. Mark had never seen one stocked like this. With lots of food he had not heard of. Foreign rubbish. There was an opened bottle of red wine and a plate of cooked chicken, wrapped up neatly in foil. He ate the chicken and drank the wine, though he did not like its dusty aftertaste. Then he smoked another cigarette and stretched back in his chair, putting his feet up on the table and letting the chair legs rock against the floor. The place was vast. Like he was in an exhibition somewhere. The Thief in the Mansion.

But he could get used to a house like this. Where you did not live on top of each other, where his music would be muffled in his room, where no-one would know what the fuck he was doing.

The wine combined with the hike across the hills and Mark began to doze. He woke with a start, spilling the last of the wine on his trousers. He stood up and shook himself, ears instinctively pricked. Stupid bloody sod. I must be getting soft, he thought. He washed the wine glass and chicken plate and placed them neatly on the wooden draining board. Above this he noticed a photograph pinned to a board on the wall, amongst assorted crap like recipes and messages. A man and a woman standing on a snowy slope, holding up skis which looked like giant pricks. The people who lived in this house. The woman was a looker, about Julie's age, but that was the only similarity. The guy was almost as pretty as her. Flawless teeth again. He ground his cigarette in his face, searing it to a blob on his shoulders. Flicking the butt at the table Mark left silently by the back door.

There were still people hanging around the club when Mark passed. It was not long after midnight and, on a Friday, they were at their most reluctant to go home. They would drink all the way through to Sunday if they could, to help them face that dead day. Mark could not understand Sunday, and did not know why they still had it. Let everything be open. Let there be two Saturdays. They said it was coming soon, and he couldn't wait.

Julie was outside with Humphries. He was pawing her, examining her plastic leather, his drunken words full of slobber and false affection. Mark let himself be seen, gliding out of the shadows with his sack over his shoulder. Humphries would not risk coming back if he saw him.

'That's your Mark innit?' Humphries said.

Julie's lurid face turned towards Mark and he saw its angry disappointment.

'Aye,' she said, 'that's him. Christ, he just appears out of nowhere.'

'Looks like he's keeping busy. Didn't know he'd got so big.'

'Over six feet now. And awkward with it.'

Humphries rubbed a hand over his face, it was not unlike Julie's. He was five foot seven in his boots, thin but wide-shouldered, as if nature had prepared him to be stocky but then changed its mind. His thinning hair brushed back to a point, and held there with gel.

'Don' mind 'im,' Julie slurred. 'Come down for a coffee if you want.' She giggled and pushed against Humphries. 'You been trying hard enough all night.'

Humphries looked across the road at Mark again. The kid was creepy, all in black like some prowler.

'Nah, I think I'll leave it. Gotta get up early tomorrow,' he said.

'Early, you.'

'Aye, going out with Dai and his dogs. Rabbiting, like.'

Julie could see his sniffing face following terriers. Humphries looked like he might crawl down a hole himself.

'I'll see you after if you like,' Humphries said. 'Come down in the afternoon.'

'Cheeky sod. I'll see how I feel. I might not be in.'

Humphries grinned. 'I'll come down.'

And he was off. Walking quickly to catch up other male stragglers.

'Waste of space,' Julie muttered.

When Emma knocked at twelve Mark was not ready. He was sat with Julie in the kitchen, she nursing another head.

'Who's that?' Julie said, worried that Humphries had come early.

'Fuck, I forgot,' Mark said. 'It's that Emma. Said I'd take her down Cardiff.'

'Oh aye, courting now, are we?'

Mark was in his usual T-shirt and shorts. The T-shirt had a drying streak of ketchup on its front.

Julie grinned through her pain.

'She'll think you're a real turn on like that,' she said.

Mark hurried upstairs.

'Let her in and give her a cuppa or something,' he shouted.

Julie brought Emma into the kitchen and made the tea. 'He won't be long, love,' she said. 'Making himself nice for you.'

Emma looked at her hands. She was shy with Julie. She had not expected to come in. No other girl had. She felt Julie's eyes on her and looked up and smiled as a mug was pushed towards her. She hated tea.

Julie watched her struggle with the tea, her dark red rosebud mouth barely touching the liquid. Emma made the last twenty years fall away. Julie saw herself. Pretty, already clocking up the men, confident with nothing to be confident about, and a baby on the way in the not-too-distant future. Emma had rings on all her fingers and a series of bangles chained her right arm.

'Been seeing Mark long?' Julie asked.

'Nuh. Just started.'

'Oh.'

There were further attempts at talk but each one dissolved after a few phrases. Julie knew there was nothing much to say.

Mark looked stylish when he came down. His black town gear made him look even taller. Emma was also tallish, with a good figure. Down Cardiff they would not stand out as being poor, not for one day anyway.

'You could have been bloody ready,' Emma said, as she walked with Mark to the bus stop. Mark's thoughts were more on his mother, and Humphries. He did not know why he had made this date with Emma. She was going to cling to him. He had taken three tenners from the tin, more than Emma could possibly expect. The tin had been raided too much recently, for women. He wanted to have five thousand stashed away by the time he was eighteen. If he did jewellery as well as videos he would get there.

An afternoon in Cardiff passed with Mark's mind working

31

inwardly. He let Emma deal with things. Shops, arcades, people swirling around paved streets meant nothing to him. This was a world for her to spend money in. She wanted to be part of it, to buy everything it had. Emma put his money with her own and when it was almost gone her mood changed.

'Christ, you don't say much,' she said, as they dawdled over coffee in a burger bar.

'Nuh.'

'I'm coming down here with the girls next week. Debbie's great at nicking. She got a lot of stuff last time.'

Mark looked at the adjoining table, where a mother struggled with a baby whilst being pawed by a toddler with food all over his face.

'Keep your voice down,' Mark said. 'That's risky, innit?'

'You can talk. It's easy, as long as there's loads of people around. How do you think I got these?'

She jangled the bands on her arm and displayed her rings. Mark knew she wanted to impress him, to be like him. Most of the girls nicked from shops now. It was their thing.

'I'll do some now, if you want,' Emma said. 'I need new jeans.'

She rummaged in her bag for a Stanley knife. 'See, if they have those beeper things you can cut the tags off with this and nothing happens. Not all the shops have them yet, anyway.'

Mark waited outside a large store whilst Emma went to work. Not too near the entrance. If she was caught he would melt away. Emma emerged and walked quickly away until she was on the next block. She opened a plastic carrier to show Mark her illicit pair of jeans.

'This isn't my scene,' he said. 'Too many tossers about.' But he was impressed, even if she was just an amateur.

'I did it though, didn' I?' Emma said.

Her face was flushed and her eyes shone with excitement. She was having a very good day but Mark was bored. There was nothing for him here. He rarely came down to the city and when he did it seemed as if he was on another planet. Everyone seemed to have money to spend. Milling around the pedestrianised centres loaded down with bags, moving like the sheep he liked to watch dogs working on the hillside. It had changed so much since Julie had first brought him down. Old stuff knocked down, new stuff built. There was always money for this down here.

'Great innit?' Emma said. 'I love the shops.'

'Come on, let's get the bus back.'

'Don' you wanna go for a drink? You can get us served easy. We got three quid left.'

'We're going home.'

'Call our poxy place home.'

Emma pouted, but did not complain further. Getting Mark to Cardiff was a triumph which she would use for weeks with the other girls.

They sat in the back of the bus. It began to rain as they passed the castle, fat drops that quickly obscured the windows.

'Have you noticed they can't talk proper down here,' Mark murmured. 'They have a tossers' way of talking, their voices go up all the time.'

'You're a moody bugger.'

Mark took his crumpled baseball cap from a pocket, straightened it and put it on, pulling its black peak down over his eyes. He slumped down in his seat. Emma sighed, lit up a cigarette and examined the contents of her plastic bags. Through the gloom Mark's slits picked out familiar landmarks. He noticed how the houses and people hardened as they neared the valley, and felt more comfortable. They passed through the shambling mess that was Pontypridd before beginning the valley climb. When they changed buses at Porth Mark began to relax. Emma wanted him to go to her place.

'Mam'll be out with her new bloke,' she said.

'I wanna get back. Got some things to sort out.'

'Like what?'

'Things. Jesus, you ask questions.'

'That's 'cos you're so bloody secretive.'

Mark shrugged his shrug. 'Take it or leave it.'

Emma thought of saying more but bit her lip.

'What we doing tonight, then?' she asked.

'I dunno. I'll see after.'

Emma asked Mark to come around at seven but he did not acknowledge her. She did not want him to go when they reached the estate. She was desperate to have him with her. If they could stay together he would be the one constant thing in her life. Nothing else would matter. But she was not sure if he would come to her tonight. Mark was so strange. You could never tell what he was thinking. She dropped her bags onto the wet pavement and leant against Mark, her hands pressing his buttocks.

'We can have fun tonight,' she murmured. 'They'll be down the club 'til twelve.'

'What about your brother?'

'He'll be in bed by nine. Jason's only six.'

Mark did not respond to her probing hands and chewing gum breath. Emma pecked at his face, trying to pin down his mouth. Boys passing shouted encouragement and advice. Mark pushed her away.

'I gotta go,' he said.

And he was off, leaving Emma to pick up her bags and walk home alone.

Humphries was on the sofa with his mother. There was a flurry of movement, clothes rearranged, limbs realigned, in the seconds Mark took to open the front door and enter the house. He stood in the doorway, his face on fire.

'Oh, hiya love,' a flustered Julie said. 'You're back early.'

'Alright, butty,' Humphries said. He stood up, and positioned himself behind Julie, smoothing back his hair. Mark could see its gel shining.

Mark's face spoke for him. His eyes were about to pop. Julie came close to him.

'Mark, love, don' be funny, right. It's not a problem.'

'S'right kid,' Humphries added.

Mark pulled Julie towards him but Humphries did not move.

'There will be a problem if he calls me tha' again,' he hissed.

'Okay, okay. *Please* Mark, don't spoil nothing,' Julie whispered. 'I haven't got much life as it is.'

Mark pushed past her and went upstairs. He threw his cap at the window and put on The Clash. Heavy guitar chords slashed out of the speakers, shaking them slightly. For a while he stood at the window, squinting at wild, red-flecked clouds. Spoil it for her? What about him?

Mark could not stand change, and things had been settled lately. There had been no men sniffing around. Why did she have to bother? Every time one pissed off she was on a downer. She was always looking for something she couldn't have.

In a break in the music he heard the front door slam. Julie's heels were on the stairs. She entered his room without knocking.

'You didn't waste much time,' Mark muttered, without turning around. As the music started up again Julie stood there, uncertain, not sure whether to placate or admonish. Hesitantly she

34

approached him, and shared his window view. They stood there in silence for a few minutes. Julie hated the windswept hillside. It was too open, too empty, and every day it told her she was trapped. But she knew it did something for Mark. He had stared at it since he was little, like there might be something there for him. And he had roamed the hills later, getting into the loner ways which scared her. When she felt guilty she thought it was because she couldn't provide him with a father. At least not anyone permanent, or worthy of the title. When Mark reached thirteen their rows had taken on another, darker dimension: he had screamed at her that he did not need anyone. That he liked the hills because they were free of useless people. Julie wasn't sure if he had meant it or not.

'Getting dark early now,' Julie murmured.

Mark did not answer.

'Look love,' Julie said, 'It won't come to nothing with Wayne. Just a bit of fun, that's all. It's not long to Christmas now.'

She did not know why she said that. It sounded so stupid, and Mark thought Christmas a waste of time anyway. Why bother? was his usual dismissal. When he was silent like this she wanted to shake him. Frustration welled up inside her and he knew it. Silence was one of Mark's weapons. He pulled the curtains and moved away from the window. Julie felt he was denying her access to his world.

'Why 'im?' Mark said, turning away to his hi-fi, where he thumbed through tapes and records.

'Wayne's not so bad. I told you. Would you rather I met someone who has a load of kids, and maybe bringing them down here?'

Mark laughed, a breathy dismissive sound that was full of threat. Julie pulled at him, reaching up to his face with her own.

'I'll tell you why 'im,' she shouted, tears starting to wash her eyes. 'Cos he's interested, that's why. And not many are now, not once they know about you.'

She held onto Mark and braced herself for the push away, but it never came. Mark stood there immobile, but letting her lean against him.

'He makes me feel a bit special,' Julie whispered. She saw the look on Mark's face. 'You'll always be the most important person in my life,' she said quickly, 'you know that.'

Mark disengaged himself, but gently.

'I'm going in the bath,' he said, making an instant decision to see Emma. He stopped at the door. 'If you have to see him, do it when I'm not around.'

'I will, I will, love. It won't be for long.'

Julie stayed in Mark's room for some minutes. She wanted to tidy up his stuff but knew better. She contented herself with putting records back in sleeves. Collecting them from around the room she cleaned each one with the sleeve of her blouse. Trying to instill just an echo of maternal presence. She turned up the storage heater under the window and peered through a gap in the curtains. The hills loomed up their black contours, natural country merging with the grassed-over slagheaps of long-gone pits. Julie shuddered a little and went downstairs.

It was half past one on Sunday. Mark was still in bed when Daniels roused him. He ignored the knocking at first but Daniels came round the back, raising his oily face up to Mark's bedroom and calling out. Bat came out and told him to shut up. Mark took his time in letting him in. First he stretched back in the bed and thrust out his long body as far as it would go. Thinking of Emma the night before. She was alright as long as he could stop her talking.

Daniels swept past as Mark opened the kitchen door. Like a bad smell.

'I seen your Mam just now,' Daniels said, 'in a car with Humphries. He's bonking her now then, is he?'

'Shut up, pizza-face.'

Daniels slumped onto the living room sofa. His eyes shone as much as his spots and he was giggly. A thin line of mucus trailed from his nose to his mouth.

'You been on the glue,' Mark said.

Daniels let his giggles answer.

'Stupid wanker,' Mark said.

Daniels had been sniffing for years. Mark had never bothered. Not with glue, pills, dope or the harder stuff that was coming onto the estate. It was all weakness and he was strong. And going somewhere. Perhaps the only one who was.

'Wipe your stupid pizza-face,' Mark said, 'you look like a fucking baby.'

Daniels began to hiccup, but did not stop giggling. One sparked off the other. He looked like some strange knobbly puppet, jerked by wires. He smelt of the glue, it was in the room with him. Mark shook him and gave him a slap across the face. He regretted this at once, regretted touching Daniels' zits. He wiped his hand in his jeans, and looked at it as if expecting instant contamination. For a second he imagined Daniels slobbering over Debbie and wondered at girls. At women. Daniels quietened for a moment, his eyes struggling to focus. Then he started up again. Mark had seen him like this before, more than few times. Soon Daniels would go spark out. Once he thought he'd died. Mark shook him again.

'Daniels. You can't stop. I'm off out.'

But Daniels was gone. Falling asleep effortlessly with a grin on his face, his undersized body melting into the sofa.

'Jesus fuck,' Mark muttered, 'why do I bother with this?'

He knew that Daniels could not be roused for a few hours. Glue was his secret world, an escape. He had a Sunday shit feeling, and had to snort it away, by squeezing glue into a plastic bag and sticking his head in it. Taking one of Julie's bingo pens Mark wrote a crude note: *Gone out. When you wake up fuck off the front way. And don't touch nothing.*

Mark's anger turned to amusement. If Humphries came back with his Mam, Daniels on the sofa might not be a bad thing. Glue-head spark out, with Humphries gagging for a shag and Julie wondering if it was all worthwhile.

Mark went out the back way, along the bank that skirted the houses. It was a bright cold day, good for scouting. He needed to set up more jobs. He walked around the perimeter of the estate, around the blackened remnants of garages and shuttered-up houses. They used steel shutters now. Wooden ones had not lasted. Near the spot he usually left the estate was the battered metal frame of a bus stop, twisting crazily. Just bare strips remained after years of car ramming and fires. Early on the council had tried to repair stuff like this. Then they realised. And the shelters were left. So was the police station. A small house had been converted into an outpost on the estate, but now it lay empty, boarded up and zapped by the spray artists, the blue police sign forlorn and lost above the door. Victory. The garages, shelter and beaten police were part of what the estate was. What Mark liked. The place was as raw as the wind, an open feeling that put a charge through him. He lived in the largest safe house in the world. Flanked by forestry plantation on one side and a craggy arrangement of rocks too small to be called a cliff on the other. A diamond shaped group of houses, which, when seen from far off on a sunny day looked like some strange display of stone, or dull jewels sunk into the ground for no good reason. A good place to hole up in, to come back to from a job, to lose yourself in. And a good place to leave when the tins were full.

He was on the open hillside in minutes, catching the wind rushing up the valley. He bent his body into it. Below him cottages reflected the sun in silver flashes. He passed the statue on this part of the hill. It looked away from the estate. A woman with a crown on her head holding a boy child, carved in a thin white pillar of stone. Religion did not touch Mark and he was not sure why the statue was there. It said *Dinistriwyd Medi 1538* on its side, but he did not know what that meant either. An old woman standing at this spot had once told him that people used to walk here long ago, to worship. It was a shrine of Mary and Jesus. No-one had ever sprayed the statue. For Mark this was the real miracle.

He walked above the golf club, a small course nestling in folds in the hillside. Years ago he had sat with Daniels and watched matchstick people play, baffled by their presence less than a mile from the estate. Baffled by the game. Now he knew that he had visited many of the people who played. They had helped fill the tin. Unlike most of the boys on the estate, he did not hate rich bastards. He knew them for what they were, and they were useful. One day he would have money himself. Real money. Walking on to the forestry Mark made a mental note to do the golf club some time.

He was in the gloom of conifers within minutes. A dark, private world. He hated it when they cut a chunk down and left land naked and exposed. It was a mass of intertwining root and branch, hard to clamber over. Sunlight lanced into the plantation for the first thirty feet then it was shut out and he was amongst familiar spongy murk. Brown dead debris soft under his feet. And the heady, piney smell he loved. There was no apparent sign of bird or animal. No sign of life at all apart from the steady push upwards of the conifers. When a bird did stray into the upper canopy of branches it flew away quickly, because there was nothing for it here. Sometimes Mark heard the odd rustle of fir, but these were interlopers, passing through like him. What was here was under the ground, burrowing, scuffling, hiding.

Mark walked on confidently, never losing his footing. His feet had always seemed to work on their own. Finding their way while his mind raced. When the tins multiplied and he went on to other things he would have a house on the edge of a place like this, where he could smell the silence and dark, covered places.

The trees thinned and he stepped out of the other side of the forest. The sun was strong now. Shafting through dirty grey clouds moving fast. Mark imagined the sun gone. The clouds congealing into a snowy mass and bringing a storm. Wind whipping snow around the conifers, enclosing them with a white wall. And him inside. A prospect that did not worry him. Since a small child he had hidden. In cupboards, under beds, wherever it was dark. It was his nature but he did not waste time thinking about it. Sometimes he imagined the sun gone forever.

Mark reached the other side of the valley. Territory he thought he might include for future work. He took a small pair of binoculars from an inside pocket. His anorak had multiple pockets, perfect for scouting and walking. He had stolen it from one of the houses, when it had began to piss down unexpectedly. Sweeping the terrain he noted the large detached houses. It was strange how they sprang up. Knackered rows of terraces then a fat rich place on its own. He fixed three such houses in his mind's eye and put them down for a visit before Christmas.

He returned on a lower road. One that snaked above the allotments of people from miners' cottages. They let their pigeons out on a Sunday and he liked to watch them. Twelve or twenty flying out of each coop in a neat arrow. Turning and twisting as one, dodging the pylons and cables that laced the valley's space. Mark had never seen a bird crash. An arrow flew over his head, its flap and flutter and whoosh loud in the still afternoon. Below he saw tiny figures calling them back, waving arms clumsily, but in control of the birds. Control was good, he thought.

He returned to the estate exhilarated, his lungs seared by the mountain air, his head cleared of all irritants. As he neared the houses he knew he was not imprisoned here, his mind not enclosed by four walls. He could leave anytime. And would.

Mark's mood evaporated when he saw Humphries' car outside the house. A large saloon from the seventies, multi-coloured panels with an exhaust system to match that of the school bus. Black fur seat covers and a bunch of crap hanging in the windscreen. Humphries was an intrusion. But Mark felt another emotion, a vague need to give his mother something, let her have a small piece of life. Like when she was ill. And Humphries was a kind of illness, a rash, a disease that she would have for a while then get clear of. Mark could stand that, until the New Year.

They were on the sofa when he came in, but this time there was no fuss of embarrassed movement. Julie must have given him the all-clear, for Humphries did not spring up like a startled hare.

'Alright, Mark,' Humphries said, reaching for a can. 'Have a lager.'

Julie followed this up with a fag. They were on their best behaviour.

'Ta,' Mark said, noting the relief on Julie's face.

'Where you been then, love?' she asked.

'Round and about.'

Humphries laughed. Too loudly.

'He don' give nothing away, do he? I like a man like that,' Humphries said.

Mark winced. 'I'm going upstairs,' he muttered, and turned away before they could say anything else.

Mark lay on his bed and looked around his room, sipping slowly from his can and flicking cigarette ash in the general direction of an ashtray. He knew each stain on the wall and remembered how it got there. The times he had thrown cans of coke and even plates of food, or shot at the ceiling with the air gun, trying to make an 'M' with the slugs, and wishing he had something more powerful. Despite the presence of Humphries he willed his mood of the hills to come back to him. Next week there was no school to hassle him, Emma was there if he wanted it, and the tin was under the floorboard. He wanted to feel good, like he usually did after a walkabout. But he heard Julie laugh downstairs, the same laugh she used on him, when she wanted to please. Humphries would stay. Mark felt bitter at having to see the man in the morning, and wondered if he could steel himself to the git's presence. He thought of Daniels, his snotty nose and racing eyes. Daniels was good training for all gits.

During half-term Mark did one of the new targets. It was a difficult job. A large, detached place, with lights that were triggered when someone approached. He had watched it for two nights and made his plan. It was impossible to prevent the light show but he was up the wall and at the alarm in two minutes, and inside the house in five. In the hall he found the light panel. The lights were a joke anyway. There was not another house in half a mile.

It was the largest place he had done. High beamed ceilings, fireplaces you could walk into, real wood everywhere. So much space, so little life. It reminded him of his old junior school. He took jewellery, men's stuff as well. It was his next step.

On Sunday The Man took it all, his white grin widening when he saw the haul.

'Fuck me, kid, what's all this shit,' The Man said, 'you expanding?'. He quickly scanned through the goods and named a price. An extra fifty pounds.

Mark shook his head instinctively. The Man was not pleased. 'We always done good business,' he said. 'Don't get greedy now.' He looked at a necklace again, rubbing it with his fat fingers and holding it up against the lay-by light. About a grand's worth, he reckoned. 'Alright, kid. I'm a fair guy. Seventy five quid for the beads, on top of the video money.'

Mark nodded. He had kept a bracelet for Julie, for Christmas. A silver band with a dull red stone in it. No-one would think it was real.

In the weeks before Christmas Mark hit several houses. He never expected any trouble, and did not get any. He even went to school a few times, though Julie did not nag him so much about it. Not now she had Humphries. Mark tried to see as little of them together as possible. It turned his stomach. But at least Daniels had made himself scarce. He had given up on school completely now that he was back on the glue, and no-one bothered with him. Emma was the only one who pestered Mark but he kept her at arm's length, stringing her along with an occasional promise and a few words he knew she liked. But as the end of term neared Emma became more insistent. The Friday before Christmas they were on the wall outside the club, sharing a can.

'I'm fed up,' Emma said. 'We haven't been nowhere tidy. An' I know you got money.'

'You must be joking.'

'Don' bullshit me, Mark. Everyone knows you goes nickin'.'

Mark gritted his teeth and breathed in deeply. He grabbed Emma's arm and squeezed.

'Everyone should mind their fucking business,' he said. He pulled her towards him.

'Gerroff me.'

Emma stumbled and spilled lager down her jeans.

'Now look what you done. You're getting more fucking strange all the time. Psycho Eyes.'

It was as if she had given him a cue. He felt his eyes starting and temper stoking up inside him. Sometimes it came quickly, after many calm weeks. Emma's face was close to him, and in it he saw Daniels, Humphries, his smiling, stupid mother. All the people who bugged him. He squeezed harder and Emma dropped the can.

'Mark, for fucksake. You're hurting me.'

But Emma did not shout out or scream. Mark's face was against hers, his breath cutting through the icy night. She saw his twisted uneven teeth, and imagined him tearing her.

'You fucking weirdo,' she gasped.

He punched her, low into the stomach. Emma broke away and tried to rake his face with her nails, but he blocked her hands. It felt as if his eyes were outside his head now, looking on. He pushed Emma against the wall and slowly his hands closed around her throat, and still she did not scream. Her eyes matched his, wild for wild. He sensed her crazy excitement. It was what stopped him. What turned his anger into lust. And they were in the same alley as before, snuffling around like animals.

Emma started to resist again.

'Mark, this is mad,' she cried, as he tried to rip at her jeans. 'I'm on.'

He knew she was saying something but her voice was so far away. A faint echo of words. Emma was saying something over and over. He shook and felt something leave him. He could understand her now. And he felt cold. His shirt had rucked up his back under the denim jacket, his flesh exposed to the wind. It rubbed him with cubes of ice. He pushed Emma away and sagged against the wall.

'Don't wind me up,' Mark murmured. 'Never.'

'Jesus fucking Christ,' Emma said, her voice gaining strength as she realised Mark's storm had subsided. 'Wind you up? You didn't even know what you were doing.'

Mark shuddered, then smiled.

'I don't like people nosing.'

He felt very tired. Whatever made him want to smash, kick out, wound, did this to him. As if he was losing something every time. He had a vague recollection of his hands reaching for Emma, but

42

it seemed a long time ago. The rest was a blur. Maybe there would come a time when he would not be able to stop, would not want to. He hated it. And now he had to go home with Humphries there. Slumped on the sofa like he belonged. His eyes glued to crap on the telly.

Emma looked up at him, trying to work him out. She liked the danger. Mark was different, and it put a quiver in her.

'You alright now?' Emma asked. 'We can go back to my place. Mam'll be out, I 'spect.'

'Nah, I'm going home.'

He wanted to say sorry, but the word would not form on his lips. It never had. Emma hung onto his arm as he turned away. He knew that she wanted him all the more now. Emma would put up with his terror, his razor's edge.

Humphries was asleep on the sofa when Mark went in. For a moment he thought it was Daniels. They were the same pathetic size. His mouth was open, working noiselessly, and Mark smelled the club. Julie came from the kitchen with a finger to her lips.

'Don' wake him, love,' she said.

'Nothing's gonna wake him. He's had a skinful.'

He saw that his mother was in a similar state. Her face red, her eyes shining. She giggled.

'We've had a few. Wayne passed out as soon as we got home.'

Julie wore her leatherette mini-skirt, a white top and a new hair style. Cut shorter, it was a strange purplish brown colour, as if something had been thrown at her.

'Your hair looks like puke,' Mark said.

He went to the fridge, and took the last can it held. Julie's giggle subsided into a half-smile, then a frown as she digested Mark's words.

'Been out with Emma, then?' she asked.

'I'm going up,' he muttered.

'Ignorant young sod,' Julie muttered, but under her breath. She went into the front room, pushed herself into a space besides Humphries and turned up the TV.

Mark stood by his bedroom window and drained the can quickly, then crumpled it in his hand. Opening the window the few inches it would move he flicked the can into Bat's garden. The usual resting place. He did not know if he could stick Humphries for much longer. And there was no sign of him going. Getting his feet warm under the table more like.

43

Daniels died two days before Christmas, on the banking behind Mark's row of houses. Bat came running into the garden in a frenzy, falling against the junk as she banged her fist on the kitchen door. Mark was at the stove, cooking his own breakfast. Julie and Humphries were still in bed.

'It's your friend,' Bat shouted, 'the spotty one. I think he must have been there all night. He's cold. Stiff. Oh my God, I touched him. I gotta get off this bloody estate. Oh my God.'

She grabbed at Mark.

'Don' you hear what I'm saying, you stupid sod. That boy Daniels. He's dead. Out there. I'm going up the club to phone.'

And she was gone. Mark turned down the gas, annoyed at the intrusion. Daniels would be asleep, he was always doing it, and Bat wouldn't know the difference, judging by the men she took up with. Mark went outside. It was bitingly cold, and he shivered in his T-shirt. Daniels was slumped against the wire fencing about twenty yards along the bank. Mark bent down and pulled him roughly by the shoulder.

'Daniels, wake up, you dozy fucker. Bat's gonna get the pigs here.'

Daniel's body yielded to Mark's hand, and turned over. Daniels stared at him. Through him. Past him. His eyes had lost their shiftiness and were unwavering. They stood out sharper than ever before. Mark felt that Daniels was looking at him clearly for the first time.

'Jesus fuck,' Mark mumbled, 'Jesus fucking fuck.'

Bat's shouting had woken Humphries. He hurried up to Mark, struggling to put on a jacket over his white vest, and tried to examine Daniels. Mark pushed him away.

'Get away from him,' he shouted, 'don't you fucking touch him.'

Mark stood up with clenched fists.

'Alright, alright. Take it easy. Is he gone?'

'Well fucking gone,' Mark said.

Other people were approaching, but hesitantly. The street was waking up to another incident.

Mark felt tears coming to his eyes. The first time in years.

'Go and get someone,' he panicked. 'Phone for an ambulance.'

No-one nearby had a phone, not currently connected. Mark noticed Julie by the back gate.

'Stay there, Mam,' he yelled. 'No, go and get a blanket.'

Neighbours gathered in a semi-circle, taking care not to slip on the banking. But they did not come too near. Mark seemed to be guarding the body. Beside Daniels were the means of his death. Two large tubes of superglue and a plastic bag. Mark knelt down again and touched his hand. It was the same temperature as the air. At the third attempt he closed his eyes, and felt a little easier.

In the fifteen minutes it took the uniforms to arrive Mark ran through his memories of Daniels. There were not many, but he remembered junior school and their time together there, when they were too young to know they had been dealt such a shit hand. Daniels had tried hard to please the young teacher from England. They all had. Latching on to something better from afar, a touch of well-bred security and order left at the school gates. That they gave up on it at ten.

Then everyone was there. Police, ambulancemen, and the early drinkers from the club, who had followed Bat down. There was a flurry of official activity. Mark was pushed to the edge of the scene. He made his way back through the crowd to his garden gate. Julie was there, holding the blanket that no-one needed. She had dressed quickly in her new shell-suit. Bright pink with decorations.

'God, who'll tell his Mam?' she murmured. 'Poor Jamie. Poor little sod.'

Mark had almost forgotten Daniels' first name.

'He was a stupid wanker,' Mark yelled, the suggestion of tears turning into a flow. He rubbed a hand quickly over his eyes and turned away from his mother. She thought about touching him, but a policeman approached.

'Don't go anywhere, son,' he said, 'We'll need a full statement from you. You found him, didn't you?'

'No, he never,' Julie said. 'It was her next door. My Mark had nothing to do with it.'

'Alright, love, calm down. I'll be back now. I'd go inside if I were you.'

Daniels was closed off in a white plastic tent. The most attention he had ever had.

It was the first time the pigs had been in the house to see him. There had been occasional visits years ago, to check out one Daddy or another. Yes, he had known Jamie Daniels all his life. No, he didn't know he done glue. He didn't know nothing. With each empty answer he built up a wall of reticence, abetted by Julie and Humphries. In this they were united, sharing a common hostility of a common enemy. Two officers left knowing that the scraps offered were all they would get. It was an open and shut case anyway. Another statistic.

Mark went up to his bedroom, where he could see down to the banking. People had begun to drift away. Some kids hung around. All with a made up story about Daniels. Mark placed a chair by the window and sat. For hours. Until they moved the bagged body of Daniels to an ambulance, and dismantled the tent, and dispersed the onlookers. It was over. Daniels was over.

Julie looked in a few times, brought him a cup of tea. Tried to talk but knew better than to try too hard. He heard Humphries on the landing, muttering about 'letting the kid be'. They had no choice.

Mark continued to stare at the ground where Daniels died until the sky darkened. He was not sure what he felt, perhaps anger more than loss. That Daniels had been a loser to the end of his short life. Mark got up from the chair when it was too dark to see. He looked through his cupboard until he found a folder of photographs. Daniels was in a few taken when they were kids, and almost the same size. He found one of them with Daniels' grandfather. The old man had been alright. He gave them a ride from junior school sometimes, in his old Cortina with seats so big you could explore in them. Smelling of pipe tobacco and whisky. Telling them about the old days, when kids played all sorts of games forgotten now. When people left washing out all night, and it was still there in the morning, and little 'uns scrabbled around the streets without anyone worrying about them. The back doors of houses left unlocked. Mark had never believed that one, not even at the age of seven. And the old man coming up the estate. Not many times. His rheumy eyes starting to cloud as he saw the housing, its bleak concrete, and muttering 'Bloody hell' as he chewed his pipe, forgetting the small boys on the seat besides him. His thick-veined blue scarred hands clenching his walking stick as he took them to Daniels' house. 'We struggled all those years for this?' And two young faces looking up at him, a little fearful at his strange words, but anxious to please, to put a smile back on the old man's face. And it came back when he noticed them again, when he realised they were there.

Mark made a pile of the photographs of Daniels and then ripped out each image of his friend. Pushing the window he

46

opened his palm and let the wind take each tiny face. Let Daniels be scattered by it. He was gone and Mark did not want any reminders.

Christmas came and went without much impact on Mark. The weather was unusually cold and fine, so he walked in the forestry, which was as dark and enclosed as his mind. Emma thought Daniels' death would make them closer, but she was mistaken. Mark did not want to know. There was no present, and no contact. Julie told him that Emma had called, several times, on Christmas Eve, but he had been out.

'I don't think she believed me,' Julie said. 'She was gutted, poor kid.'

Usually, his mother would have berated him, called him a heartless sod, but he was protected by Daniels' death. He was useful at last.

Due to the inquest and Christmas the funeral was delayed until the second week of January. Mark made a last minute decision to attend. He stood as near to the exit of the Crem as he could, and ignored Emma, who was with a scattering of school kids and a few teachers from the Comp. When her pinched face looked for his he turned into stone.

Mark was amazed at the turnout. There were the usual gawking, nosing estate tossers, full of gossip and mock concern. Eager to be part of the action. The ones that turned up at everything. None of them would have given Daniels the time of day when he was alive. Julie and Humphries sat with Mrs Daniels, and the meagre Daniels family. Daniels' skinny little mother looked as if she had died with him. Julie said they had given her pills.

A vicar who had never known anyone like Daniels read some words, something he had prepared about 'Jamie'. They meant nothing to Mark and he switched off after he heard 'tragic loss'. Mark was lost in the past, with the smiling healthy face of Daniels with his grandfather. He came out of his thoughts as the last ragged chorus of a hymn was sung. Daniels was on his last trip. His chipboard box with polished veneer slid through the doors to the burner. Mark was the first to leave. As they were herded outside another bunch were coming in through the other doors, for their twenty minute slice of the farewell action, like shoppers at a big store sale.

Julie struggled to catch him up outside, almost tripping on her new heels. Humphries trailed behind her. He wore a black suit from the seventies, with large lapels and flapping trousers.

'You could have worn that black tie,' Julie whispered. 'Wayne got it special for you.'

'What for?'

'What for? It's what people do. To show respect, like.'

'It's not what I do. It's all fucking nonsense.'

'Don't swear, not here, Mark.'

Mark gripped her arm.

'Mam, no-one here ever bothered about Daniels, apart from his old girl. I hardly bothered about him myself, this last year. So why pretend with all this crap?'

Julie dabbed at her eyes.

'It's what people do,' she repeated, but much quieter this time. Humphries nodded agreement.

'It must have cost a few bob,' he said.

'She had a loan off the social,' Julie said. 'Them words were lovely from the vicar.'

Humphries nodded again. Mark offered them his most sullen glare and got into the back of Humphries' car.

'That boy,' Humphries muttered, 'he'll be worse than ever after this.'

On the way up to the estate Julie felt unwell. Humphries stopped on the hill road. Julie just made the grass verge, where she threw up over the seat placed to catch the divide in the valley. Today low cloud hung over the hilltops, the colour of dirty smoke. Mark had idled on the seat many times with Daniels. Humphries hovered around Julie, reminding Mark of the scavenging garden crows in his ridiculous suit.

'Alright now, love?' Humphries called out, without getting too close to Julie. She waved him away and he got back behind the driving wheel. Mark had not left the car.

'Your Mam's sensitive, see kid,' Humphries said. 'It's all been a bit much for her, like.'

Mark looked at him with disdain. Humphries did not know his mother at all.

Julie woke Mark at twelve thirty on giro day. It was two days after the funeral, well into the new school term. He had not attended at all since Christmas. Julie stood over him, slowly coming into focus as he rubbed his eyes.

'You seen Wayne?' Julie asked.

'You woke me up to ask me that?'

Julie sat on the edge of the bed.

'I thought he'd gone out early,' she said, 'not that he ever has before. Likes his kip even more than you.'

Mark rolled over and tried to bury himself in the bedclothes.

'His clothes are gone,' Julie said. 'All of them.'

Mark's ears pricked up. He emerged from his den of sheets and sat up.

'What you on about?' Mark said.

'I think he's pissed off,' Julie said, trying to control the tremor in her voice.

Mark fought down the temptation to shout out *good!*. His face remained expressionless.

'If he hadn't took all his clothes I wouldn't be sure,' Julie said quietly. 'But he has, and I am. He won't be coming back.'

Mark's face was still blank. Julie might just as well have been talking about the weather.

'Just don't care, do you,' Julie shouted. 'An' don't do that shrug of yours.'

But he already had.

'He was a tosser,' Mark muttered. 'You're well rid.'

Julie slapped his face, a stinging blow that took him by surprise. He had not received one in years. Julie began to sob.

'He was company,' she said. 'And who am I anyway, the Queen of bloody Sheba?'

Mark fingered his cheek.

'You could have done better than 'im,' Mark said. 'He was like an older Daniels.'

'That's right, make me feel worse.'

Julie's sobs lessened. She sat wringing her hands. She was about to draw into herself, her one defence. Mark knew the signs. It was like looking at himself.

'I knew he wouldn't stay,' Julie mumbled. 'Not once he knew. But I had to tell him. I've done it again. Stupid useless bloody cow.'

'Done what?' Mark asked. 'What you on about?'

It was Julie's turn to be blank-faced. But hers was streaked with tears and twin black trickles of mascara making their way down her overdone rouge.

'Done what?' Mark repeated.

49

'Oh shut up. I'm fed up of talking. I talked to him long enough last night. Begged the bastard.'

Mark did not press her. It was enough that Humphries had slung his hook.

'I'm going to bed for a lie down. Leave me be for a bit. Get down that school if you want to do something useful.'

Mark did not go to school. He had no intention of going again, but he did take Julie a cup of tea, in the middle of the afternoon. There had been time to think. With Humphries gone things would return to normal. Just the two of them. Julie might not bother with anyone again, or by the time she did he might be long gone.

Julie was lying on the bed in her clothes, her blue eyes fixed on the wall. On her small display of photographs. Mark as a baby; a young boy; his first day at the Comp in the uniform the social had bought; with the grandparents he had so rarely seen.

'Here, have a cup of tea,' Mark said. He felt awkward suddenly, as if he was intruding on a secret place. Where Humphries had been, making his mother moan and wail in the night. She couldn't do anything quietly.

Julie turned over to face him. Her red-rimmed eyes fighting blue eye make-up, her tears smudging it into a mess.

'Is he gone for good, then?' Mark said.

'Looks like it.'

Mark was hopeless at pretence, so he did not try. He could only hide his pleasure at Humphries' leaving with silence. Julie sat up and held the mug in her hands. They trembled slightly, as if cold, though the bedroom was at its usual baking, window-streaming best. Julie could not bear the cold and Mark had to top up her heating bills with money from the tin.

She put the cup down and reached for Mark. He let himself be pulled towards her, but he was sweating and wanted to go.

'You might as well know now,' Julie said. 'Why Wayne's gone.'

'I know why. He was a tosser.'

'No, you don' know. He's got me pregnant. I been sure since before the funeral.'

It was a silence so tangible it could be cut into pieces. As if their time together, all its tribulations, had congealed into a thick wall. Julie looked up at him, her tearful, fearful eyes searching his blank, white face.

'Well, say something, for Christsake,' she said.

50

She saw Mark's hands clenched into fists, but they hung use-lessly at his side. Julie wanted his support. She needed it desper-ately. A spark in the gloom that had taken her over. The past fif-teen years would start again. She knew it would be a boy. It had to be. That was the way her life had always gone. Would always go.

Mark felt cold, despite his wet brow. Victory had been snatched from him so quickly. Humphries had gone, but he had left something behind. Something that Mark could not yet com-prehend. But he knew his future plans might be under threat. Jealousy surged through him, that his mother might be taken from him again. He avoided her hand. Her streaming, begging eyes only fuelled his anger. He found his voice.

'Stupid cow,' he shouted. 'I don't believe you. You'll have to get rid of it. Get rid of it!'

He swept out of the room, kicking at furniture as he went. Julie tried to call him back. But in minutes he was kitted up and out of the house. Striding over the dying-ground of Daniels without giving it a thought, his eyes fixed on the frost bound hills, as if they held something more for him than bitter emptiness. His self-pity stoking his anger.

Julie heard the back door slam. The crack in the glass would get worse. 'Getting rid of it' was the first thought that had come into her mind. Turning the clock back sixteen years, to the pleas of her parents, and the realisation that it was an easy solution for them, not her. She had not taken it then and would not take it now. Julie could lay out all the arguments in her mind, each one sensible, the obvious thing to do. And each one rejected by her inability to seriously consider abortion. No matter what. She would be fifty when the child got to Mark's age. And where would Mark be then? What would he be? Time had dripped away slowly with Mark, a long struggle surviving on pittances, supplied by people who lived on another planet, far from her own. Now it would start again.

Mark was not sure how far he had walked over the washed-out landscape. It was almost dark. He might have done anything in the last few hours. Fetched up on the mountain behind the pigeon lofts his senses cleared. He had homed to this spot just like the birds. He was also a creature of instinct, but the birds were not flying today. They had more sense.

He shivered in his denim jacket, as cold damp settled into his bones. He thought of Humphries, about to start a night's drinking, his weasel face flushed, his eyes shifty, telling his butties about Julie, how he had gotten away from the slag, now that she had a bun. Bastard cunt. Julie would get no money from him, Mark knew Humphries would make sure he never had any. Not that it would get as far as that. Julie would never name him. Women like her would take a lot from men, and they were always men like Daniels. Mark could not understand this, and he did not respect what he did not understand.

It began to pick with rain, but Mark did not want to go home. To her pleading cow eyes. He remembered there was a house to be done here, not more than a few hundred yards away. Beyond the pigeon fanciers' terraces. It would be crazy. He was not prepared, not tooled up, not in his protective comforting black. And it was tea-time. He had never worked so early. But he did not care. He wanted action. To do something he was good at, to confirm his usefulness. What kept him apart from Humphries, and the thousand of tossers like him.

The house was one of a pair of semi-detached Victorian villas. It had a name – Brynhyfryd – on a plaque outside. Crap like this annoyed Mark. He had never met anyone who could speak Welsh, yet it was still all around the place, as if it belonged. The name-plate encouraged him.

There was light upstairs and down in the house next door but his target was in darkness. And no alarm. In bushes he found a handy sized brick which he wrapped in a rag someone had thrown away. The back door of the house was solid wood so it would have to be a window job.

Mark heard kids shouting in the adjacent house as he climbed through the window. They were complaining about something, wanting their mother to sort it out. She told them to wait until their father got home. His target was an untidy house, stuff was strewn around and it looked like someone had left in a hurry that morning. Breakfast dishes were still on the table, and a crumpled newspaper. People with jobs lived here.

There was no video. Mark could not believe it. He felt cheated. And the telly was old, a black and white bastard. Books were everywhere. On the floor-to-ceiling shelves and in piles in the corners of the spacious rooms he surveyed. Why didn't they have the same as everyone else? For the first time Mark understood why other nickers trashed houses. He too felt the need to destroy, to tear things down. To leave his mark. Anything to relieve the pressures in his head, and blot out the leering image of Humphries. Fire came to his mind, the thought of all these books going up in flames.

Mark sensed there would not be much in the way of jewellery here. Hesitantly, as if it might snap at him, Mark took out a heavy book from a shelf. It had pictures of old pits in it, the black and white former days of the valleys. He recognised his own area as he flipped the pages, and was interested despite himself. The outline had not changed much. The terraces were still there, and the upper slopes of the hillsides. Only the clusters of smoking industry had gone.

He found a photograph of the pit nearest to the estate site. He knew it from a framed picture in a classroom in the comp. It was in full flow, fed by steam trains, their smoke spouting out in circles as they hauled the long lines of trucks. Where they had built the estate was mountain turf, dotted with sheep. There was no sign of the forestry. Everything was open, and dirtily busy.

Mark had never been interested in the past, had never seen a working pit. But the old geezers talked about them as if they were still around. Daniels' grandfather had. All the time. With a mixture of hatred and affection, nostalgia and venom. Mark knew one thing about those days. That they had led to nothing, to the nothing of the estate, and the many like it in the valleys. But he decided to take the book, and was leaving by the back door when challenged.

A man appeared out of the night to block his path.

'What's your game?' he shouted.

He was large, and not too old. Mark hit him with the book, a solid blow to the side of the head, but he did not go down. He grabbed at Mark's jacket and wrestled him to the ground. Mark was desperate to get away. He twisted, turned, bit and scratched. He took a punch to his face and felt blood flow from his nose. The man was calling out for help when Mark connected with his balls, ramming his knee into his crotch as violently as he could. The man gasped and loosened his grip, allowing Mark to wrench his body away and get up. Light from next door lit his opponent's face. It was dazed with pain and would stay with him. A guy about forty, who looked as if he read books.

Mark ran into the bushes and through them. Something

53

scratched at his face, adding to the punishment of the man's fists. He scaled the hillside without looking back, knowing he had to be in a safe place before the blue lights came. Eventually he sank down into the wet undergrowth. His lungs were bursting, and every breath had to be fought for. He cursed the pain that shot through him. There was blood on his T-shirt, his own, his hands were cut and his ribs hurt where that fucker had planted his size tens.

He looked down on the now distant houses and saw the beams of torches ineffectually probing the bushes. They were too late, but Mark shouted at himself inwardly, a silent mouthing of castigation. You stupid sod. Useless cunt. Letting your concentration wander, because of a book, for Christsake. Acting like any tosser off the estate. Like Humphries.

Mark had let Julie and her pathetic problems affect his work. It would not happen again. He lay on his back, ignoring the mulchy remains of fern that squelched under him. It had stopped raining and was turning much colder. A few flinty stars pricked the gaps in the clouds, competing with the orange sheen of the road lights. He watched them for a time, trying to imagine the cold black distance between their light and his eyes.

He stayed like this for an hour or so, until he was sure everything had quietened down. The pigs would cruise the estate, looking for someone marked up. Checking those on their lists. But they didn't know him, and they wouldn't call, and the man couldn't have got any sort of look at him. Not whilst scrabbling around in a dark garden.

Mark startled Julie when he opened the kitchen door noiselessly. She spilt the coffee she was making.

'Jesus, Mark, don' do that,' Julie said. Her tipsy eyes struggled to focus on him. 'Oh my God. What you done? Are you hurt?'

She tried to examine Mark's face but he pushed her away.

'Leave it,' he said. 'I'm alright.'

'Aye, you look alright. You're covered in blood. Oh Christ, you haven't been after Wayne, have you?'

'That wanker? You must be joking.'

Relief flooded Julie's face but she soon showed renewed concern.

Julie advanced on him again and this time Mark let her touch his battered face, wincing as her fingers probed.

'Bruises more than cuts,' she murmured, 'nothing needs stitching anyhow.'

Mark sat down on the plastic chair and let Julie clean him up. She ran hot water into a bowl and sponged his face with a tea towel. It was the closest he had let her get in years. Even as a youngster he had not liked being touched. But now it was comforting, for one short speck of time it seemed to make sense. Something other families did. Mark began to enjoy the stinging touch and the pumping heat of the kitchen.

Everything was over the top with Julie. Her emotions, her choices, the way she decorated the house, the heat she insisted on. Her slight body leant against him as she washed his eyes. There was a small cut in his right eyebrow which made her cry as she wiped fresh blood away.

'What am I supposed to do?' she sobbed. 'I can't cope with all this. It's not fair. Not bloody fair.'

Mark touched her arm, almost patting it.

'Mam, when was it ever fair for the likes of us? Fair belongs to money, I've worked that much out. Anyway, you've coped. All this time.'

'Oh aye, mother of the bloody year I am. With a perfect bloody son. I'm useless, a dead loss. And I can't keep a fella, even when *they're* bloody useless. And you run wild.'

Mark was not good at words of comfort, and none came.

'I was just messing about with the boys,' Mark said. 'That's all you need to know.'

Julie looked at him dubiously. He looked frail to her now, long-framed but wafer thin. And his eyes more lost than angry. The danger washed out of them for a while.

'The pigs aren't going to come round about this, are they?' she asked.

'Don't keep on. I already said.'

'Okay, love.'

Julie did not push further. She wanted to savour this rare intimacy with her son, and dared to rest Mark's head against her. He tensed, but did not object. It seemed moments ago that he was a child in her arms.

'Don' worry,' she murmured, 'it's just you and me now.'

Mark was exhausted. He wanted to soak his aches away in a deep bath, then count out the contents of the tin. For the hundredth time. Each note a small reassurance of his future. Being caught by that man was the price of Humphries leaving. And maybe Daniels too.

Mark thought in terms of punishment and retribution, but his judgement was clouded now. He hoped things might settle down again if there were no more disturbances, and felt a lessening of the anger within him. For a moment he felt like the normal son of a normal mother.

Later that night, as he lay nose deep in bathwater, watching the steam make rivulets on the window, Mark made a New Year's resolution. Not to be caught again. Tonight had been a warning which he would take.

Mark kept away from school for the rest of that winter. Like Daniels and Humphries, school was the past. And he tried to keep away from Emma. Now Humphries had gone she did not seem necessary. He let Julie make excuses for weeks, but Emma kept trying to see him. Turning up in all weathers in tiny skirts, with a garish, anxious face. Sometimes he watched her from upstairs, squinting through the gap in the curtains.

Emma caught up with him at the end of January. He was coming back from a scout over the hillside, hunched up against the shrieking, ball-busting wind, which seemed to stroke each of his ribs with ice. Emma stepped out from behind the white statue, which caught the raw sun and threw it into his eyes. She had been hidden behind the wall flanking the shrine but Mark was still disgusted at his inability to sense someone watching him. Since the fight his instinct had been awry.

'I been watching you coming,' said Emma. 'You was walking funny, always looking around, like a shifty bastard. On the nick all the time.'

She stood before him in a short orange fur-like jacket, her wind-whipped face all defiance and scorn.

Mark leaned against the statue, the Welsh words rubbing against his shoulder.

'Bloody cold, innit?' he said.

'Don't talk about the bloody weather to me,' Emma shouted, 'as if you only seen me yesterday. Bloody sod, Mark Richards.'

'That's not news, is it?'

'You aven' even got the guts to tell me you don' wanna see me again.'

Mark shrugged, and watched Emma's hands warily.

'Been busy,' he muttered.

'Aye, busy doing fuck-all. You haven't been to school once.'

'What's the point?'

Emma wanted to shout and scream, to pound Mark's chest with her hands. Anything to get a reaction, a sign of emotion. Silence got to her. It was threatening, strange and there was so little of it in her world. Mark was a master of silence. He looked weird slouched against the statue, his head blocking out the sun, his face dark and shadowy. As if he had never been in her life. She knew she had been used but something made her hang on, despite the beating her pride took. Mark was different and, for Emma that was a kind of hope. And he was right about school. Her anger dissolved into pleading. She tried to link her arm with his.

'I know you been down about Daniels,' she murmured. 'He was a nice boy.'

Mark glared at her.

'Leave it out. You couldn't stand him. And I don' wanna talk about him anyway.'

Emma sensed a softening in Mark's body and pressed against him.

'Come on, les' still go out together,' she said, 'you know it makes sense.'

She was rubbing against him now, trying to find his chest with her breasts. Her face looked for his.

'Aw, for fucksake,' Mark said.

'Come on home with me,' Emma said, 'there's no-one there.'

Mark felt nothing for Emma, apart from his control over her, but he let it start up again, realising that there was lust if nothing else. He let her lead him to her house on the estate, and felt her relief as she pushed him in through the front door.

Emma's house was just like his own, higher up on the estate, within shouting distance of the pub and club, and the few services built into the concrete heart of the place. But there was two women's clutter here. Tights, leggings, shoes, magazines and other assorted crap lay around, and, hanging in the air, Emma's mother's perfume. So heavy it got to Mark's chest, making his breathing tight, while his eyes smarted after the cold air of the hillside. He knew this would be a one-off.

'She's got a new fella,' Emma said, as she made a half-hearted attempt to tidy up. 'Lush looking bugger, but I wouldn't trust him an inch. I don' like the way he looks at me.'

Mark sat on a lumpy sofa which had once been pink but was now mottled with stains.

'Me and Debs party on this,' Emma said. 'It's seen some sights.'

She started to mouth his face, short sharp kisses that were mini bites, exciting herself whilst he remained impassive. Having got him on her ground Emma was oblivious to his coldness. She could imagine Mark as she wanted him to be. Sweeping her off her feet with sex and money. Taking her away from the estate to a place where she could be safe, warm and rich.

Julie's pregnancy was common knowledge in her street by the spring. It was not news enough to travel further. The estate was awash with similar cases. Bat had been the first to notice, in the garden as they put out washing on their lines. Julie's swelling was easy to spot against her skinny body as she stretched up to peg clothes.

'Jesus Christ,' Bat said, 'you've caught. You're up the bloody stick.'

A sneer began to form on her face.

'I wondered why that Wayne pissed off so quick. About half-way gone, are you?'

Bat put down her clothes basket and approached a gap in the wooden fence. It was mainly gaps. Her stance demanded information and for once Julie did not feel like a scene. She hoped for a quiet time in the next few months, even if there was little chance of it.

'No point in saying different,' Julie said. 'I could never keep it secret anyhow, not with my figure. Aye, that bastard's got me pregnant.'

Some of the venom went out of Bat's crinkly face. She adjusted her scarf over her curlers.

'You should have learnt with your Mark,' she muttered, 'but we never do. Men – they're a waste of space.'

Julie was grateful for the 'we'.

'Tell me about it,' Julie said, more to herself than Bat.

'You don't have the hips for kids,' Bat said. 'There's nothing of you, mun. You'll have to have a caesar.'

'No I won't. I didn't with Mark, an' he was nearly eight pound.'

Bat looked at her in disbelief.

'Maybe it'll be a girl,' Bat muttered, as she went back to her washing. It was the nearest they had been to civility for years. Julie found that she liked this. Female friendship had not played much part in her life. Her mother had always been more of a rival for her father's affection, with no other children to take the strain. And telling her about Mark had been difficult. Accusations instead of support, blame not sympathy, and the old man absenting himself to his garden shed with a tut and a cough. Then her history paraded, the men. All the men. Her mother remembered their names better than she did. And the rapid escape from hot maternal words, feeling even more defeated and alone, her father's bemused and helpless face watching her go. Confirmation of her situation. Steel shutters snapping shut on her future. Steel shutters snapping shut as she struggled off the bus with her shopping. Steel shutters snapping shut as she turned the key in the front door. The door a flaking orange; pathetic colour. Winking at dominant grey.

Mark watched Julie talking to Bat. It annoyed him. He did not want any barriers broken down. He sat at the kitchen table, waiting for his dinner. Chips bubbled and spat in a pan, filling the room with pungent fat to which he added his smoke. He went through a pack a day now, trying to adjust his young lungs to what he thought was manhood. Likewise his stomach and copious amounts of lager. Stuff strong enough to give him an instant kick. A jolt to the head as he felt its cold on his brow, then seeping warm spreading as he drained a can and opened another. His thoughts becoming light and hazy, his plans alive with success. That he could and would be someone.

His mother looked so small next to Bat. A girl. Bat with her curlers and brawny red hands, built like a Sumo wrestler, her fur-collared red anorak looking like another skin. Her hanging tits too big for anything other than a hammock. They seemed to be talking, not shouting. That was worrying. Julie came back in.

'It's brass monkey weather out there,' she said, 'don' this wind ever drop?'

'Whadyou expect. We're on top of a bloody hill. Exposed, they said on that telly programme. Remember?'

'Aye, made us all look like morons, that did.'

'What were you talking to Bat for?'

'Why can't you get on with people? I need someone to talk to. I might need a bit of help when the baby comes.'

'From 'er? I'm here, an' I?'

Julie looked at Mark doubtfully.

'Well I am,' he reiterated. 'Anyway, if you'd got rid of it we wouldn't have no problem.'

Julie's face flushed and she gripped the end of the table, where the plastic coating was coming away from the Formica top.

'I told you not to say that again. I didn't and tha's that.'

Mark returned her anger with a glower.

'Don' you look at me like that,' Julie shouted. 'You're still a kid, no matter what you think. Christ, you're not even sixteen yet.'

She turned away from him and adjusted the gas under the chip pan. When she faced him again she was calmer, but tearful.

'Look love, I know girls who done that. They're never the same after, even the hard cows. Something like that stays with you. Forever. I'd rather have it, no matter what. Anyway, we'll be better off with the social. It'll make up for you turning sixteen.'

The baby was one more grey area for Mark. The house only had two bedrooms for a start and it would be filled with more crap. Julie stood over him, her wet eyes pleading. He knew she must be desperate to start talking to Bat. What the hell, he would be gone before the kid started walking.

'Aye, alright,' Mark said.

'I'll get your eggs on,' Julie said. 'You can have three if you like.'

Mark learned his lesson well. Each target was checked out many times before he struck. He was not caught again. Now he stole anything, videos and jewellery, small ornaments and anything that was portable, and looked valuable. Once he took a set of golf clubs, lugging them over the black hillside to his stash place. This was a hole he had dug out in the forestry two years ago. He had waterproofed it as well as he could and it was adequate if he didn't leave stuff there for long.

The Man took all his stuff, eager to use Mark's enterprise. The tin was full by May, full, sealed and pushed further under the floorboards to make space for another, an old tea caddy he had taken from the grandest house yet. It was silver coated and had caught his eye as he prowled a huge kitchen. He was getting a taste for fine things and occasionally The Man gave him hints. He learned that what glittered the most was not necessarily the most valuable. The Man was alright for stuff like this. Mark noticed his cool clothes now, the way his hands were manicured, his neat fingernails pale white moons in the gloom when they met. He wanted all this and more.

On the eve of his sixteenth birthday Mark had twelve hundred illicit pounds to his name and Emma available on tap when and if he wanted her. School was becoming just a memory. And he had adjusted to the prospect of another Richards. Julie was two months away from babytime but he no longer viewed it with angry dread. Future plans crowded his mind and he had re-evaluated the news of the baby. It would give Julie something to do when he left home. This was logical to Mark, and reasonable.

In late May Mark began a series of jobs in a new area, a few miles further up the valley, where a small development of detached housing had been built. New estates like this were magnets for nickers and the houses came with alarms and lights but Mark did not mind this. Amateurs were put off. He called his new target Wankerville but it intrigued him. The way it was enclosed by a wooden fence. He probed its perimeter, but discreetly. Always with a made-up name and address to hand, to be given in his best voice if challenged.

He sat on the slope above the houses, scanning the estate with binoculars which fitted snugly into hand or pocket. They had foreign words around the lenses and were old, but shit hot quality. He felt power when he used them, picking out individual houses, noting which ones he would visit. Promising them a visit. Who would he turn the glasses on next? So many waited for him. The valley was riddled with nickers of all ages, most of them dopeheads, but he was the best. If there was a championship he would win. No problem. All his points were in the tins. He was content as he stretched out in the sun.

Mark planned to do at least two houses on the new site. Despite the fine Sunday there were few kids about. As far as he could tell, the couples here were at the pram stage, or had not started at all. He picked out the houses with the plushest motors in their drives. Some were being washed now, hosed down by their owners then buffed up proudly, as if they were prizes. These goons would have expensive black goods, lots of overpriced pieces of ponce waiting for him. He would do them next Friday night.

Life felt good. He'd give Emma a tug later, and get some cans and a curry in for Julie. She had stopped going to bingo, or anywhere else, and had been sick on and off for months. He heard

61

her in the mornings, saw her coming out of the bathroom, her worn face even more pinched than usual. Dark smudges under her red-rimmed eyes as she sat at the kitchen table, stirring her tea with one hand and reaching for her first fag with the other. 'They told me down the clinic to cut out smoking,' she said, 'but I can't. I didn't when I was having you. No fags would kill me.' She asked him to go to the clinic with her once. She had to go there a lot, 'because of her age'. 'Cheeky sods. An' me only thirty four. Said they gotta monitor me more, like. Things have changed a lot since I had you.'

He had gone with her, at the third time of asking. All the time wondering if anyone thought he was Julie's old man. He was sure one old bint did, as she smiled at them encouragingly. When Julie was called in to see someone Mark sat scrunched up and head down, counting the minutes. He hated the place, full of lumbering women. What was it with women and babies? They all seemed to go gooey-gooey-gaga for a while, then spent the next twenty years worrying. He recognised a girl from school, younger than him, walking along with a fat cow he supposed was her mother, her face tear-stained and frightened. Mark drilled the floor with his eyes and willed the girl not to see him. It had been his first and last time at the clinic.

Mark lay back in the hollow he'd found. Small birds were fooling around on the warm air currents. This year's crop, he guessed. Dashing specks of new life dark against the sky, flitting on the wind with tiny, overworked wings. They swooped low over him, making his hand involuntarily reach up for them. He preferred the homing pigeons, birds with a purpose. This lot were clowns tossing about all day, getting nowhere.

He dozed for a while, the sun welcome after the penetrating winter winds. When he woke and got up he knew the place was ripe for him, even if it lacked cover. There was no forestry to sink into here. The mountainside did not have the curves for it. It was shale and scrubby turf, and straight up to a rocky finish. Even in sunshine it looked grey.

Mark was with Emma until nine the following Friday evening. Taking advantage of her mother's absence. He looked through her schoolbooks and old examination papers while she made him food. Upstairs her young brother ran amok. Mark heard things fall about but did not raise his head. From the kitchen Emma shouted at Jason to go to bed. She'd told Mark that her brother was hyperactive, whatever that meant. He thought it meant a complete pain in the arse.

Emma brought him a tray and he opened the can that was on it. He did not mind drinking before a job now. The work came so easily to him.

'Still bothering with this crap, then,' Mark said, flicking through the papers with his fingers.

'It keeps Mam happy. I haven't done no work though,' Emma added quickly.

'You was sixteen in March. Should've left then.'

'I wanna go to the Tec down Ponty. Maybe. Do a hairdresser's course.'

'Hairdressing. Jesus Christ.'

Mark forked the chips into his mouth and offered her one of his best withering glares.

Emma hated Mark's attitude, his constant put-downs, but she knew he might go at anytime and did not want that. His contempt was mixed with an anger which rarely left him. It was exciting and frightening, and she could not manage life on the estate without him.

'I gotta do something,' Emma said. 'Mam's got no money and she can't keep a fella for more than a few months.'

'What about that oily ponce?'

'Gone. She's got another one on the go now. Runty-face. He looks a bit like that Wayne Humphries.'

'Don' mention that fucker.'

'Sorry. Your Mam's not got long to go now, has she?'

'Stupid cow.'

'Might be nice for you. A little brother or sister.'

He glared at her.

Emma winced. It was a constant battle to say the right thing. Her angrywords at the shrine were long forgotten, a brave one-off she could not repeat. Mark was on a job tonight, she knew the signs now. Even more irritable, a fist-clenching restlessness, and an ability to see her only as someone to snap at. Maybe a replacement for his mother. After a job he could be better, almost kind. He'd given her the odd tenner then. The other girls told her she needed her head read to go with him but she knew they were jealous. Mark was different, even if it was an angry, dismissive difference. He was alive, real. He was her drug.

Mark scooped up his beans quickly.

'Christ,' Emma said, 'you'd think you'd never seen food before'.

'Gotta go. Gemme another can.'

'You sure? When you're working?' She knew he liked her to use this word.

'Course I am.' Mark clicked his fingers and pointed to the kitchen.

Emma was putting on weight, around her hips and arse. And her tits were getting bigger too. Mark imagined her in ten years time, shagged out before she was thirty. He had made her go on the pill; she told him this was the reason for the weight increase.

He forked his last chip, looked round the room and winced. He hadn't thought anyone could crap up a place worse than Julie. A pink settee and lime green carpet, Jasonified. And an oversized telly stuck in the corner like a big fat eye. The video had gone back to the hire shop but he was deaf to Emma's pleas to get her one. None of his goods went back to the estate.

Mark downed the can quickly, and allowed Emma to slobber over his face for a minute. She made soft mewing noises of affection but his mind was on the work ahead. An hour's brisk walk over the mountain to his targets.

'Be careful,' Emma said, as she stood in the front doorway.

'I was born careful. See you.'

Emma watched him glide away into an alleyway. With his black gear on he seemed a part of the night itself. She shivered in the keen wind but was thrilled.

It was a fine night, two-thirds of a new moon sitting on the hill-tops, yellow and streaked with blue-grey shadows, giving off too much light for Mark's liking. When he reached the houses he crouched in darkness beyond the perimeter and waited for the moon to go down, cupping a cigarette in his hands so that it glowed secretly, warm against his palms. He noted with satisfaction that no lights showed in his chosen houses. He wanted two videos tonight and whatever shinies came his way.

He put on his balaclava and black fingerless gloves, checked his tools and advanced on the estate, skirting the rear gardens. Waiting for no moon had been a waste of time. This was the brightest place he had operated in. Six months ago he would have shit out, told himself there were safer pickings. But he wanted to get in here, to penetrate these poxy boxes. He activated the intruder lights of one house and quickly faded back into darkness. No-one came out. They never did.

The first house had been singled out because it was built at an angle to the main estate, its rear in convenient shadow, and facing the hillside. It had a simple alarm, standard stuff, something he had learned to disable at fourteen. These new places had walls made for him. He was able to work hands into their uneven mortar and crab his way to the alarm. This was danger time. To be caught half way up the wall would be tricky but he loved the charge that ran through him. His every sense on fire. He was inside the house in five minutes and nothing had stirred around him.

It did not take long to check it out. He was amazed at the size of it, how it gave an illusion of space outside but surrounded you when you entered. Eighty grand for a doll's house. He'd have something better. Much better. He bagged the video but found nothing else of interest.

He left the house and made his way to the second target, wincing at the cruel glare of the street lights. The video was stashed in a hedge. It was getting close to pub stop tap, so time was pressing. He thought of the long trek back with his load, and the raid no longer seemed such a good idea. It was always the same: adrenalin rush then a vague disappointment, that whatever good he felt would not last for long. If he had not let his thoughts slacken he might have heard the dog coming at him.

It padded out of the darkness quite silently, to catch him halfway across someone's garden. He was knocked down and pinned to the lawn, the dog barking a warning. Mark didn't know what breed it was, but it was a big bastard, with yellow teeth snapping close to his face. He felt its eagerness to chew him, admired it even, and it took all his strength to hold it off. He got a hand on either side of its neck, the steel studs in its collar cold and sharp. He didn't dare to free either hand to look for his knife but he had never wanted to use it more. To plunge it into the pulsating strength of this fucker. Mark could not believe his luck. The rare guard dog he had come across had always been spotted and the house left.

People came running. He sensed them all around him but could not see anything clearly. His senses were a whirl of excited, angry words and excited, angry dog, and his vision a slanted mix of houses, street lights and the faces that were beginning to surround him. He heard someone shout out 'phone the police'. The dog was pulled from him and he ceased to struggle. Blood flowed from cuts on his hands and something had jarred his back. A number of men stood around him, all youngish and fit. As his eyes cleared he saw their women standing in the light of doorways.

'I wasn't doing nothing,' Mark said instinctively, 'jus' walking through. This bloody dog should be kept chained up.'

Then he realised he still had his balaclava on.

One of the men made to grab him. 'Thieving bastard,' he shouted. An older man restrained him. 'Alright, Dave, leave the police handle it.' Mark was able to decipher their words as his head cleared. 'I've had a bloody 'nough of it. This is the third time since we bought the place.' 'Bloody scum, they're all on drugs. This one don't look more than eighteen.' 'Bloody good kicking they need.' This last remark came from the man anxious for action. Mark was not sure whether to lay down and whimper if they started, or to make sure he destroyed the bastard's balls. The first idea was the most sensible but the second was more attractive. What the fuck? He had crapped up bad.

But he didn't do either. The blue lights arrived. He was united with them at last. Mark stood quietly in a circle of light, flashlights probing his face and body. Flung open front doors added their light to the spectacle, making the lawn's dewy grass look freshly painted. Possible explanations raced through his mind but his sense shot them down. They would search around and find the video. Go through his pockets and find all his gear. And the balaclava. How the fuck could he explain that? Fashion wear? No, best tell them it was his first job. Play the snivelling kid coming clean. Then he thought of the tins. Would they find them? They'd bound to search the house. And Julie seven months gone. Fuck it.

Outraged householders spilled out their tale for the police. They were a little and large affair. One shortish, but built like a tank. Beefy shoulders, arms and legs. Beefy red face. Angry dangerous face. The other was about six two, the athletic fancy-itself type. Mark knew he'd be all threat and no menace.

'What we got here,' Beefy said, 'the SAS?'

'Take that thing off,' Lanky added, yanking at the balaclava.

When asked, Mark gave his name and address. He saw no reason not to. The estate was instantly recognised by the gathering, the name taken up and spat out as if it was poison. Mark concentrated, harder than he ever had, and let the noise from these prats wash over him, not into him. He repeated that he had done nothing as he was cautioned and led to the police car. Beefy sat with him while Lanky searched around until he found the video. He brought it to the car proudly: 'Got you all ends up now, kid,' he said. All the while the dog kept up its bark, but half-heartedly. Its fun had been taken away. Lanky put the video on the seat beside him and radioed in before he drove off. Mark was an 'incident' now. In its plastic bag the video looked pathetic, useless, like something that had died. Evidence.

The police car passed the turning off the main valley road to the estate, and its images slotted obediently into Mark's mind. Its battered lay-out. Angry faces. Useless faces. Julie, Emma, Daniels. Lost faces. Yet despite this he still felt a kinship with it all. Something he did not despise.

Daniels' face stayed with him until the station. Perhaps Daniels had taken the right road after all. Got the fuck out. Life is shit then you die. Suddenly Mark felt very cold. He wanted someone with him. The father he had never known. The mother Julie never was. His mind went back a decade, to the times he had crouched on the landing, small, white-knuckled hands grasping the banister, listening to Julie and whatever fella rowing downstairs. Wanting the noises to stop. All the sounds, smells and sights of his early childhood came back to him, but there was no warmth in them.

Beefy was prodding him again.

'Come on, sunshine. Time to get out of the car.'

And he was inside. The station strip lit, and awash with customers. Friday night specials. Beefy and Lanky stood him in front of the desk sergeant. If a man could look harassed and bored at the same time the sergeant did.

'Jesus Christ, what we got here, the Milk Tray man?'

Other bored-harassed eyes glanced over at Mark, and a drunk tittered from a seat in the corner.

'Caught him at it, sarge,' Lanky said. 'Doing houses on that new estate.'

He deposited the video on the desk.

'One house had been entered,' Beefy said. 'Good little job, too. Neat like. We've got a statement from the householder, Mr

67

Griffiths. He'd just come home. I reckon Mark here could tell us lots. Lots and lots, sarge.'

Mark was asked to turn out his pockets, and the sergeant's face beamed as he did so.

'Good God. Now it's the Mafia. Tooled up or what? Bet you've done a lot of previous, son. But we don't know you, do we?'

He took a closer look at Mark's face.

'Nope. New kid on the block. Right, take him to room two. A detective will be along shortly.'

Mark sat down on one side of a table, an empty chair opposite him and an officer stood by the door, impassive, immobile, uninterested. Not much older than himself. He wished he had his fags. Never had he craved them more. Something to hold in his hands, to concentrate on. The yellow spots on his fingers taunted him. Stick to your story, he told himself. Admit the job but keep telling them it was your first. No matter what. He tried to remember how he had left his bedroom, if the carpet had been put back carefully over the floorboards. He thought of The Man waiting for him in the lay-by on Sunday, his BMW softly purring, his black hands tapping on the leather steering wheel.

The door opened and a plain clothes man entered. Shortish, and fat. Bleary-eyed, stubble-faced.. He sat down opposite Mark.

'So, Mark Richards, is it? Been busy, butt, have you?'

He turned on a small tape recorder and told it the date, time and Mark's name. He was being made official.

Detective Morgan introduced himself. He was going to be the chatty, friendly type, Mark decided, seeking to catch him out.

'So,' Morgan said, 'still "haven't done nothing", then?'

'Can I have my fags?' Mark said.

'Later, maybe, if you're old enough to smoke, that is.'

'I am.'

He knew he must not lose his temper. No Psycho Eyes here. He was not known to them, that was his ace in the hole and he was sure he had not left fingerprints anywhere. Watching Morgan through slitted lids he decided to answer each question with as much snivelling lying as he could muster. Perform, you bastard, he shouted to himself. He wished he knew how to cry, that might help.

'So, when did you start, Mark?' Morgan asked. 'We can probably clear up lots of stuff between us. The more you tell us, the better it'll be for you. You know it makes sense. A young pro like you. Tooled up like you were.'

Mark was being flattered, in the hope his tongue might be loosened, to fly away on bragging nonsense. He wondered how thick the usual people they questioned were. He rubbed his eyes with his fists and played his hand.

'I haven't done no jobs before tonight, right. That's why you don' know me. My Mam's having a baby. She's been dumped by some tosser so we got no money. I had to do something.'

Even the man at the door smiled.

'Sweet Jesus,' Morgan said, 'spare me. I've trod in better bullshit in a field. So, you just knew how to do an alarm, break in no fuss, no mess, stash a video and move on to the next house? I'm hurt that you think I'm so stupid, Mark. Really hurt, I am.'

Morgan stopped the tape recorder and smiled.

'It's gonna be a long night, Mark, if we carry on like this. The boys will be up your house soon, with a warrant. Now you and me know that they'll find a load of stuff, and you'll be deeper in the shit. Especially with me.'

Oh no they won't, you fat bastard, Mark thought, as he dug his fists further into his eyes, in the hope that they might water. It all depended on the tins.

'I'm telling you right,' Mark said. 'I just listened to the boys on the estate. They told me what to do.'

'What boys?'

'Leave it out.'

'I think you're the one leaving it out, Mark. Leaving fucking everything out.'

Morgan switched on the machine again.

'So, you're telling me, that on this, your first job, you walked three miles up the valley to get a few videos. Gonna walk back with them, were you?'

'Spose so. I dunno. I haven't been thinking straight.'

It was time to bring in Daniels.

'I haven't been right since my mate died,' Mark murmured.

Morgan looked up. The doorman's attention was also caught.

'Mate?' Morgan said.

'You know about it. Daniels, a few months ago. He was my best mate.'

'Oh aye. You do glue then?'

'Nuh. Not interested.'

Morgan looked at him closely. At his eyes. His hands.

'No, I don't think you are,' he said. 'See, I believe you, kid. Right, let's start again...'

And so it went on, for another hour. Mark kept hold of his story, stuck to it. Like glue. He regained some pride. When Morgan's friends returned from his house empty-handed he knew he was winning. In the early hours of morning he was locked in a cell without further talk. And still no fags.

The knocking made Julie wake with a start. It couldn't be Mark. He'd come round the back if he didn't have his key. Not that he ever forgot it. He was too careful. She got up from the sofa with difficulty. She had been dozing in front of the television, unable to concentrate on the film. The baby kicked and she gasped a little. It crossed her mind that it might be Wayne at the door. Pissed and declaring undying devotion. Others had done that before. She felt hope and hated herself for it. For dreaming. Someone was calling out her name. A man's voice. A man she did not know. She stood at the front window and peered through a chink in the curtains. Police. Two uniforms on the front porch, another man in a raincoat standing by a car. Bat was already out, hands on hips, eyes eager for a feast.

Julie felt cold inside as she went to the front door. Her heart pumped wildly and her thoughts raced. It was Mark. Something had happened to him. He was dead. Like his friend Daniels. In the seconds it took to open the door she was shaking and found it hard to breathe.

Beefy handed her the warrant.

'Mrs Richards?'

Lanky was already past her and up the stairs. Accompanied by a detective.

'Wa's going on?' Julie said. 'Wa's happened? Is it my Mark?'

Beefy stared at her, his eyes fixing on the baby inside her.

'Better go through, love. So you can sit down.'

Julie let herself be led back to the sofa. Mark had been killed. She was losing it. She felt the need to scream. Anything to relieve the pressure. To turn on a tap and let it all flow out and away.

'For God's sake tell me,' she shouted.

'Nothing's happened to your Mark. Well, not the way you think anyway. He's been caught thieving. Trying to break into houses up the valley.'

Julie sat down heavily. Relief flooded through her, as instantly as horror had. She felt weak and could not stop shaking. But what joy. Even this overweight pig looked kind and beautiful. For a moment. She made an effort to calm herself. She realised why they were upstairs. What the warrant was for. But they wouldn't find anything. Even his records were bought and paid for. Good boy.

'You alright?' Beefy asked.

'What are you talking about?' Julie said. 'Mark? He'd never do anything like that. He's never been in trouble in his life.'

'Well he is now.'

Beefy's eyes were everywhere, but each glance drew a blank. Julie was in control of herself now. Her eyes were dry and her mind was in gear. And her natural hostility to the police had reasserted itself. Lanky and the detective came back downstairs. The detective shook his head. 'Clean,' he muttered, 'too bloody clean'.

'You better not have made a mess,' Julie said.

'Check the kitchen,' the detective said to Lanky, 'I'll do the garden'.

Julie was left with Beefy. She did not like his bull-like neck, or the clumps of black hair on his red, fleshy hands. She imagined them pounding Mark.

'Who says he's been nicking?' Julie asked.

'He's admitted it. Didn't have much choice. Caught in the act, he was.'

Beefy stood up, wandered round the room, looked out the window, casually, with his hands in his pockets.

'Your neighbour's gone back in then,' he murmured. He turned to face Julie. 'Look love, you'd be doing him a favour if you helped us. He's a new face. If we can stop him now he might have a chance later. To do something useful, like.'

Julie thought only of protection.

'Don't give me that crap,' she said. 'A chance? Up here? Gonna give him a job are you? On the force? Look, you know there's nothing up here for the kids. Just the name of this place is enough to put people off. Anyway, Mark don't need no favours. You've found bugger all here, 'cos he's never nicked nothing before, right. If he's done something stupid tonight it's 'cos of me. You can see how I am.'

'Where's the father?'

'How the hell would I know?'

'I see.'

'Aye, you see a lot, mister. See it all, you do.'

Lanky and the detective's faces registered the same disappointment when they returned. Looking at Julie, sitting on her pathetic, hand-me-down furniture, Beefy wondered if it might be true. A spark in him even wanted it to be. He thought of his own two young sons, asleep only a few miles away, in another world, another lifestyle. Then he saw the balaclava-faced Mark, caught in his flashlight, all natural cunning and cool. And knew that if the kid had done one house, he had done fifty.

'He'll get bail in the morning,' the detective said, 'you'll have to come down. He'll go before the juvenile panel. They'll decide what's to be done. He is sixteen, isn't he?'

'Last week.'

'Gave himself a good present tonight.'

Julie struggled up from the sofa.

'You're gonna keep him in overnight?' she shouted. 'He's only a kid.'

But her words fell on their backs. They wanted to be gone. There was nothing in the house for them, and not much in the case. Beefy let the others go ahead.

'Think on what I've said, love,' he said.

Julie slammed the door after him, and was sobbing again before she hit the sofa.

As the cell door shut Mark closed his eyes and tried to imagine himself in the heart of the forestry. The truest heart he knew. The hard bunk with its stained cover became moist earth, the glare of the light screwed into the ceiling faded to the comforting gloom he knew well. The drunken shouts and groans from other cells became the wind brushing the tops of the conifers. The frightened cry that roused him in the early hours was the call of a rare forestry bird, sweeping the trees as it journeyed to a better place.

Mark soared over the valley with this bird, a crow, no, a hawk, landscape flashing through his mind, the aerial photographs of that old book mixed with the cleaner emptiness of recent times, seen with pin sharp vision. He was proud that he knew his patch so well. It was time to get real again. Thinking of the forestry had steadied him, taken him away from the immediate shock of capture. Back to his inner world. His inner strength.

They had taken the laces from his Doc Martens, and his belt, which made Mark wonder. What sad wanker would want to end it all here? Giving them the ultimate satisfaction. When the metal plate was slid back from the observation hole he did not turn towards it.

He knew they had found nothing at the house, or they would be at him again. They would have to settle for one offence, done by a mixed up kid desperate to help his mother.

Mark lay back on the bunk, testing the pillow with his head. Inches from his face were scrawled a variety of names, slogans and messages. The wall was cut up with them at this level. People reaching up from the bunk, everyone looking to make a sign. Some asked him for his solidarity, asked him to join them in their defiance. One scribbler offered Jesus. Others told him to give in. But he never would. The tossers who did were the same as the pigs. Part of the game. The system. He would stay outside it all. The cells had gone quiet, and Mark felt he could sleep. Despite the light. A small triumph to finish a bleak night.

Julie felt sick as she travelled down the valley. Smoke from the bus's exhaust worked its way inside. At each stop the bus shot out another cloud, which billowed around the window then away into the following traffic. And it still reeked with Friday night cigarettes, and Friday night curry and lager. Even its No Smoking signs were stained yellow. Julie had cut down to ten a day. She opened a packet now, despite the churning in her stomach and the guilt she felt about the baby. Guilt was becoming her middle name. About her whole lousy life. And Mark was the one who pricked it. In another place and another family he would go far. And without breaking the bloody law. She was sure of this. He was ten times sharper than her. Julie gnawed at her fingers, working them mechanically into her mouth, chewing on flaking cuticles, feeling the flaking blue nail polish in her teeth.

The bus pulled into a lay-by to pick up two old women. Seventysomething, gnarled, yellow wrinkled skin worn by an age of struggle. Fattish masses close to the ground. One with glasses which made her owl-like, but not wise. Both piss-poor like herself. Julie felt their hard lives in each struggling movement as they hauled themselves up the steps of the bus. Scrabbling in oversized bags for their bus passes, which they waved at the uninterested driver.

It was not right, Julie thought. Not right, this valley. Not right the lives these old women had to live. Not right her own.

Mark was with a solicitor when Julie reached the station. He had known how to arrange this himself. Ten times sharper than her. She met Mark's eyes, but he barely acknowledged her. They were focused inwards. Julie knew the signs. Being nicked would be a huge blow to his pride.

Maule, the solicitor introduced himself. Young, clean, well dressed, limp handshake. Julie let the hand fall through her own.

'You alright?' she asked Mark.

'Course I am,' he answered. 'Don't fuss.'

'I've gone over the procedure, Mrs Richards,' the solicitor said. 'At Mark's age, the case will be considered by a Juvenile Panel.'

Julie remembered the detective mentioning it.

'What's that?' she said.

'It's like a committee. Various people sit on it. The police, social workers, maybe somebody from Mark's school.'

'I've left,' Mark said.

He could sense Maule's distaste. At being around people like him but needing the work.

'An' what happens with this panel?' Julie asked.

'They'll decide if Mark's case goes to court or not.'

'You mean there's a chance it won't?'

'It is a first offence. But then again, burglary is serious. I wouldn't want to raise your hopes. Ten years ago Mark would have got off with a police caution but things are different now.'

'Tell me about it.'

Julie took a cigarette from her packet and lit it. Ignoring the plea in Mark's eyes.

'When will we know?' she said.

'In a few weeks. But once you've signed the bail forms Mark is free to go.'

Maule guided her out of the detention room. She felt his arm nudge hers, pinstripe against cheap anorak, and wondered what it would be like to be with someone like this. She saw the gold band on his finger. His missus would have the lot. She wouldn't wake up in the morning feeling like a piece of shit. The solicitor hovered over her and she signed where he pressed his finger.

'It would help if Mark stayed on at school,' the solicitor said. 'I want to paint as positive a picture as I can for the panel.'

Julie almost laughed in his face.

'Fat chance of that,' she said. 'He was out of there as soon as he was old enough.'

'No exams?'

'Nope. He didn't see the point.'

She knew it was a waste of time to lie.

Mark fumbled with his cigarettes on the steps of the police station, his hands tearing the packet in his haste. They had given the fags back but kept everything else as evidence. He had also been fingerprinted, which meant he'd have to be extra careful in the future. And there would be a future. At no time in the last twelve hours had he doubted that.

They were awkward and a silence lasted a few minutes, as they concentrated on their smoking. They walked to the bus stop. Two dams barely holding. Julie could contain herself no longer. She threw the stump of her smoke away and grabbed Mark.

'Alright, alright,' Mark said. 'Leave it out, Mam. Them bastards are probably watching us.'

Julie struggled against the tears which welled up and her lips quivered with the strain.

'What happened, then?' she asked shakily.

'Someone got lucky. Look, I don' wanna talk about it. Please, Mam.'

Julie's quaking face was inches from his own.

'Ta for coming down,' he mumbled.

'But they treated you alright, in there?'

'No-one touched me, if that's what you mean. What about up the house?'

'Three of them come in. Frightened me half to death. They looked everywhere, even in the garden. Found nothing.'

'There's nothing to find.'

Mark wondered where the bracelet was, and made a decision to get rid of it. He'd buy Julie something else. Something from a shop. As they sat on the back seat of the bus, out of place amongst the coughing, spluttering, gabbing or gloomily silent pensioners Mark realised he had been fortunate. If they had found the tins everything would have been blown apart. A warm glow spread through him as he thought of the notes neatly squashed in those tins. Each a ticket out. That bastard dog. He imagined going back to that estate, and firing the houses one by one. Watching from the hillside as they lit up the night. The dog's barks useless as it ran itself into a frazzle.

'What you thinking?' Julie asked.

'What a stupid twat I am,' he answered. Mad twat, he thought.

Mark's star was rising on the estate. Men acknowledged him. That he had been caught did not diminish him. Glory lay in being a nicker, a serious, professional thief. A performer, a dude, cool in dress and action. Someone who didn't give a fuck. What could be more attractive than that?

Julie's pregnancy was handy now. Handy cover. He was able to play the good son for that dumb solicitor. For the first time ever he decorated Julie's bedroom, painting out the old pink with a clean white. And, after days of thought, he gave her a hundred pounds from a tin. To buy baby stuff with. Bat next door came up with an old buggy. A few months ago she had hated Julie.

A week after being caught Mark signed on at the dole. Not that there was any money. They had stopped giving money to sixteen year olds. He was not bothered. Not about *their* money. Going down, 'looking' for work, talking to the sad geezers there, was all part of the act. And he wanted to keep his head down, until he came to court. This would be in August, the solicitor said. The Juvenile Panel had decided. The solicitor told him that attitude was important now. Mark tried not to glare at him too much, and kept his eyes deadpan. The thicker the man thought him the better. At times he almost felt sorry for Maule. With his crap ties, shiny, well-scrubbed skin and slick-me-down hair. The man had no power at all. No real knowledge of people like him. He wrote down what Mark said. The crap about Julie, which Mark had polished up until he almost believed it himself. Then he went to his books and made up a tale which he called 'the defence'.

The Man had been told what had happened. He clicked his teeth in pissed-off sympathy when Mark phoned the contact number.

'I'll be back in a few months,' Mark said, 'once the heat's off.'

He almost missed the nigger. Their monthly meetings had been a solid part of his life. Every time that electric window opened he felt he was winning. Every time that smooth black wallet appeared was a victory.

Mark spent some of June and July scouting from the hillsides. His natural vigilance was honed to new keenness. He tried to pick out

76

future targets. Ones that had no dogs, no alarms and were close to cover. To be a pro was to learn from experience. He told himself this every day.

For Mark the forestry was at its best this time of year. When the sun was out it was even darker inside. He liked to get right in there. Sit down with his back against a trunk and watch the sun shaft its way into the first ten feet of forest. Punching holes of light until the trees thickened and cast it out. Smelling the thick, earthy soil.

He took Emma with him once. She had been coming down the house a lot lately. Julie seemed to like having her around, now she was having the baby. She wanted women with her. Even a kid like Emma. And Bat had actually sat down and smoked a fag in their living room. If it wasn't for the court case Mark would not have allowed it.

The walk tired Emma.

'God,' she puffed, 'how can you do this all the time? I can't wait for you to get a car.'

'I'm not seventeen 'til next year, and don' hold your breath anyway. Cars can't climb hillsides, or haven't you noticed?'

'Don' go sarky on me. We could go lots of places if we get a car. You will take me places, won' you?'

Mark did not answer. They had walked less than a mile, but ascended steeply. Emma's exertions were starting to bug him. She had long legs, but bred for the street and the insides of clubs. For show, not work.

'Can't we stop for a bit?' Emma asked.

'Jesus Christ, alright. Anything to stop you moaning.'

He led her to a slab of stone that edged the forestry. It was furred by lichen and flat-topped. Mark had often used it as a table.

'Park your arse on that,' he said, 'an' open a can.'

He handed her the canvas bag he was carrying. Emma sat down and tried to pull him down with her, seeking his face with her wet lips. He shrugged her off.

'Stop messing. And give me a bloody can.'

He was in one of his moods but Emma knew better than to sulk. She tried to ignore the way he treated her as much as she could. In the hope that one day it might change.

'It's a lovely day,' she murmured. 'Look how small the estate looks down there. Toy people.' She opened one of the four cans of lager, letting it froth down its side.

'Give it here, for Christsake.'

It was warm but he drank greedily. He sat down beside Emma and offered her the can. A group of pigeons was curving away from the forestry. They swooped low overhead, their pumping wings sounded like paper tearing.

'Look at that lot go,' Mark said. 'Like one bird. Free.'

Emma followed them into the sun, her eyes screwing up against the glare.

'My grancha used to keep pigeons,' she said. 'His shed was always full of shit. An I don' see how they're so free. They always go back to their cages.'

Mark scowled at her as he offered the can.

'Stupid tart,' he muttered. 'Don' you understand nothing? That's the joy of it, see, the pigeons have an arrangement. They go back of their own free will.'

Emma wasn't interested. Mark took the can and drained it.

'You'll be pissed,' Emma said.

He watched the arrow disappear into the yellow haze. In minutes the pigeons would be back in their loft, stuffing themselves.

'Fit now?' Mark asked. 'We're going into the forestry.'

'No, Mark, I don' like the look of it. It's so dingy. And quiet.'

'Think the Bogeyman's gonna get you?'

He took her hands and pulled her to her feet.

'I got news for you,' he said, lowering his voice as much as he could, 'I'm the Bogeyman round here.'

Emma laughed as he squeezed and tickled her but it was an uneasy laughter. She couldn't truly relax with Mark, but he *had* changed. Become more open somehow. Maybe it was the baby. Julie had told her that Mark 'don't show things like I do, but I think he likes the idea of having a little brother. Coming round to it, like'. Emma was not sure. It was impossible to work Mark out. His way of thinking was different to anyone she knew. He loved secrets.

Mark led her along the edge of the trees, and she knew she'd have to go in. These great slabs of man-made green had always frightened her. Secret worlds she had shied away from as a child. Her mother's tales of 'funny buggers' being 'up there' had struck home. But Mark was fascinated by the place. *He* was a funny bugger, a mad bastard, the other girls said. He treated her like shit at times, lots of times, but something shot through her when it was good. Better than any pills. And he was getting to be even more lush looking, and filling out a bit. Even more of a man. She thought he looked a lot like Mel Gibson, only bigger all round. Bigger dick too, probably. Emma smiled, despite the encroaching gloom. As they entered the trees she locked her arm with his.

As Emma shivered nervously, Mark knew she could sense the change in him. That this place, weird and dark to her, was part of him. He guided her confidently through the undergrowth, pulling her over obstructions. It was the first time he had been in the forestry with anyone and he felt like he was showing off his home. His world. The rock on which he had chiselled his initials, M.R. 1990, the gaps in the trees which acted as windows on the valley below. He was oblivious to Emma's lack of response. She saw only gloom and danger and an unnerving lack of people. That somewhere could be so empty yet so close to the estate.

Mark led her to a glade, more a gash in the trees, which had been grubbed out by a JCB, and they stopped on the edge of a bank. The remains of a wall threaded a loose stone way through the scrub. One of the many that had been obliterated by the plantation. Once he had found the caved-in stones of a house, a dark and mossy mound almost a natural part of the forest yet still able to evoke a past Mark knew so little about. He wondered if its owner had gone willingly.

Emma was glad to stop.

'You're like a monkey round this place, aren't you?' she said. 'The way you walk over the ground, like you don' have to look where you're going.'

Mark pulled her to him.

'It's my eyes,' he cried, 'they're like radar. Psycho Eyes.'

His raised voice sounded strange, an invasion of the heavy silence of the trees.

'Get that blanket out,' Mark said. He had packed an old one, knowing what he intended to do, and knowing that forestry ground was always damp, even in a spell of summer weather.

They sat down and opened another cans. Emma glanced back into the trees and gave an involuntary shudder.

'No-one there,' Mark muttered. 'No-one's ever there.'

'What about the forestry workers?'

'Once in a blue moon. That lot only appear when there's clearing to be done.'

Emma lay back, can in one hand, the other behind her head. Mark lit a cigarette and smoked as he looked down the valley. The twisting snake of development that disappeared into the haze. Further down a faint smear of coastline and a grey smudge of sea beyond it. This was their calmest moment together so far. Emma wanted more of it. She wanted to go down the Tec, become a hairdresser, have a nice house and two nice kids. With Mark. With a nice Mark. She wanted to reach up and grab him, keep him, mould him. Wanted his nature to be as sweet as his looks. But as he turned towards her, blowing smoke out like Mr Cool, Mr Iceman, something told her these hopes were forlorn.

Emma tried to snuggle up against him. Beyond the wall a straying sheep coughed, making her start. Mark grinned, and knocked out the fire from his cigarette.

'Thought someone was coming?' he said. 'It's only a sheep. They always cough like that, specially in winter, when it's cold and misty. Sounds just like an old geezer, don' it?'

He noticed the curve of Emma's breasts. They pushed against her white T-shirt, inviting his hands. He wanted her, here in his forestry. To set the seal on his ownership. Mark couldn't see the relationship in any other way. He dived on Emma and worked quickly with his hands.

'Do you love me?' Emma asked, as Mark rapidly undressed her.

He did not answer. Mark enjoyed himself. He felt today was important. For him, bringing Emma into the forestry was the closest he could come to sharing. It was the most of himself that he could give. In two years he planned to be away, on to better things. To be like The Man. Another role model. Emma's noise, and terms of affection washed over him. Words from afar, unable to penetrate his unshakeable belief in his own worth. That he was better than them all.

They shared the last can.

'I'm half pissed,' Emma said, 'an' cold.'

It was early evening, and a chill wind blew through the trees.

'It's never too warm up here,' Mark said, 'even on a day like this. It's softer down there.'

He gestured to the horizon where the sea now glinted silver as it stored up the last of the sun.

When Mark got home the house was empty, but Bat was soon there, knocking on the kitchen window with her fat fist. Mark let her in.

'Julie's gone in,' she cried, 'to hospital. She's gone into labour. Gonna have it quick, I think. Early, like. You better get down there, she might have had it already.'

And the mood was broken. His control broken. He was back in the lousy real world of struggle. And skint people rushing nowhere. And babies.

'Do you wan' me to come with you?' Bat asked, mistaking his silence for worry.

He struggled to get his mind back in this place.

'No, no need,' he said.

If he met Humphries now, he might kill him.

But Bat was wrong. It was not quick. Not at all. More a long, stretched out night of waiting. Following the slow hands of the wall clock under the harsh light of the waiting room. Hospital night silence, punctuated by the occasional movement of something somewhere else. Cold polished corridor floors showing up the worn yellow-cream of the walls.

It had taken him a long time to get down to the hospital, a large centralised one ten miles away, safely out of the valley. An old place, built in another age, for another age. It had the same knackered, hanging-on air as his school.

Mark sat. And sat. Sometimes his eyes clashed with other peoples'. Hushed-voice nurses gliding past on their flat shoes. Silent running. Wondering if a 'kid' like him was about to be a daddy. He knew plenty who already were. There was no-one else in the waiting room.

Julie had been moved from the main ward to a smaller room. A quieter place. Where she would have the kid, Mark supposed. Some time after his arrival he was allowed to see her. She looked tiny in the hospital bed. Tiny and lost. Her forehead filmed with sweat, her eyes jumping with pain. Alive with it. She reached for his arm and pulled him down on the bed. He sat on an edge awkwardly, not wanting to touch in this public place. An oxygen cylinder by the bed. It looked weird, like a kind of weapon.

'It's for the pain,' Julie said. 'You breathe it.'

He wondered if it was anything like glue. Daniels' dead-staring eyes came to him. He saw them appear in Julie's face, and was afraid. He should not be here. He was her son, for Christsake. Mark felt responsibility being thrust on him, and did not like it. It was a threat. Something dark moving towards his future. Something that was starting here, in this lousy hospital.

Julie's hand was insistent. He felt her fingers probing. Asking. Pleading. She needed him now. He was all she had got. Her parents were not here, Mark realised. They probably didn't even know. He never thought of them as his grandparents. They had given him no reason to.

'Is it bad, then?' he finally managed to ask.

Julie clenched her teeth in answer, as another contraction passed through her. Why does it have to be so damn hard, he asked himself. So much pain and mess. A nurse tapped him on the shoulder.

'Better go back to the waiting room now,' she said. 'Give your mam a bit of peace.'

Julie smiled weakly at him as he left. She looked like a baby herself.

So he sat again. And waited again. His arse numbing on the hard plastic chair. A huddled figure. Alone. This was the place he had been born in. Maybe in the room where Julie was now. It could not have been much different for her then. Or maybe she thought he was a one-off mistake, and that her life would get back on track. It hadn't even left the station.

Mark thought back as early as he could. He got back twelve years, to his first major accident. A four year old running full tilt into the yawning front window of the living room. Julie had left it open on a warm summer day. It was a low window, and it jutted out into his path, an unexpected barrier, as he triked himself around the small square of garden. He remembered that long panicky second of awareness, and the instant knowledge that something bad was going to happen. Then a black fist of darkness. He was out for more than an hour. Bat had told him, years later, how Julie had wailed hysterically, waiting for the ambulance.

A nurse approached him. A heavy, bespectacled woman, but treading lightly. She spoke softly, tiredness in her voice.

'Do you want a cup of tea, love? There's a machine round there.'

She pointed to the end of the corridor.

He saw the glint of her band of gold, solid and safe on her pudgy finger. Her declaration, her badge of belonging. She patted his shoulder, in a practical, motherly way. He did not know whether to recoil or give her a hug. He was confused, unable to take refuge in his usual anger. There hadn't been a 'turn' for a while now and part of him missed the feeling.

Mark almost managed to smile at the nurse as he got up. Like the hospital, the drinks machine was almost on stop. For his money he received a scalding squirt of lightly browned water, which he did not bother to take. As he went back to his seat he passed the open door of the nurses' room. The fat one was talking to a younger nurse. Pretty and not long in the job, he thought. Her figure showed no sign of lifting, fetching, carrying. It was still optimistic. He thought the old nurse-mother would see him tea-less and offer to make him a cup but she said nothing as he glanced in.

He sat again. Another man was being whisked through the waiting room, the nurse at his side trying to calm his hectic questioning chatter. A daddy present and accounted for. This was all such a long way from the forest.

Dawn came. Seeping in through the high windows. Its natural grey light competing with man-made yellow until it gained the upper hand. The day shift arrived and the place busied as the noise and clutter of breakfast began. Mark could not believe how early they had it. His gut rumbled, and he remembered the small shop in the hospital foyer.

'Won't be open 'til nine, love,' a passing nurse told him.

He tried to think of this as a long job, a nicking expedition, and fought down his hunger. Laughed off the need to sleep by swilling his face in a washroom. A spot had appeared at the side of his nose. He squashed it and again saw Daniels. This time staring at him from the mirror. His smiling, crying, zit-shining face. The dead were harder to get rid of than he thought.

A nurse was waiting for him when he came out. More real than the night staff.

'Mark Richards? Your mother's had the baby.'

He stared at her blankly, suddenly feeling there was bad news.

'Everything's fine,' the nurse said. 'But she's very tired. You've got an eight pound baby brother – Shane.'

He winced at the name.

'Amazing for a woman your mother's size,' the nurse continued. 'You can see her in a bit. But only for a few minutes.'

A few minutes would be long enough.

She took in Mark's reddened eyes and pale face, and the bloody smear of the spot.

'Been here all night, have you? Why don't you get yourself a cup of tea. There's a machine down there.'

This time he tried the coffee. It was hot, and smelt like coffee. Now the corridors were jumping with people. White coats, blue coats, brown coats, cleaners, porters. The contrast to the quiet night was striking. Mark was glad he had waited through a night, rather than a day. A gaping, full-of-people day. He steeled himself to the shit coffee, downed it, and went to see his mother.

Julie was propped up in bed, fat pillows looking more wholesome than her. Despite its shortness her hair was matted by hours of sweaty struggle, her face yellow-pale with tiredness, but the pain was gone from her eyes. She held a blanket-wrapped bundle in her arms. Mark stood frozen in the doorway. Inside was an alien world. Julie beckoned to him to come in. He felt like he was looking in on his own past. His own start. And he felt helpless. Powerless to help his mother any more than she had been able to help him. A nurse pushed past him into the room, making it easier for him to move. Julie motioned to the edge of the bed.

'Sit down,' she said. 'Come and look at him. Little Shane.'

He hated the nurse being there. The openness of it all. She attended to something and left, beaming him a smile. Hesitantly, he approached the bed, and the baby in his mother's arms. A pink-red screwed up face smaller than his fist in a nest of blankets. He could see nothing else. Shane looked up at him calmly, the barely blinking eyes too large for its face, he thought. A sprig of black hair on top. He had expected it to be bawling.

'Shane,' Julie murmured proudly. 'I always loved the name, ever since I seen the film. In he great? Bloody perfect. Just like you was.' She freed one of the baby's hands. Immediately it began to look for something to hold, the hand opening and closing instinctively. 'Look how tiny he is. Tiny and bloody perfect. Hard to think he'll grow up to be your size. Bigger, maybe.'

Mark thought of the runtish Humphries and doubted it. His own father must have been tall.

'Want to hold your baby brother?' Julie asked.

He was surprised she'd trust him, but Julie was high on emotion. On her triumph. All that counted, for a while, was having had the baby.

'No, better not,' Mark said.

The thought unnerved him. He did not like the steadiness of the baby's stare. As if it knew all about him. As if it was claiming its place in the family.

'Quiet, innit?' Mark said.

84

'Don't call him "it", love. He's Shane. Shane Lee Richards.'

'What happens now?'

'I'll be in for a few days. Then home. I got everything ready. Shane'll be alright in with me for a few years, then we'll have to see about swapping for a three bedroom.'

She thought he would be staying. The nurse came back in.

'Your mam has to rest,' she said 'She's had a hard time. Come back early in the evening, if you want.'

Mark did not want, but could not deny Julie's pleading eyes. She gave him a list of things she needed. Again he felt husband, father, provider.

The baby sniffed and gurgled, clenching and unclenching its hands. Instinctively, Mark prodded a finger at one and it curled around it. He felt Shane's hold on him.

Bat came round as soon as he got home. Bombarding him with questions about the baby. Acting as if she had always liked him, as if years of animosity could be swept under the carpet by the birth. Mark still despised her, all the more for having changed, but he was too tired to be rude. He had nodded off on the bus up, waking with a start as it clanked through gears on the estate hill. He answered Bat's questions briefly.

'Shane. It's a lovely name,' Bat said. 'I bet he'll be a right little cowboy.'

Mark edged her out of the house, voicing his need for sleep. And he did sleep. Soundly on the sofa, his long legs hanging over the end. Knocking roused him five hours later. It was Emma.

'I come down before,' she said, 'but I couldn't get an answer. The old girl next door told me about it.'

Bat had spouted off, but he knew that Emma would demand more. They all dived head-first into this baby club. Excited and sticking together like glue. Emma wanted to wring each moment of the experience from him.

'Christ, you look knackered.'

'I been up all night. Down that poxy place.'

Emma wanted to touch him but he pushed off her hands and turned to the window. Scanning the hills with aching eyes, as though the night at the hospital had deprived him of them.

'Look,' he said, 'I gotta get some air.'

He remembered Julie's list.

'Here. Sort this lot out, if you wanna help. Have this tenner.'

As an afterthought he added another note. This was an expensive time. Money was flowing from the tins and not being replenished.

'When you coming back?' Emma asked.

'Meet me at the bus stop at six,' he said.

'You mean I can come? Come to the hospital with you?'

Emma hugged him before he had a chance to step back. Her eyes shone, and Mark could read the transparent workings of her mind. Julie-baby, Mark-Emma-baby. All living happily ever after. That would be the day.

'Thanks, love,' Emma said, 'I can't wait to see little Shane.'

He stood on the doorstep and watched her flit away. Excited, happy, her figure at its turn-on best. Her jeans another skin for her arse. Dreaming of some future for them both. Fooling herself, and being fooled by him. Without him even trying. It was enough he was there.

He went upstairs, washed quickly, and was on the hillside in twenty minutes. Sat on one of his stone slabs looking down at the valley. This was more like it. Space to breathe. No people, no noise apart from the faint drone of the valley road. He lay back and breathed deeply, sucking in his escape. A jet made its way across the valley, fuselage flashing silver. It seemed to exist in its own time and space. Free. He did not want to think it was controlled by someone. It passed overhead noiselessly, slipstream fanning out like a feather.

Mark lay against the stone, face warmed by the intermittent sun. The stone was also warm. The pigeons flew over. Their weekend workout. They dipped a collective wing at him. He slept, and did not wake until the sun was resting on the far hillside. It was some time past six o'clock.

Emma stood at the bus stop with the bag, the realisation that Mark was not going to show slowly dawning on her. She pursed her rosebud mouth and tasted her wine red lipstick. It would be no use going to his house. He wouldn't be there. She looked across to the hills and cursed him. He thought more of them than anybody, she knew. Mark was strange with people. With her. With his mother. As if he didn't belong, or was part of another race. The Psycho Eyes People. She shuddered at the thought of a world of Marks. Each one as cold and cruel as the next. Yet even this thought turned her on. Anything about him did.

She was not too upset. Without Mark she could be herself when she saw Shane for the first time. The baby made her feel more sure of her position. Mark would have to stay now. Even he wouldn't leave his mother alone with a baby. Any doubts she had were evaporated by the sun. It had been shining all day. A warm, hopeful day, when even the estate did not look so knackered.

Julie was disappointed by Mark's absence, but not surprised.

'He stayed all night,' Julie said, 'he's probably had a gutsful.'

'Probably,' Emma agreed. 'He went walking. Him and his bloody forestry.'

'Say no more, then. That boy is a right wanderer.'

Emma stood by Julie's bed, suddenly shy. Julie looked as if she had been through a wringer. Her pinched face did not seem much bigger than the baby's. Small, creased, not much hope in her eyes. Emma felt too made-up. Too young. She smelt her liberal appliance of the expensive perfume she had stolen a few months ago. It was out of place.

'Sit down,' Julie said.

'I got your stuff,' Emma said, offering the bag.

'At least he didn't forget that.' Julie rummaged through it as Shane slept at her side. 'Good. He got the fags. I've been gagging for one. You have to have a drag in the toilet here.'

Emma smiled. She wanted to hold Shane. To snatch him up and hug him. To imagine him hers and Mark's, the seal on their future together. She could not believe anything so perfect could have been made by a prat like Wayne Humphries.

'You can hold him if you like,' Julie said.

'He might wake up.'

'Go on. It's okay.'

She felt Julie's need to share, and gingerly picked Shane up. He did not stir. His lids remained closed and his face peaceful. There was no trouble in it. Yet.

'Suits you,' Julie murmured.

Emma blushed.

'I wan' lots and lots of kids,' she said. She could not resist giving Shane a kiss. For one mad moment she imagined herself running out with him. Keeping this image of peace and safety for herself.

Julie guessed what was going through Emma's mind. This one was easy to work out. To reach. To share something with. Nothing like Mark. With him she was always chipping away at a hard surface, being rebuffed, teased or just ignored. Very occasionally getting through to something warmer.

Emma put Shane down.

'Was Mark like this?' she asked.

'More or less. Hard to believe, innit?'

Emma played with the rings on her fingers, her shyness lessening.

'I never thought he'd get caught,' she said, and bit her lip immediately. She was not sure how much Julie knew.

'He got too cocky,' Julie said. 'I think he's learned his lesson.' And pigs might fly, she told herself. But she did not want to talk against Mark. Though now she had another child she wanted his help and needed his support. Emma might be a useful ally. She watched her study Shane. Wide-eyed and innocent-young. Life on the estate had not yet crushed that out of her.

'What'll happen to him?' Emma asked.

'Won't be long before it goes to court now. He'll get a fine probably, for first offence. Community service maybe, the solicitor said. Christ, that'll crease him, Mark helping anybody.'

Secretly, Julie hoped he would get community service. He would hate it, but that might not be a bad thing. Take some of the arrogance out of him, perhaps show him another way.

Emma stayed for an hour, until Julie got tired.

'Want me to come down tomorrow?' Emma said.

'If you like. See if you can bring Psycho Eyes with you.'

Emma laughed nervously, surprised that Julie knew Mark's nickname. And that she didn't seem to mind.

'Post this for me on your way home,' Julie said, handing Emma an envelope. It was a note to her parents, informing them of Shane's birth. She could not run to a letter. They'd respond with a card but they wouldn't visit. Maybe her mother would show up at the house in a few weeks, nervous, and anxious to be gone before she set foot in the place. Her life had become one long embarrassment to her parents, distancing them. She would have liked Shane to have one set of grandparents, at least. As Emma left, Julie lay back, stroking Shane. Gently sifting the strands of his hair with her hand. All the love she had left to give in her touch.

Mark did not hurry back from the mountain. He enjoyed the end of the day, pleased by the convenience of his sleep. After the bustling hospital he was comforted. Even the familiar, wasted closeness of the estate as he re-entered it was alright. For him its dereliction had always been there. Smashed houses, chaotic lay-out, shitty streets had always been his environment. So why should he give a fuck? What was the point? The estate could be cleansed away any time by the forestry and the hillsides. And blown away completely by the grandeur of his future plans.

He stopped off in the club to phone the hospital. There was a public phone in the entrance, the only phone on the estate that could be relied on to work. Opposite it an old man who passed as a steward dozed in a glass booth. Fat, droopy moustache, droopy eyes, droopy brain. A glass of ageing bitter in his hand. As flat as the old geezer's life. He was one of the few really old men on the estate. Most were young or middle aged. The new crop.

A harassed nurse on his mother's ward took the call. He kept it short. 'Tell her I couldn't make it,' he said. 'I'll come down tomorrow.' He hoped he could get away with just one more visit. Mark stayed in the club for a while. He could get served now. He stood at the long, empty bar and drank two pints of subsidised lager. For him it tasted better out of cans. He missed the cold of the metal on his lips and doubted if he would ever have much time for pubs. Unless he owned one someday, and could watch people spend in it. He glanced at a paper lying on the bar. Two estate tossers had been jailed, for running amok with a shotgun and machete. He remembered the incident from last winter. It had amused him. Showed some people still had imagination.

He was slightly pissed when he got home. It was strange for the house to be empty. Soon Julie would be bringing extra noise to the place. He looked in on her room, where a second-hand cot lay waiting. Expectant. Demanding. He shut the door firmly and went to his own bedroom, tapping a hello to the tins with his boot. The sky was on fire. Crimson soaked the hills. He sat and watched until it grew dark, smoking and playing something unusually quiet on the hi-fi. Knowing that change was coming and there was nothing he could do about it.

Julie came home at midday on Monday. As Mark paid for the taxi, he made a mental note to get back to business as soon as things settled. Emma was with them. Anxious to help. To join the

Richards family. As they travelled from the hospital, Shane asleep in his mother's arms, Mark thought through possibilities. Use everything, The Man had once told him. Shane might be useful. With him being watched now, having a sprog around could be handy. A handy cover, and a steady girlfriend with no record to go with it. Signs that he had 'changed'. To show that he had gone off the rails just the once. Not over a hundred times.

Mark planned to do a job just before he went to court. It would be a good way to get his retaliation in first. Of fucking Beefy and the other pigs. A matter of pride. And nerve. Proof that years of work and learning had not been wasted. He had already phoned The Man to confirm his return, and had tooled up again. Very secretively. Going down the valley and beyond to get stuff, and leaving it at his old stash point in the forestry. It would not come near the house.

He left Julie and Emma to their baby club and went off to scout. A pair of semis on the far side of the golf club. Showy places that looked out of place against that bleak part of the mountain. It would be a pleasure doing them. Emma had said goodbye, shutting the kitchen door as if it was her house. It would be if he gave her half a chance. Bat bustled past him in the garden. Eager to see Shane.

As he passed the shrine he breathed in deeply and touched the white stone with his hand. So often the woman had pointed the way to another job. He stopped for a moment to see if the stone child was anything like Shane. He was bloody quieter, that was for sure. Before long the roofs of his targets glinted invitingly. The game was about to start again, and he felt good.

Mark's solicitor sat in the living room. Robert Thomas Maule. Too much name for a wanker, Mark thought. He enjoyed the man's discomfort. The way his eyes flitted around the room, as though the furniture might attack him, or bugs might leap on him from the carpet. Shane bawled in the kitchen, fussed over by Julie. It was three days before the court case.

'We got no money to pay a fine,' Mark said. 'Specially with little Shane here now.'

'Quite,' Maule said, pushing back a stray strand of hair. One that had escaped from its binding gel. With his black, swept-back hair and fidgety unseeing eyes he *was* a mole, Mark thought.

'So it will almost certainly be community service,' Maule

continued. 'Once the Panel has decided on a court appearance it is always on the cards.'

'How long?' Mark asked.

'A hundred and fifty hours is the usual, for cases like yours.'

Mark tried to look eager. Pleased. Good practice for the big appearance.

'It'll mean you'll have a criminal record,' Maule said, 'but if you keep your nose clean in future that will fade. Your age will be in your favour. Of course, the magistrate will be aware of police suspicions. That you did seem very well equipped for your first job.'

Mark shrugged.

'It was a one-off. You know that.'

There was a silence. Maule's face was blank, his sea-green eyes non-committal. Mark met his stare with complete confidence.

Julie joined them. Carrying a red-faced, grumpy Shane.

'He's a bit under the weather today,' she said.

Maule stood up and clipped his case shut. He thought of touching Shane, then thought again.

It was court time, Mark squirming in shirt and tie. The tie pressing around his neck like tiny hands. It was the first time he had ever worn one outside of school. Not even Daniels' funeral had made him do it. His neck itched under his shirt collar and his face beaded with sweat. It made him conform. Outwardly. It was a warm day and there was plenty of glass in the court building to catch the sun. It was new, its stone façade not yet blasted by pollution. There was a fancy council crest outside, and other designs which shouted out its importance. Begged for it.

'This place must have cost millions,' Julie muttered as they entered. 'There's always money for stuff like this.'

'There's always plenty of customers, Mam.'

By ten the reception area was already steaming, and filling with the odour of its congregation. Mark walked around, trying to keep his hands out of his pockets. His mind thinking. Churning. Julie sat on a chair against the wall, in demure outfit and restrained make-up. Maule fussed around them. Checking his papers, his hair and his tie with his podgy, busy hands.

Mark's name was called out. Mark Dean Richards. He'd almost forgotten his middle name. There was no need for it. They were only thirty minutes behind their appointed time. Maule said this was very good. Mark walked in behind the solicitor, ignoring the reaching hand of Julie. Emma was looking after Shane. The women thought they were almost a family of four now. Emma using the court case as a way to get her foot in the door. Mark using her as cover. And everyone using Shane.

They sat where Maule pointed and Mark took in the scene. Various suits fiddling about, a few pigs – he recognised the detective who had interviewed him – and the magistrates. Two men and a woman. The woman in the middle and sitting higher. Boss lady. Grey old dogs either side of her, looking as if they should have been put down long ago. One had small, square-cut gold-framed glasses which sat on his nose. Made him look simple. Mark fought down a smile as he wondered if he had done any of these.

It did not take more than twenty minutes and Mark did not get much involved. He cut himself off, fed off an instinctive hatred for everything these tossers represented. Their rules, laws, conventions, wants, needs, were all shit to him. But he could still act. He said his piece. He had rehearsed it until it was a polished jewel of lies. Stuck to it in the face of questioning. Enjoying the irritation on the detective's face. He looked ashamed at the right time. When he spoke Mark put a falter in his voice at planned places, looking mainly at the polished new wood of the floor, but occasionally raising his head and looking directly into the woman's face. She wore a nice necklace, he noticed. Real pearls.

It went as Maule had predicted. One hundred and fifty hours community service and a long, boring warning from the old girl. Something she had said a thousand times before. Maule looked pleased, as if he had done something. Dick. Julie was also pleased. Her face shone with relief as they shuffled out of court, their places taken by the next punter. A druggie Mark recognised. They exchanged knowing glances. He wanted to identify with Mark. To be a comrade. A brother in the struggle to tell the world to fuck off. Mark ignored him. He was pleased with his performance but pissed off at the thought of painting walls and the like.

Maule was thrusting a hand in his. Moist and pink. He felt the man's cuff links rub against him.

'We couldn't have expected anything better,' Maule said, 'but, considering the gravity of the charge, it might have been a lot worse. We can be well pleased, I think.'

'I am,' Julie said. 'Well pleased.'

'What happens now?' Mark asked.

'The community service people will be in touch. As the magistrate said, you must attend regularly, or they'll bring you back to court. It would mean a young offenders' place then.'

'He'll attend,' Julie said, more in hope than determination. 'Won' you, Mark?'

'Course, Mam.'

They walked out into the sunshine, Maule leaving them on the steps of the building. Mark allowed Julie a quick peck.

'Jesus Christ, I'm glad that's all over,' she said.

Mark dug her gently in the ribs.

'Was I good, Mam?' he said.

'You're an awful young sod,' she said. 'Come on, let's get out of here.'

They stood at the bus stop and smoked, each looking up to the estate.

Emma was waiting for them on the doorstep when they got home. She wore a postage stamp skirt the same colour as her lipstick, and her legs had browned up in the fair summer.

'How's Shane been?' Julie asked.

'Good as gold. He's really cute. I love him to bits.'

Mark went to the fridge and took out three cans. Rubbing one against his brow.

'Aye. Les' have a drink,' Julie said. 'I need one. Mark got away with it.'

'With what? I was done for one job. My one job. Don' no-one forget that.'

There was a moment of silent conspiracy then three cans pinged open. Shane slept in his pram, rocked gently by Julie. Angelic face nestled in blankets, plastic rattle in one hand. Mark wondered how his brother would be when he was sixteen. He felt a faint stirring of envy. Shane would have two people to know.

Mark felt the long first chapter of his life closing. His brush with the law was his coming of age. He had been noticed by the system. Noticed and logged. His crime lying forever in computer land. Able to be called up in a moment. He was proud and pissed at the same time. He was one down but it was just starting.

TWO

Late September. Mark's favourite time. The green hillsides shot through with brown. Everything heavy. Wilting, dropping, dying. And the nights shortening, bringing with them welcoming, enveloping dark. It was his first week of community service. Painting the outside walls of a welfare hall. Long bastards. He wore overalls and white-spattered shades to fight the glare. The sun had gone ape since he started the job. From the first day it had bounced off the wall into his face. He went home with a head like a bucket and a blazing anger which he used up on Emma.

Community service had one immediate benefit. While he was doing this the tossers down the dole would stay off his back. Signing on was like a continuation of school. Just as useless. Going to the same nowhere. Lots of talk by people paid to talk. About courses, schemes, qualifications, work experience. All a crock of shit. Shuffling the lads of the estate like a pack of cards. Losers' cards. There was no real work. His first time down there, while he waited for what they called an 'interview' he had tried to think of one boy from his year who had got anything. And couldn't. Most were where he was. A few pushed brushes somewhere, their 'experience', others had gone back to school. Cold turkeys. Some had got in trouble, like himself. The smart ones, who knew this was the only way out. Nicking. If they were useless and blew it what the fuck. They were no worse off. Unemployable before and after.

Once they knew about his record they stopped hassling him. 'Better serve that out first,' some tosser told him, 'then we'll see about getting you on a placement scheme.' Mark thought about doing the dole office. Computers were all the rage now. But they were not neat enough to get away, and too big to store safely. If he had not been known he'd have taken one for himself. Might be useful for the future. He was not interested in the stuff, not even the games but did not want to get left behind. 'Be open to everything,' The Man had once told him. 'Take everything going.'

Mark adjusted to the painting. Working a roller over a wall, a brush into smaller places, had a rhythm of its own and he went with it. His anger of the first morning was over. That was stupid, a waste of time. This had to be done. It was nothing to do with the pigs. This was not their price, or that smug old cow with the pearls. It was his. For being so stupid. This work allowed his mind to roam free. That would always be out of their reach. Of everyone's.

The tosser in charge of the service liked the sound of his own voice. Even if it was squeaky and ineffective. Mark commandeered the painting job. None of the others could remotely challenge him, and he was left alone to paint. The second day he brought his Walkman in. No-one told him to take it off.

It was a three way street for his brain. Raucous, private music, soft mechanical work and a free rein for his thoughts, which lurched everywhere. He'd do thirty five hours in the first week. More than a fifth of his sentence. It was a piece of piss, and would be over before the first frost bit. And the job might be useful, a good cover for scouting, even if he was working amongst his own kind. The poor.

A woman about Julie's age began to bring him tea. Her house overlooked the Welfare Hall, part of an estate that was a smaller version of Mark's. The same problems, the same people, but shrunk down, nutters and nickers thinner on the ground. This woman fancied him. Each day she tried to look smarter. A bit more make-up, a bit more fuss with her clothes. She probably thought he was older than he was so he told her he was twenty. She appeared on Friday afternoon, at clocking off time, and asked him over to her house.

It was like Emma's place. Bright-coloured crap. Evidence of young kids. She told him she had two under six, and a vanished husband. Offering him a smoke and coffee she said her name was Brenda, which sounded like something from another age to him. He said his name was Dean. Brenda was a blonde. A real blonde. Her hair a dirtyish yellow, cut short. With her blue eyes and holding-on figure he guessed she had been a puller in her time. She wanted to pull now.

'My mother's got the kids today,' Brenda said. 'She has them every Friday. Likes to spoil them.'

Mark nodded and smoked. He had never felt so cool but he wasn't sure what he was doing here. Breaking a pattern maybe. He'd been going home the same time every day with Walkman and sandwich box. With Julie and Shane and Emma there to meet him as often as not. It was a routine, his first, and it made him feel like a provider. And for him that was a trap.

He could almost smell Brenda's eagerness. Her excitement at having got him into her house. The day before he had stripped off to the waist when the white wall joined forces with the sun. Her eyes had drilled him and he had enjoyed it. Enjoyed what was going on. That she was hanging it on a line for him.

'You got a girlfriend?' Brenda asked. 'Yeah, you must have, good looking fella like you.'

They were sitting at a small round table in the kitchen. Plastic coming away from its edge.

'Want another cup?' Brenda asked, getting up from the table.

It was an excuse for her to circle around it. She had crammed herself into jeans. Mark thought that if he'd pop the top button everything would come flowing out. He touched her as she brushed past him.

'No more coffee,' he said.

The touch was light, and nowhere important, but it was the signal she needed. She was all over him in seconds despite the twenty years between them. He let her half-drag him upstairs and they did it in her double bed.

Brenda was energetic but Mark was detached, he moved out of himself and view what was going on from a distance. As Brenda squirmed and sighed and wailed and screwed on top of him his eyes fixed on the window. It was a small window with a small view, the slanting roofs of the houses opposite, and above these a blue and white patch of sky.

He lay there. It was all Brenda required. For him to be there and function, which he managed. He did not have to bullshit her. She did this to herself, letting her dreams wash over him. Brenda's body rippled over his and she began a series of small screams, working at his chest with her mouth.

After, he sat up in the bed and smoked, Brenda wrapped around him, almost burrowing into him. There was a photograph of her and her husband on the dresser, in a heart-shaped gold-effect metal frame. It had been taken some time ago, before the kids came and he went, but Mark knew why she kept it. The photograph drove him out.

'I gotta go now,' Mark said. 'Got things to do.'

'Stay a bit longer. I could do you some food. The kids won't be back 'til seven.'

'Nah. I got a lot on.'

He dressed quickly. He had only boots, jeans and T-shirt to put on.

'When will I see you again?' Brenda asked.

He barely glanced at her as she propped herself up in the bed with her elbows, breasts large and flat.

'I'll give you a ring,' he muttered, and was gone before she could tell him she didn't have a phone.

Mark walked up to the estate, having missed the Community Service van. He felt strange, unsure of the past hour. Brenda had been there and that was about it. As Emma was there. Forced presences. He could not imagine himself looking for a woman. So far it had not been necessary. Yet he wondered at his difference. Around him lads not much older were getting engaged. Hitching onto the system. They seemed to have an inbuilt need to start another family, even if their own had been blown apart. Perhaps that was why.

He stopped at the shrine for a smoke. The sun was still strong and highlighted the statue's outline, making the stone glossy. He was not sure whether he hated the thing or not, but it had always been there, to see him off on a job, to welcome him back. Constant.

He sat at its base, stretching out his long legs and enjoying the smoke. Brenda would be doing the same, still in bed, and wondering if he'd come back. Psyching herself to come back down to reality and deal with the kids. He had been careful, as he always was with Emma. Not that she minded. A baby would be fine by her. She'd think she'd got him then. Despite the examples all around her. The Julies and Brendas who lived in every other house on the estate. Her own mother. They always thought it would be different for them. That they had latched on to any man who was not a useless wanker. All chasing down blind alleys for bits of comfort. Clinging to the rare long-term. Bits of dream. Mark had no doubt he'd do a runner if ever Emma did catch. As his own father had, and now Humphries. It was tradition.

Mark lived in a place of women and kids, whilst the men shuffled around from one estate to another, leaving kids scattered in their wake. He could identify with the fathers but judge them at the same time. He saw no conflict in it.

He smoked the cigarette down to its cork tip. He liked to feel its heat on his fingers, and the smoke sear his eyes. A yellow haze was settling in the valley below, terraced rows drifting in and out of sight. Their roofs reflected back a thousand diamond glints, like sun on a grey sea. The estate was in a desirable spot, if you ignored the weather. They'd love to knock it down and build ponce boxes on it. Just right for the golf club. Perhaps the estate was having the last laugh. Plonked smack dab in the middle of fine landscape like a scab. Crapping it up with its people.

He picked at the paint on his hands, under his nails. He had been given an insight into what low-paid work would mean. The biggest fucking trap of all, what the school used as a threat to get them going. Working outside on the wall he was able to connect with the hillside and the forestry. Check out his world. Tell it he'd be back soon. But next week he was working inside. Why did people stomach it? Because they had to, that's why. Steel shutters snapping shut.

Emma's face replaced Brenda in his thoughts. He imagined the look on it if she ever found out about his toyboy hour. Emma had got into the Tec with her two GCSEs. Bubbling with excitement when she had told him earlier in the summer. Thinking she was going somewhere, and taking him with her maybe. She was already practising on Julie's hair. They had sessions in the kitchen, Julie as daft as Emma as they squealed and giggled. He stayed well out of it, and his hair likewise. Sometimes he'd sit out the back with Shane. He didn't mind him when he was quiet. He'd rock the pram back and forth with his foot as he sprawled on an old blanket, protection from the lumpy garden. Working his way through a few cans and getting brown for the first time. Shane sucking fingers, gurgling, sleeping, protected from the sun by his shade. If Shane was his he'd feel panic, the need to run, but Julie dealt with his mess, and the responsibility. He could just chill out with his brother. For now.

Working inside was not so cool for Mark. He stood on the planked surface of a scaffold, working a long-handled roller onto the ceiling of the Welfare Hall. Turning tobacco-yellow into fresh green. Someone had worked out that white was not a good idea. No matter how careful he was paint flicked back into his face. He felt it in his hair, on his eyebrows. His back ached, a tug deep down his spine that tickled him with pain whenever he loaded the roller. His arms were tired.

By midday he was seriously pissed off. He sat in a corner in his Walkman world, nodding to Stiff Little Fingers, and cursing Emma's sandwiches. She had taken over from Julie, but was just as useless. Cheese or ham. But he was not going to make anything for himself, or buy anything. Brenda did not show up with any tea. She knew. She'd had the weekend to get real.

He was surrounded by age. The main hall was soaked in it. Wooden walls worn to a burnt orange, hung with various plaques and shields. Their gold-leafed words tarnished and flaking. This was a place out of the book he had stolen. It smelled secure and safe but that was false. He was painting a shell, a symbol of a world of work and complete families. It had all been blown away. Mark knew this much. The evidence was all around him. He was part of it.

He took a cigarette from his spattered packet. Tosser, the foreman, stood in the entrance and whined at him.

'Oi, you can't smoke in here, dozy young sod. You're surrounded by open paint cans. Shouldn't be smoking anyway.'

Mark did not react, which made Tosser's face glow redder. He thought of ripping Mark's phones from his ears, but Mark stopped him with a glare. He smiled, and made a display of crushing the cigarette in his hands, making a ball out of the loose tobacco and flicking it away.

'Get back on it,' Tosser said. 'You've had your break.'

Mark climbed back up to his work place and looked at the unpainted half of ceiling. A mocking bastard dome of cracked and peeling once-white emulsion. Like a large egg above him. He saw Beefy's face there and slapped the roller at it. He had been seeing a lot of faces lately and was having trouble sleeping at night. Having trouble adjusting to the change in the household. And having dreams. Bad fuckers. Daniels was always in them. He had been able to block him out in day to day thoughts but the little bugger got him at night. Just as hanging-on in death as he was alive.

One nightmare became constant. The time they used to go scrambling over the old mine workings. Not much older than ten. The colliery site adjacent to the estate had been demolished and landscaped but it had been a crap job. Only a scrubby yellow grass ever seemed to grow. Bits and pieces were left, if you knew where to look. They found an opening once as they clambered over the barren remains. It was not much bigger than a rabbit hole but Mark had messed about and threatened to squash Daniels down it. Getting Daniels' head in an armlock. Terrifying his friend – which had never been hard to do. Feeling him go limp in his arms. Like a rabbit.

'Bogeymen down there,' Mark said, 'ghosts of all them miners.'

When he got free, Daniels had backed away and had been chased all the way home, Mark whooping and shouting after him. He had enjoyed his timid friend's tears and was unable to stay his actions, even though something in his ten-year-old head told him it was wrong.

The dream changed all this. Turned the table on Mark. Made him the victim. Daniels' face shooting out of that black hole to smother his. Swirling around it like smoke, entering his eyes, his nose, everywhere. Twice he woke up in a sweat, hands gripping the sheets. The second time Daniels drove him out of bed. He sat in the window, smoking and looking out at the moonlit hillside.

Now he was thinking about it in the day. Stupid sod. He shook his head and specks of paint flew from it. Grasping the roller firmly he attacked the ceiling, painting out Daniels' face. Ghosts would not win with him.

Community Service came and went quickly. A blip. Mark did not miss a day and Tosser had to give him a good report. He was a first time offender who had learned his lesson. Once out of the hands of the system he began planning for new business immediately. Phoning The Man and arranging to meet in the usual place. For the first time Mark was invited to sit in the front seat of a new Merc. Enveloped by leather. Sinking into it, as if it was a large purse and he was money.

'Much better motor that the BMW,' The Man said. 'I'll drive around for a bit. Don't want to be seen here, not now the pigs have made you.'

Mark winced and felt his failure.

They purred around the valley. Mark knew the nigger was showing off for him, parading his success, but it did not bother him. He was still a nigger. Viewed from inside the Mercedes his world seemed different. Smaller. He was able to see it with new eyes. Mercedes eyes. And he saw a sad nothing.

The Man stopped on a hill looking onto the down-curve of the valley. Lights were coming on to prick the dusk. At the touch of a button a window slid down and Mark felt like he was being shown his past on a TV-sized screen. Inside the car was his future.

'Thing is,' The Man said, 'you got not to be greedy. Not at first.'

He stretched back in his seat, flashing his rings.

'We done good business together for two years,' he said, 'but you're still young. How old you now?'

'Sixteen.'

'Fuck me. You done good. But you also been done. I wasn't 'til I was nineteen. And even then I was set up. Pigs can't usually do nothing theirselves. I learnt to be cool. Don' rush in. Don' trust.'

'I don't,' Mark said.

The Man grinned.

'Yeah, I noticed, that's why you're in this car. You learn quick. Same with me, down the docks. When they sees me down there now, back for a visit, sees the car and the gear I wear, they knows I'm The Man.'

The Man scanned the valley, its contours sinking quickly into night.

'You must be bustin' a gut to get out of this place,' he said. 'See this.' He waved a ringed finger in front of Mark's nose. It caught the glow of street lights and added silver fire to orange light, its cluster of stones flashing into life. 'The old man would have had to work a lifetime to pay for this. Not that I knows who he was anyway.'

Mark laughed with The Man, forgetting his colour in a moment of identity.

'You gotta keep on doing what you're doing,' The Man continued. 'You don' know shit about cars, so there's only dope left. An' you have to deal with the dregs then. Strung-out arseholes who could jump any way. Not nice people like me.'

'I don' feel the same about doing houses no-more,' Mark muttered.

'Feeling stale, eh? That's just a bit of feedback after the pigs. You got caught so don' get fuckin' caught again. If we're still doing business in a few years maybe I'll suggest something else for you.'

Mark knew this was bullshit. The Man wanted to keep him sweet and steady. A reliable source of goods. But the advice was still cool.

This was how the next year went. Steady business. Steady nicking. A stream of houses done, and the occasional business for an extra challenge. There were a few scares but no-one came close to catching him again. Dreams still troubled him and there were times when he felt his old black rage gnaw away deep inside, inviting him to jump right in and have fun, but he fought it off. And Daniels faded. His snotty face became less clear with each passing month. When Mark turned seventeen his friend no longer appeared out of holes in the ground.

Things settled. With Shane around Julie seemed to lose interest in men. She was too knackered, even though the kid was no trouble at first. Sleeping, crapping and crying was his day. But Mark hated the new female presence in the house. Emma was around too often and a string of women off the estate dropped in to see Shane.

Julie sat with Mark in the kitchen. It was coming up to Shane's first birthday. A rare fine day in what had been a sodden summer. Spring slinking in after winter and now summer and all three wet.

'I was gutted at first,' Julie said, as she shared Mark's can. 'Didn't think I could ever cope with it again. But it's been alright. The first year anyhow. Shane gives me something to do, and I got money off the social for another sixteen years. If you get a job we'll be quids in.'

'What about Humphries?' he asked.

'Forget him. I have. Shane Mark Richards is on your brother's birth certificate. I want no part of Humphries at all. No sign of him. Nothing from him. Which is just as well, for he was good for sod all.'

'I hear he's living down the bottom estate now,' Mark said, 'shacked up with another woman.'

Julie flinched slightly but her face did not alter.

'Aye, I heard that as well, down Bingo. Poor cow. He'll probably get her up the stick as well.'

Mark knew that she hadn't heard, but was glad she was able to shake the tosser off.

'Why'd you wanna call him Mark?' he asked.

'Well, it's only his middle name. I wanted you to be part of him. Christ, it only seems like yesterday you was like him.'

She gestured to Shane, asleep in his buggy, waiting to be collected by Emma for a turn around the estate. Mark flexed his muscles, stretching out in his black vest.

'Up to fourteen stone now, Mam, and six foot one and three quarters. Shane'll never be that big, if you think of Humphries.'

'Aye, he was a bit of a runt. I don' know what I was up to there.'

She reached out a hand for Mark's but he pulled away. Force of habit. He gave her the can instead.

'You hate being touched, don' you?' Julie said. 'Your father was like that. Wanna know about him?'

Julie was feeling mellow.

Mark shrugged. 'What for? Bit late now anyway, innit?'

'You never asked nothing. Well, he was tall like you.'

'How old was I when he pissed off?'

'Three. The last time.'

Julie looked out to the garden.

'He used to throw you up into the air out there. I was always afraid he'd drop you, but he never did.'

Her watery blue eyes turned to Shane.

'Seems like last week,' she murmured.

Mark knew she was about to blub, to go into what-might-have-been mode.

'I don' wanna know anything else, Mam.'

His voice came out as a shout, which he had not intended. He softened it. 'Look, it's cool, right? It doesn't worry me.'

'But I feel so guilty sometimes, love.'

'Why? You didn't leave nobody. Nah, I'm better off. Don' think I'd want an old man like the tossers round here, do you?'

For once he let her catch his hand. Hers was moist, and trembling.

'What about you and Emma?' Julie said.

'What about us?'

'I never thought she'd last this long. She's bonkers about you. An' she's the best looking kid on the estate.'

Mark shrugged again.

'She'll be hairdressing next year. That's a tidy job.'

Talk of Emma irritated him, but he was surprised that he had let Emma hang around for this long too. He'd let it drift, with one eye on the pigs. They had checked him out for a few months after the court case, he'd sensed it, so having a steady girlfriend was a good move. He had kept his head down, as far as they were concerned. Putting up with the crap down the dole, and keeping away from the estate tossers. Nicking farther afield. Now he was sure he was out of the frame. They had too many others to look out for, dopehead crazies who'd do anything to get money for a fix, and were easy to catch.

Two days after his seventeenth birthday Mark took a major gamble. Each job was a risk, but this was different, something he'd thought about for a year, and planned for weeks. He wanted to do the old house where he had been surprised by its owner. The one with all the books. A deep-seated need outweighed his natural caution. That night had foretold of his capture, a warning that he was about to fail. Going back would be a way of releasing the hold that memory had on him. The man's face was fixed in his mind. Not nailed there, like the dead-eyed clock of Daniels, but persistent. A back-up floater for his nightmares. And it had been his first fight. His only fight. Despite his attitude, Mark's life as a teenager had been violence-free. His size and the figure he cut on had been enough. Since junior school he had always been the biggest in his group. Numero uno.

The thought of raiding that chocolate box collection of new houses again also had strong appeal, but it could never be on. It had to be the house of books. It was important that the place was done, and done properly. It would be proof that he wasn't going soft. For a year he'd been pulled into the Shane scene. Having to note every moment in his life: his hair, his first crawl, the appearance of the tooth that made him wail most of the night, Shane's row greeting him as he slipped in from a job. Each thing Julie celebrated. Happy families was acted out, Julie aided by Emma and whatever woman she brought back from bingo. He knew it was all nonsense. The shit had stopped flying and the fan turning for a while, that was all. Anything else was not real for the Richards. It might last until Shane got out and about or he left Julie to look after him on her own. Julie would get interested in men again.

Mark did not understand happy. It annoyed him, described things he had always looked into from the outside. Shut out. As much by his own character as by circumstance. Something channelled him down a different path and yet sometimes, when he watched Julie, Emma and Shane in their gurgling ensemble, a tiny part of him wanted to join in. To accept the small, instant pleasures which came their way. All that their lives offered them. Accept the estate. But he shook this off angrily and cursed himself. That sort of thinking was reason enough to go back to that house.

He was extra careful scouting it, making four trips to the adjacent hillside. He saw the man come and go several times. In an old estate car filled with boxes of files. No-one else seemed to be around. Some sort of pen pusher obviously. Perhaps a college geezer. He dressed like one. Green corduroys, joking jumper, too much hair. Wanker. Looked like something you'd pick off a tree in the forestry.

On two consecutive Fridays the man went out. On the third Mark went in. The same way as before. The house had not been alarmed. It seemed even bigger and there was a video and new telly. Good boy. Almost as if the git was making him an offering. I've been done so let's get a video in. He could scarcely believe it.

Mark was in no hurry. He scanned the books like before. Pulled out a few from their slots. This was his test. To sit here, looking at old photographs, like it was a library. Edgy but calm too. For fifteen minutes he scanned pages, the longest time he had ever been in a house. His ears pricked, senses on stalks. Enjoying the buzz. Then he went upstairs and looked around. More books and untidiness. No sign of a woman or kids, though on a bookcase there was a photo of the man with his arm around a woman. He was younger, and bearded, but Mark recognised him. That face had been thrust up against his own. The woman was overweight and dressed as crappily as the man. Yeah, this would be his piece, Mark thought. They looked right for each other, even if she wasn't around now. He turned the photograph to the wall and went back downstairs, where he bagged the video and a few books. Books might be dangerous to keep but he wanted something as a trophy of his return. His comeback.

He slipped out of the house. This time there was no challenge. Music came from next door and he heard the voices of women. Fighting down caution he stayed, sitting on the mountainside until the man returned. Watched him park his car and carry a box inside. The lights going on, then the back door flung open. And his victim appearing in the garden, thick set, hands on hip, scanning the back with his eyes. Looking directly up to Mark's spot but seeing nothing in the blackness. His were useless eyes, without power. The man went next door and the music cut off. This was his cue to leave. He'd take his time stashing the video. The pigs would have a hundred more recent suspects to consider. His crime would be lost in the crowd.

He walked up to the forestry, picking his way over uneven ground. A section of trees had been felled recently, leaving a knotty mess. In the moonlight logs seemed to glow white, weird, misshapen twists of wood which would have given Emma the shits. They comforted him. He left one book with the video, to look at

108

when he came back on Sunday. Every page turned would be a celebration.

Julie was up with Shane when he got back.

'Shss,' Julie said, 'I've just put him down. He's been bawling for hours with his teeth.' She scanned Mark up and down. 'Don' say nothing. I don' wanna know. Christ, if you get caught again.'

'What, caught going out for a walk?'

Julie saw the book.

'What you got there?'

'A computer. What does it look like?'

'I never seen you with a book before.'

'Well you have now. It's about the old days. Round here.'

'Christ, the new days are bad enough.'

Mark stood over Shane, who was sleeping on the sofa.

'Might as well get us a brew,' he said, 'as you're up.'

'Alright, but keep your voice down.' Julie rearranged the blankets around Shane. 'Don' he look nice. As if butter wouldn't melt in his mouth. Wouldn't think he had a pair of lungs from hell.'

'Was I a yeller?' Mark asked.

'No. You were so quiet I thought something was wrong with you. Got you checked by the doctors.'

'You never told me that.'

'I'd forgotten. Having Shane has brought back them days.'

She went to the kitchen. Mark sat down next to Shane and pressed a finger at his soft pink hand. Shane murmured but did not wake. He was helpless. It would be years before he'd fend for himself. Most animals were up and going in weeks. Mark saw Julie in that hospital bed, pissed off, afraid and excited. It had been a hard start for Shane and things would not get much easier unless Mark paid for it. He couldn't imagine the estate when Shane was sixteen. It had always seemed old, even though it had only been built twenty years ago. It had aged instantly and fallen apart almost as quick. All he could remember was things crumbling. He'd heard that they were already knocking down places like this and he wondered what happened to the people. Did they herd them somewhere else so they could shit it up all over again, or were they split up, to disappear quietly?

'Here's your tea,' Julie said. 'You haven't woken him up, have you?'

'Nah. He's spark out.'

'Is it safe, having that book in here?'

'It's nothing to worry about.'

'I need you here, Mark. With Shane now I –'

'Mam, don't start. They'll never get me again. Never.'

Julie's face registered doubt but she let the matter drop. She knew she could do nothing else. He'd clam up. Go sullen. Get nasty. Her eldest son had a range of devices to hide behind, and she had never been able to break down any of them. Her eldest son. The phrase sounded strange in her head. That she now had two of them. She turned her attention back to Shane.

'Aw, look at him sleeping,' she said. 'If only he could stay like this. Forever.'

'Soft bugger,' Mark murmured, but Julie did not hear him. She was lost in her baby world. Her Shane world. Mark felt a flush of anger which he did not know was jealousy. He had felt it before, in the quieter moments that Julie fussed over Shane. When no-one else was around to blunt the scene. He felt a need to break the mood. To come out with something nasty or sarcastic. An echo of the old black rages, now absent for some time. He missed the peaceful feeling that came in their wake, when he was calm and fulfilled and for a brief moment everything was right in his life. This was not a world he wanted to come back to. It chaffed against his restlessness. The rush of a job, particularly tonight's, clashed with the softness of this scene. He slurped his tea and just about kept quiet but Julie picked up his mood.

'What's the matter with you?', she asked. 'You got a face like thunder.'

'Nothing's the matter. I'm going up. An' I've been in all night, right?'

'Aye, I know. You've told me often enough.'

Julie heard him clump up the stairs, sensing the anger in each step. As Mark grew older, she understood him less. What he did at night in the last few years terrified her, and made her feel guilty for providing him with the life all nickers seemed to have. She had heard the same things for years down the bingo. "He'd be alright if his father was there." "He needs a man in the house to control him." "He won't listen to me." She imagined Shane in cahoots with Mark but quickly put the thought out of her mind.

Upstairs, Mark thought of playing something loud. Very loud. Slicing through the crap with piercing sound. A scream of music that would serve as his. Waking everyone on the estate. All the dummies. But he did nothing, just smoked and looked out of the window, sitting in his chair with his boot-heels on the windowsill. Cats prowled around outside, their silhouettes against the moonlight. The toms walking stiffly with tails erect. Looking for a fuck.

Something had been building up in him for months. During the day when Emma and others were about, when Julie fussed over Shane, it was alright, but at still times like this he felt Julie's love pouring out for someone else. It had always been all his, no matter what tosser came along. Now there was Shane, and increasingly he didn't like it. Something was being taken from him.

Mark counted out his money. The notes were fanned-out on his bed. Each one a tiny piece of security. He enjoyed the touch and feel of them, the way their soft colours blended together. Green on blue on brown. When he'd made it he'd have shirts made with pictures of bank notes on them. Mark Money Man. The second tin had filled nicely. He had almost three grand now, and was probably the richest bloke on the estate. Easily the richest his age. He put the money back in the tins, facing each note the same way, crushing them in a tight wad. A happy family. He'd need another tin soon. Julie called him.

'Mark, will you look after Shane for an hour? I want to go down the shops.'

He went downstairs. It was late spring, warm and airless. It was the one thing he would always remember. How still it was. Usually it blew strongly all through May, clouds shooting across the sky, the edge of the sun competing with the keenness of the wind. But today was different. Strange. It was warm and heavy, and the estate was sleepy and chilled-out.

Mark had taken on the mood. He was chilled-out himself, satisfied with his recent work. It went like clockwork now. Job, The Man, money. He had not been within a sniff of trouble as he ghosted his way in and out of houses. The buzz was not the same, but he had lost the downer that the court case had brought on.

Today Shane was out the back, playing in the pile of sand there. The council were doing bits and pieces around the estate. Papering over the cracks, ignoring the fact that the houses hadn't fallen apart on their own, responding to the growing press the estate was having. Its name had begun to serve as an example of all the knackered places in the valley. And there were lots. When

Mark read his nicked books he realised the estates had replaced the pits. *They* were the sign of the times. And people thieving and doing drugs had taken the place of men going underground. But old and new equally trapped by systems forced on them. They thought if they did up the estate the people on it would change magically. Dream on, Mark thought, as he got a can from the fridge. Here it's dog eat dog, and tosser eat tosser.

'Don' be long,' he shouted after Julie, his mother already disappearing out the front. She had got her figure back and was confident again. Ready to make all the same mistakes in her orange mini-skirt and white heels.

Shane could walk now, if a teeter-totter lurch could be called walking. He was almost two and getting to the bugging age for Mark. He'd learned to keep his bedroom door shut. Shane had got in there, advancing with purpose on his belly towards the hi-fi.

The sand had been there for weeks. Dumped by the council to rebuild the back fences. Work hadn't started and the sand had taken on a life of its own. Rained on, shat on by any passing animal, and delighted in by Shane. He played in it for hours, if the weather was right and Julie had cleared away the crap. Today was fine.

Mark sat on the kitchen step with his can, smoking and watching Shane root around in the sand. He sprayed it into the air with an old tablespoon, which he preferred to his bucket and spade. He gurgled with pleasure at his invention, turning to Mark and inviting him to join in. Shane couldn't get his name right, the 'k' was always left off. Now he shouted 'Mar' over and over. Reluctantly Mark went over to the sand, to shut Shane up as much as anything. He drained his can and flicked his cigarette butt into Bat's garden and sat at the edge of the sand on an old chair Julie had thrown out. It rocked unsteadily and he had to balance his weight on one side. Shane was delighted with the attention and offered Mark his spoon.

'Mar, Mar-ga,' Shane cried, digging into the looser sand and flicking it at Mark. A grain caught his eye and made it water. He dug a boot in the sand and showered Shane with it. His brother loved it and tottered around him excitedly, falling over and struggling up immediately, the spoon flashing silver in his hand. He had a blond thatch of hair now, which made him look like a girl.

Mark played with Shane for a while, the first time he had really bothered. He was taken back to his own early days, when innocence meant each day was an adventure. Wrestling around with Daniels on this very spot. It had always been easy to overpower his puny friend, and frighten him when he got on top and pinned him to the ground. His liking for control must have started here. He picked Shane up and dangled him over the sand. This was what his old man had done with him, Julie said. Shane was swung from side to side, squealing with joy and fear. He wondered how far he'd fly if he let him go. Shane a blond, tubby missile.

'Oi, you'll hurt him like that.'

It was Bat, leaning on the dividing fence. Mark felt the mood puncture, bringing him back to the adult world. The world which held him now and which he would always be a part of. That he had so joined quickly.

'He's alright,' Mark said. 'He's loving it.'

He righted Shane and held him steady until his giddiness faded.

'See, right as rain,' he said.

'Poor little bugger, you'll shake his brains loose like that.'

'Well, he'll be like everyone else up here then, won' he.'

He imagined himself snatching Bat up, swirling *her* around and letting her fly. A fifteen stone flying Bat.

'Where's Julie then?' Bat said.

'Out.'

Bat stayed at the fence, talking to Shane and trying to get him on her side but he wasn't interested. He had eyes only for his brother. She gave up and went inside.

'You should be out working,' she muttered.

Shane sat down on top of the sand and found his spoon again. He played quietly now, mumbling to himself as he made shapes. Mark sat in the chair again, and winked at him. He sensed their connection. A few minutes when life didn't seem stupid or point-less. When perhaps it wasn't all shit and then you die. That Shane might be someone he could protect and care for. Not just con-trol. Christ, he was thinking like Emma talked. Bat had brought the real world to him, in all its bitching, spying ways. He felt she had caught him naked for a second. She'd not wait long to tell Julie how he was swinging Shane around. By the time she finished telling it, it would seem like he was attacking him.

The phone rang, the sound carrying strongly from the house. He had paid for it six months ago, an acknowledgement of the need to move on in his business. It was easier to deal with The Man. Shane heard it too. 'Bone,' he shouted, pointing the spoon at the house. His face was quizzical, his eyes blended with the blue of his dungarees, his hand reached out as if to grab the noise. Joy puckering his face. Mark's last image of him.

It was The Man calling. Checking about business. Mark had supplied him with stuff two Sundays a month for almost a year since court. Nicking had become a steady job. If any doubts did surface, or he thought he might be running out of targets, he visualised that Welfare Hall ceiling waiting to be painted. Community Service had worked for him alright.

The Man took his time. He asked for specific things now, a shopping list. CDs were becoming popular, a new thing to nick. The phone was in the living room. Mark lay on his back on the sofa with his feet sprawled, looking up at the clear sky beyond the window and the twisting lines of the top houses. The Man called him Mark now, not kid. He knew he was knocking on eighteen. Perhaps he'd suggest a change of the work then. Mark made a mental list of the things wanted and put down the phone. It wasn't until he went into the kitchen to get another can that he thought about Shane. And the fact that he was no longer in the garden.

He stood on the step and shouted for him. Shane was hiding somewhere, he did it all the time. Crawling into spaces and keeping quiet. Enjoying Julie's panic. He sat down and opened the can, sucking up the froth before it spilled. Screwing up his eyes against the sun he wondered if he was getting any colour in his face. Despite his tanned body his face had proven stubborn. He had grown sideburns, razored down flush to his cheeks and fanning out at the bottom like crescents. They made his face thinner. Meaner. Emma and Julie hated them.

He slurped and shouted for Shane alternately. Pissed off that he would have to look for him. After a few minutes, when Shane did not appear, he got up and looked around the garden. Which took all of ten seconds. The rubbish bin and sand heap were the only cover. He went out onto the banking, stood on Daniels' dying place and scanned the open ground before the hillside. There was not much cover here either, but it was crazy thinking Shane could have got that far. He had to be inside. If he'd got amongst his records...

In such a small house he'd covered all possible hiding places in a few minutes. He went out to the front and shouted. His brother's name dying in the still hot air. Nothing. No-one about. It was one of those holiday days when kids seemed to disappear, leaving a boring, nothing-happening quiet in their wake. Shane could not have got far in a few minutes, not at his age. He searched the house again, looked in the same places again, shouted again. Anxiety seeped into his mind.

His shouting had alerted Bat. She came round the back way.

'What's the row,' she asked, 'shouting at little Shane, are you?'

'I'm shouting for him, right. The little bugger's disappeared.'

'What you mean, disappeared?'

'I was on the phone.'

Bat gave him a strange look which Mark countered with a glare. This was bloody stupid. It gave him an inkling of the trouble Shane might be later.

Soon everybody in the street was out looking. Turned out with sleepy sun-dazed eyes, roused from their daytime telly by Bat's piercing calls. Mark was amongst a group of women who fanned out back and front and took up the name of Shane. The air was thick with his brother.

Anxiety turned to alarm. Mark mouthed answers to his neighbours' questions: 'I only left him for a minute.' It was closer to ten. To twenty, maybe. And to himself, 'come on Shane for fucksake, stop messing about'.

He checked the house a third time, looking in impossibly small places, willing Shane to appear from one of them. Outside someone mentioned the police and Mark felt his guts churn. This was crazy. It didn't make sense. He felt the old blackness build up. The need to disperse the crowd, to punch his way out of this mess. To tell everyone to fuck off and have Shane appear back on the sand.

'A minute is all it takes,' Bat murmured, 'these days.'

'Shouldn't have been left with the kid,' another voice added, 'nutter like him.'

His brain started to bounce around in his head when Julie got off the bus, struggling with her plastic bags and looking puzzled at the crowd of women. Bat scuttled towards her, words flying from her mouth. Alarm turned to panic.

'Wa's up?' Julie asked, as soon as she reached Mark. Her question was the cue for a dozen pairs of accusing female eyes to focus on him. 'What have you done?' she asked again.

'It's not me. It's Shane. We can't find him. But don' worry, he's around here somewhere.'

The 'we' sounded a lot safer. Less responsible. It took a moment for Julie to understand. Then her face began to crumple. Mark saw panic strike, but not gradually, as it had with him. Julie's emotions were instant. An unseen force rearranged her features. Widening the eyes, lining the face, pitching the voice to a higher level.

'I don' understand,' Julie said, 'disappeared? But you were with him.'

She shook Mark, and wheeled around to the other women, who circled them.

'Calm down, love,' Bat said. 'He's got lost but we'll find him now.'

'I was on the phone,' Mark said. 'When I come back out he was gone. Gone from the garden.'

'He couldn't have gone, not on his own. Oh my God, someone's took him. Took my little Shane.'

Julie's face was rearranged further. Terror showed in it now. She wailed, sobbed, shouted for Shane. Pulled at Mark.

'Mam, take it easy.'

'Take it easy? Take it easy? What are you on about, you stupid sod. How could you leave him?' She turned to the other women. 'Has anyone seen him? My Shane?'

There was a chorus of no.

'Have you looked everywhere?'

Julie dashed into the house. Mark knew she'd look in all the places he had. But her panic calmed him. He tried to think. Maybe Julie was right. Somebody had taken him. There was no other solution. It happened all the time. The papers and telly were full of stories of missing kids. And they were usually from estates like his. And they were usually found dead. He thought of all the dopehead crazies, the older tossers like Humphries, and people much worse. He thought of his own black moods which he did not understand and felt copper tinged saliva trickle down his throat into his tight guts.

'Better call the police,' Bat said, 'on that phone of yours. He's nowhere near the house.'

She joined the other women, became part of their low murmur. Julie appeared in the front doorway.

'I can't find him,' she shouted, 'oh my God, I want my Shane.'

She shouted this with her head turned skyward. There's no answers there, Mark thought. Julie sank down on the step and began to lose it in earnest. Bat went to her and Mark slipped past them to the phone. The police were involved within twenty minutes.

'So, let's go through it once again.'

The inspector was a new face to Mark. One that needed another shave by mid-afternoon. A man in his early forties, with thinning black hair slicked back from a thin face. A pock-marked face. This geezer would have had lots of spots once, like Daniels. But he was a shrewd bastard. Something up top besides the hat.

He'd been at the station for three hours. It was early evening. Hundreds were now out searching for Shane, he'd been told. Half the estate. Probably the first thing the people there had ever done together, apart from drink and crap up.

Nash, the inspector, flicked the pages of a file. Mark's file. There couldn't be much in it, Mark thought. Just one bust. Yet Nash kept looking at it, studying it as if answers might spring from its thin pages. Tapping it with his pen. Glancing up at Mark then back down at the file.

He'd kept silent as much as possible, maintaining his cool. Being caught nicking was nothing compared to this. What they were thinking or maybe pretending to think was something huge. Something Mark could not think himself. If he did, he'd start raging. And he couldn't treat these bastards like Emma or Julie. They had power.

They'd quickly split him up from Julie at the house. When it looked certain that Shane was not going to be easily found. He had not seen her since. He'd asked Nash if she was also at the station and was told no. She wouldn't be. They would have checked out her story. Lots of people would have seen her down the shops. As Bat had seen him with Shane. The last he had seen of Julie she was being engulfed by police, who shepherded neighbours away and cleared the area outside the house. A van had pulled up with dogs in it. He was surprised by the speed of the police reaction. It was like a bit of news on the telly, except that he was part of it. He imagined a thousand pigs with their snouts in his business. They'd soon have his 'make' in a way they never bothered before. Psycho Eyes, Emma, Daniels, Humphries, it would all be found out. They'd root amongst it all. Thinking anything. Yet he could tell them nothing but the truth. Shane in the garden, the phone call. He could only tell them this and had done to Nash, over and over for three hours. The phone call was a problem.

'Who were you talking to?' was one of the first things Nash asked.

'Just some bloke.'

'Who?'

'Just some bloke I met down Cardiff. He said he might be able to get me work painting.'

'Name? Address? Number?'

'I dunno. I gave him *my* number.'

'Where'd you meet him?'

'In a pub. We just got talking.'

'I don't think so. I don't think you just "get talking" with anyone, Mark.'

'He's called John.'

'White, black, yellow?'

'White, of course.'

'What pub?'

'I can't remember. Somewhere in the city centre. Look, I'd had a few. What does any of this matter? What's it got to do with Shane going missing?'

'Everything, maybe. If there was no phone call.'

Nash let the words hang in the heavy air, and offered Mark one of his own cigarettes. Another man stood at the door, hands behind his back, red-faced and sweating. His eyes boring into Mark in unison with Nash's. The recorder faintly whirring.

'You can check the call,' Mark said. The Man would have to deal with his side of it if they got to him. They would know how long it was, which was to his advantage but he took no comfort from this. Nash was trying to draw something out of him. Something that wasn't there. Mark retreated into himself. Farther than he ever had before. Nash's questions became distant and his own answers faint. He blinked an eye and Shane was in the garden. He blinked again and there was only the spoon, stuck in the sand. A small metal flag catching the sun. Witness to everything.

What was happening here? He was drifting away from this scene, shutting out Nash. Shutting out everyone. Daniels was with him. And his father: the tall man with a blank face. No matter how much he tried he could not see the face. It taunted him, invited him to try again. Then he was pushing Daniels down that hole. Crushing him into the blackness. Ignoring his pleading screams which climaxed as he fell. Someone was touching him, pushing his shoulder.

'Are you leaving us, Mark?' Nash said. 'You look groggy.'

'Uh?'

'Alright, I think that's enough for now. But we'll have another chat in the morning.'

Mark regained his wits. Got himself back from wherever he had drifted. He got his second wind and had never felt sharper. He could sense the tick of the electric wall clock, feel the slight vibration of its hands echo in his head. He could hear Nash thinking. That Mark had done something to Shane. Something bad. That the whole estate had done something and that it should be sunk into the ground.

'Where's my mother?' Mark asked.

'Back at your house.'

'Talked to her about me, have you?'

Nash did not answer, but Mark knew he had. One of the times he had been left alone in the interview room. They'd all be out talking, digging dirt. Self-preservation clashed with worry, but he was too tired to worry about either.

'Are they still out looking?' he asked.

'Of course. They will be until dark. We've got a helicopter on it now. We'll find Shane.'

Mark felt there was more threat than hope in this.

Nash turned off the tape recorder. Mark couldn't recall the hours of repeated questions. Each time he went through it the telling became more blurred. And it only took a few minutes to tell.

The man at the door led him out. He was in the new central police station down the valley. Near the court he had attended. He breathed in deeply as he stood on the steps, filling his lungs with the fumes of the car-clogged road. The sun was almost done but the day still held its warmth and despite the traffic the quiet of the garden hadn't left him. Its atmosphere clogged his thoughts, he felt like he was swimming through warm soup, with each sensation of the garden clinging to him. Beefy was approaching. He detached himself from other men entering the station.

'I heard about your brother,' he said.

He was the last person Mark wanted to talk to.

'You gonna have a go, an' all?' Mark said.

'No, I'm not. They fixed you up with a lift home then?'

'Didn't want one.'

'I could drop you up, if you want.'

Beefy had put on weight, if that was possible. A second chin had rolled into place. Mark wondered that the force put up with such a fat git. Was he a plant? Someone acting nice outside the nick. To see if he would open up. Caution and hostility returned. He thought about the tins. Would they search the house that much? They were not looking for something so small.

'No, I'll make my own way.'

Beefy held his arm as he made to go.

'Look kid, I'm sorry about your brother. He'll turn up okay. They'll find him.'

His face was close. A trace of beer on his breath, stubble bristling through his pink cheeks.

'Aye. Sure.'

Mark pulled away, before he said more. Did he want a lift, be fucked. He didn't even want to go home. To a house full of Julie. Her tears, anger, panic, and accusation. Emma might be around. Bat too, probably. He'd be surrounded by women, either lashing him with their tongues or denouncing him with their eyes.

For once he felt powerless. Psycho Eyes fucked. On the bus he tried to examine the day. Each jolt of the road and grind of a gear spurred a fragment of memory. He'd told Nash he'd left Shane for ten minutes, but he knew it was closer to twenty. Time enough for any arsehole to come along. Humphries came to mind. Nah, that little shit wasn't capable. But he'd seen enough telly to know that they often weren't, on the surface. Runtish, anoraked little bastards looking for a high.

The bus brought him to the estate. Several police cars were parked in the street and some vans down at the roundabout. Every villain around the place must be getting the wind up.

Julie was on her own as he entered the house. He saw Bat leaving through the back door. Clearing the way for him. At least there was no Emma. Julie was sitting on the sofa, her orange skirt merging with it. She looked wasted, as if the last few hours had lasted twenty years for her. Dark smudges fanned her red and swollen eyes, and the lines which had appeared in the last few years had taken on extra depth. They cut her face now. But she wasn't crying.

'He's gone,' she said, 'I know he's gone for good. I can feel it.'

His mouth was dry, his tongue stuck in a desert, spit hard to come by.

'He'll turn up,' he mumbled. 'Bound to.'

This was a pathetic attempt at calming, at togetherness, and it dried on his lips. He sensed the need in Julie to love him now, to channel everything to him but she sprang up from the sofa and ran at him. Pounding him with her tiny fists. He felt the imprint of her grandmother's wedding ring, but he did not try to stop her or brush her away. He just stood there, an upright drum for her to beat.

'Where were you?' Julie cried. 'Why'd you take your eyes off him? Someone's got him. I know they have. Got my little Shane.'

Her words were mangled by emotion and her sobbing mouth. She pulled his face down to hers then slowly sank to the floor, sliding down his legs. 'Don' let nothing happen to him, Mark. Don' let no-one have him.'

'Okay, Mam, okay. Come and sit down.'

She broke away from him, her shaking increasing, looking at him with the same strange look he had seen cross Bat's face. He felt her eyes probing his but did not meet their stare.

'Mark, *you* haven't done nothing to him, have you? Have you?'

He feared another attack but her voice trailed away and she sank down on the sofa. Anger was no longer an option. He was too shocked for anger. Too shocked by the simmering day and its one uncontrollable event. For once Julie had centre stage. This was *her* anger, *her* despair. And it was all coming his way.

'Well, answer me,' she sobbed. 'I don' know what's been going on.'

'You're not thinking straight,' he said.

'What are you fucking talking about? My son's gone. Your brother. And you're talking about thinking straight.'

He stood over her, breathing as deeply and evenly as he could. Feeling useless, unable to do or say anything that would help.

'I'll make some tea.'

Pathetic, what every useless fucker did in times like this, but Julie let him go into the kitchen with the question unanswered.

She was calmer when he came back with the tea, exhausted, sunk in the cushions of the sofa. Hugging herself and rocking slowly, like a doll, or one of the nutters he used to watch come home on their special school bus. Again he felt helpless. This was the unknown.

'Here, drink this.'

Julie took the mug but he stayed close, thinking that she might let it drop. Her shaking made tea spill down the sides of the mug over her clenched hands, and onto her lap. Uneasily he sat down beside her and took the mug back.

'I'll put it down here,' he said, resting the mug on the floor, away from her feet.

He resisted the urge to protest his innocence. He thought it might set her off again.

'They'll find him, Mam. We'll hear anytime now.'

She looked at him as if just acknowledging his presence, just recognising him. And slowly leant against his stiff body. Trying to burrow into it, as if *she* was a child. He was embarrassed and lost as her tears began to dampen his shirt. Her bony body felt so frail as he patted it lightly. It was hard to believe he had come from her.

Julie cried quietly for a few minutes, twisting her fingers into his T-shirt, then she pulled away from him and looked carefully into his face.

'You never wanted me to have him. You wanted me to get rid of him. An' you hated Humphries.'

'He needed hating. Look Mam, this is us here, right. And we've done nothing. I've done nothing. You're all mixed up, that's all.'

'You left him.'

'I know, I know. But only in the garden, for a few minutes. Jesus, kids not much older than him go around on their own all the time up here.'

He almost said it was 'just one of those things', but he stopped himself in time. Her gaze was steady, but uncertain.

'They'll tell us as soon as they find him,' he added. 'You better try and get some sleep.'

She buried her head in his chest again.

'I'm sorry, love,' she said, 'I know you never did nothing. I know you'll never do nothing really bad. I dunno what I'm saying.'

'Go up and have a lie down. I'll stay by the phone.'

She looked at the phone and her face twisted. Her doubts would resurface in the morning, if the police did not come before then. Doubt would always be there until Shane was found. The Richards family had fucked up completely this time, without doing anything.

She went upstairs though he knew she wouldn't sleep. She'd lie there and go over her whole life, and each episode would be a blow to her. And Shane vanishing was the big one. The cream to go on her cake of shit. A thousand times worse than any man leaving her.

He waited until he heard her bedroom door shut, a slow, resigned closing, as if she never wanted to come out again, then took a can from the fridge. Slumping down on a kitchen chair he looked out at the garden. The weather was changing. It was a misty, damp night. No stars out. No moon. Just a thick orange-tinged murk hanging low. The odd car noise from the bottom road cutting through occasionally. The sand was a dull, shapeless mound that looked like something had died in the garden.

He would not even try to sleep. His senses were raw, honed down to fine, nervous points. He was surprised Emma hadn't shown, but not sorry. Perhaps she was afraid. She would have heard all the rumours. How he'd been alone with the kid, how there was no explanation for it. He thought of explanations himself. Someone must have taken Shane. If he'd toddled off he would have been quickly found. The estate had never been a dangerous place, not for kids his age. It was tossers messing with other tossers usually. That was its history, not stuff like this. His thoughts lightened for a moment. It might be some piece desperate to have a baby. He'd read about them. Shane might be looked after okay and then found. Nah, get real, he told himself. Shane is a Richards. Nothing ends well for us. Kids like Shane were taken for scumbag reasons. Some evil bastard had seen his chance and got him. Someone who had been looking around for weeks maybe, treating kids like he did houses. Targets.

He imagined the newspapers pouring all over the streets, looking for 'angles' or whatever fucking word they used. The police had kept him away today, but in the morning it would start. Everything would start again.

His head felt light and empty even though it almost burst with his thoughts. A bastard of a headache was starting up, racing from the back of his head to gather behind his eyes. Wanting to punch its way out.

It had been just one lousy phone call. The more he went over it the more dreamlike it became. As if he hadn't been there at all. He downed the can and opened another, wanting to feed the headache, to take it as far as it would go. Pulling the ring seemed

123

unnaturally loud. The first half of this day had been so quiet. So nothing. Yet something had happened. Something big and dark, and out of control.

Mark woke with a start, spilling some drink on his jeans. He had slept with his head sunk on his chest, despite the headache, despite his intentions. Instinctively he stood up and scanned the hillside. A fine rain fell softly, stealthily through mist. Shane might be up there, somewhere in the forestry. His head throbbed but he welcomed it. He deserved each beat.

He went up to his room, for once not thinking to check the floorboards. Money had been forgotten, for the first time in his life.

It was the same routine in the morning. Police and volunteers searching the hills, people hanging round street corners, excited by the new action. A bit like a street party. Something different on the estate. Kids trying to outdo each other with tales of Psycho Eyes and what he might have done. What he must have done. Media tossers camped down by the roundabout, waiting for their chance. He recognised them by their clothes, and the way they glanced nervously around the houses. And Nash again. Coming to the house at ten o'clock. To check Mark out on his home ground.

Julie was like a ghost by this time. Almost enveloped by a grey shell-suit. Her eyes sunk into dark pools by a sleepless night. But Mark had slept his few hours. Woke thinking it was a dream. Took a few minutes to click his mind into gear. A glorious few minutes, a big soft comfort to sink into, a place where Shane was alive and well. Then he'd heard police radios outside, dogs barking and someone shouting out orders – 'today we're going to search beyond the golf course, I want you all to...' Shane screamed back into his head.

Nash had done his homework. He wanted to talk about Humphries this time.

'Couldn't have been easy for you,' Nash said, as he sat opposite him at the kitchen table, 'having a bloke like that come to stop.'

'A bloke like what?'

Mark's wall was in place.

'Humphries, he left your Mam in the lurch, didn't he?'

Mark shrugged.

124

'A baby on the way. Little Shane. He *is* Shane's father, isn't he?'

He would not react. Anger was dangerous. It loosened tongues, made them wag on their own. Nash did not seem to mind his silence.

'He might have wanted to come back,' Nash continued, 'to come and see Shane. He might have wanted to come back permanently.'

'I wouldn't know,' Mark said, 'but you already do. Humphries must have been the first person you talked to, after me and Mam.'

Nash smiled. 'If Shane wasn't here he'd have no reason to come back,' Nash said.

Mark looked at him with disdain. Nash offered him a cigarette. He'd bought the packet just for him. Nash must think he was dealing with a cretin. He seethed.

'Don't you think it's strange, that with all the people round here, no-one saw a thing? No-one saw Shane wander off. No-one stopped him and brought him back.'

'I think it's strange you haven't found him.'

'Maybe he's in a place where it's hard to find him.'

They sat within feet of the sand. Each man looked out at it in silence, Mark smoking the cigarette he'd been given. Julie was in the living room with a police woman and social worker. Everyone was getting in on the act. The estate would be overdosing on regular news coverage. National news. Tossers gathered under the wall-mounted telly down the club. Pointing out their houses like big kids. Thinking their dark thoughts, making their crazy suggestions. The worst of them wanting it to end badly, even if they didn't realise it. So that they could hang onto the fame for a little longer.

Julie entered the kitchen. She stood behind Mark with her hands on the back of his chair. Torn between re-surfacing doubts and loyalty. She hated it all being so public. And staying public, whatever happened. The night had been long, each minute dripping reluctantly away. She had imagined herself in the sand, counting every bloody grain of it. If the council hadn't left it there, if Mark hadn't been on the phone. And where had Bat been? Stupid, useless cow. The eyes of the street had been blind when they had been needed most. She wanted Shane. Back in her arms. She'd never shout at him again. She'd worship him. Do anything if she could have him back. She stifled a sob with difficulty. She didn't want to cry in front of the copper.

'You've questioned him enough, haven't you?' Julie said. 'What more can he tell you? Or me either, for that matter. You should be out looking with the rest of them.'

She sat down on the third chair. They had never made up the set. Her eyes strayed to Mark's briefly then darted away. She did not want to look at him, afraid of what she'd see in that secret face.

'We have over a hundred people out today,' Nash said.

'And how long will that go on?' Julie asked.

'As long as necessary.'

But it wouldn't. She'd seen it often enough on the box. Too bloody often. If a kid was not found alive in the first few days they tailed off. Usually until a body was found. The image of a small, torn bundle dumped somewhere on the hillside, amongst Mark's beloved trees flashed into her head. It cut into her. She put her hands to her mouth to control herself. Gnawed at her fingers. She got up quickly and began to shake. Nash stopped her from falling.

'Better sit back down. I'll get the social worker to phone your doctor. He'll drop in to see you.'

'I don't want a bloody doctor. I want Shane back. I want my son.'

Mark knew it should be him settling Julie down, getting the doctor.

'Okay, that's all for now,' Nash said to him. 'We're going to search another section of hillside today. Shane's photograph has gone out all over the country. There's every chance we'll find him.'

Aye, and every chance you won't, Mark thought. The doctor would give Julie pills and she'd probably never come off them. The estate was awash with women like that. Legalised druggies, their wrecked lives propped up with dope. An image of The Man in his sleek car came to him. He wanted to reach out and grab his life, exchange his own for it.

As Nash left, Emma came in. He could see that she'd been crying. All this emotion, but getting them nowhere. Emma wanted to hug him but he turned aside. He had no time for it.

'Don't you start,' he said, 'it's hard enough as it is.'

'I been thinking about it all night,' Emma said, 'poor little mite. I couldn't go to Tec.'

'Thanks for being here, love,' Julie said. 'I dunno if I'm coming or going. I keep getting these awful thoughts.'

Emma sat down next to Julie. Mark lit a cigarette for his mother and she cupped it in her trembling hands, inhaling deeply.

'Filthy habit, this is,' she murmured, 'an' look at him, smoking like a trooper and not yet eighteen. What a mother I've been.'

'Don' say that,' Emma said, 'you been a good mother.'

Julie smiled, a thin, humourless, bitter curve of her mouth.

'You have,' Emma reiterated, 'Shane didn't want for nothing.'

She realised immediately that she'd used the past tense, but the words were out. Julie didn't seem to notice, but Mark did. He looked up from his own smoking and glared at her.

'Aye, nothing 'cept a father and a decent place to live,' Julie said.

'There's lots of good people up here,' Emma said hesitantly, 'not everyone is a waster. I'll be getting a job in August, after Tec. I've fixed it up already. On Monday, before all this happened.'

Her voice trailed to a halt. She realised how useless she sounded. How out of place. Julie could not take much in. She had two things on her mind: what had happened to Shane and who had taken him. People were talking about Mark. About how strange he was. A loner. She'd rowed with her own mother last night. Turned on her when she'd tried to suggest Mark had done something. She knew about his rages but he wasn't capable of anything like this. He couldn't be. If she ever thought such a thing herself they'd be finished as a couple, but she hated it that other people did. She drank her coffee and wished she was away from the estate for good.

Mark's face was as pale as Julie's and his eyes darker than ever. She hoped Julie wouldn't start crying again. It might set her off and Mark would split then. And she wanted to be near him. How she wanted to grab hold of Mark, to grieve for Shane with him. But he wouldn't have it. Not even in private. Things were locked inside him and she hadn't found the key. Not yet. She caught his eyes on her. Looking at her through slitted lids in that secret way of his. Drilling her hopes, making them shrivel up. If Shane was not found where would that leave them?

'Make yourself a cup of coffee if you want,' Julie said.

Emma was glad to have something to do and took as long over it as she could. Through the kitchen window she saw the police and volunteers fan out over the hillside, dogs ranging ahead, men prodding undergrowth with sticks, skirting the golf course. No-one played during the search. The course was a bright, deserted strip of green.

'They won' let Mark go looking with them,' Julie muttered. 'Think it might cause trouble with the people round here. Her next door's gone back to her old ways. Seen her just now, outside with the other crows. Spreading muck about Mark. Me an' all probably.'

'They'll be sorry when Shane is found,' Emma said quietly.

Mark was stuck with women again. Locked in by his thoughts and fears. And nicking seemed so long ago now, so easy and free. Just two days ago. 'When Shane is found.' Emma was wrong. It would be much worse then. They'd be looking for someone for murder and they'd be looking straight at him. He didn't trust the bastards not to find a way of proving he did it, just to close the case.

Emma handed him a mug of tea. He felt her warm fingers linger on his. Julie looked at them, sucking down on the last of her cigarette. He could work out her thoughts. She was thinking that he *might* have done something, hating herself for it, then thinking it again. Concentrating on Shane, going over every inch of his memory, then coming back to her eldest son. Chasing her thoughts around in circles, a roundabout she desperately wanted to get off, so she could meet Nash coming in through the door with Shane. So she could take him and nestle him in her arms and cover his chubby face with kisses. But it would not let her go, and Mark could not make it let her go.

'I'm going up to my room,' he said. Emma made to follow him. 'No, you stay down here with Mam.'

She had never heard him call Julie this before.

He closed the bedroom curtains but their uneven join still let the sun in. It cut a swathe through the gap, a line of light over the boards above the tins. Without knowing why he got them out and counted the notes. With police all around him. He imagined himself running out into the front garden and throwing twenties to the crowd. Making it a real party. Watching all those who thought he'd done something to Shane fight over his money.

Each note calmed him. All he had to hold on to, that didn't talk and look and accuse. Something he could still control and which might yet lead somewhere. He arranged the notes on the bed, his semi-circle of achievement. He spelt out an 'S' for Shane in tenners. As if he might buy him back. If Emma came in now she'd think him cracked. Julie probably did already. There was a knock at the front door. He went to the front window and looked down. It was Julie's mother. His gran. He couldn't remember the last time he'd seen her. He scooped the money up and squashed it untidily back in the tins.

Linda, Julie's mother, was an even slighter version of her daughter. Julie thirty years on, natural slimness turning to bony hardness, a woman on the edge of a pension. But she did not seem so old to Mark. She did not seem anything. His only memories of her were fleeting – a figure hovering over him. He remembered Daniels' grandfather better.

Linda sat down on the sofa. She managed to sniff as she looked around the room, nerves merging with judgement. She took in the large photograph of Shane on the television. A smiling laughing Shane, framed in gold. A smaller one of Mark in his school uniform stood next to it.

Emma stood awkwardly with Mark, who lounged in the doorway. Julie sat down opposite her mother, legs drawn together, hands on knees.

'You've come then,' Julie said.

'Aye. Your father wouldn't. Said he wouldn't feel right. Coming now, after all this time.'

Mark could feel each woman tensing for what might happen. They were his family, he realised. He'd come from Julie and she from Linda. And they were all strangers. For the first time it occurred to him how odd it was that Julie never saw her parents. They had abandoned her in a way she would never have him. Yet he could tell Julie wanted her mother here and had asked her to come. Without talking to him. She needed something from her past to hold onto, something that had once been good. It wasn't just a few days she wanted to turn the clock back.

Julie started another cigarette and tossed the packet to Mark. They both smoked. Linda sniffed again. Holding a fag was the only way his mother could keep her hands under control. They wanted to perform on their own, to wring themselves stupid and snatch at the air. To snatch Shane out of it.

'Been a long time, Mam,' Julie said.

'Yes.'

More silence.

'Look, there's no point arguing now,' Linda said. 'What's happened in the past has happened, but I want to see that little lad found safe and well as much as anyone. And your father does.'

'Aye, but he haven't come up here though.'

Mark left them to it. He didn't trust his tongue. He joined Emma in the kitchen. For once he was glad she was there.

'God, have they never bothered?' Emma asked.

'Not that I know of. They never liked Mam's boyfriends. And when she had me we moved up here. End of story.'

'But that's not fair on you. You're their grandson.'

He shrugged. 'Who needs a pair of old wankers.'

Emma began to cry and fell against Mark's chest. Praying he wouldn't push her away. He didn't. He stood there uneasily, but held her lightly. She began to see why he was the way he was. She didn't know a family as distant as the Richards. Usually it was the other way around. Everyone living in each other's pockets, nosing, bitching, angling. Playing mind games. But with Mark's lot there was nothing. No contact.

'Better make the old crow some tea,' Mark said.

He wondered if the police had been to see his grandparents. Maybe. Maybe that was why she was here. Distrust flared up again. He longed to be out, on the hillside. Not looking for Shane but just away from it all.

'He was a beautiful little boy,' Julie said. She sat drinking tea with her mother, glad that Mark was keeping out of the way.

Linda nodded to the photograph.

'I can see,' she said. 'It doesn't seem yesterday that you were that age. Doesn't seem long at all.'

'It does to me,' Julie murmured.

'Billy had just come out the army when I had you,' Linda continued. 'He stayed on after his national service. Another seven years. We had it all ahead of us then, and I wanted lots of kids.'

Had she come to talk about herself, Julie wondered, at a time like this? Was this her mother's way of showing concern? 'When I was in the army' had been one of the catchphrases of her early childhood. She had thought of the army as some strange kind of other world, hell maybe, often used as a threat by her father.

'And you only had me,' Julie said.

'If only you'd listened to us more,' Linda said, 'in the early days. There were lots of decent lads around then.'

'Mam, I don' need this. Mark is right. It is too late. Far too late.'

'We saw about him in the paper. The court case.'

'Aye, you would.'

Julie got up quickly.

'Look, if this is all you're going to talk about you'd better go. It's not helping at all.'

Linda put up a hand.

'No, you're right. It's hard to know what to say at a time like this. No mother should have to go through what you're going through. And I'm still a mother too, remember, no matter how we've been.'

Her voice trembled. Julie saw how time had marched all over her face. Lines bursting through her powder, refusing to be hidden, eyes weak and watery, and her hands showing signs of arthritis. Her knuckles starting to knot and one finger going away from the others at an angle. Julie could not remember Linda's exact age. Sixty three or four, a few years older than Billy. Could not remember her own mother's age. That said it all.

'If I can help in any way,' Linda whispered.

Julie was confused and felt the need to open up to her, to sweep away the last two barren decades. To be hugged and comforted by someone who was not trying to use her. To be a real daughter. Yet she knew she shouldn't have phoned, and regretted her weakness. Linda did not deserve to be involved with them in any way. She had made her choice years ago. A quiet life with a quiet selfish husband. Whose quiet selfish ways had locked her up and stolen her soul. Julie's voice thickened with emotion and she struggled for words.

'I don' know what to say either, Mam. I'm going crazy waiting for news. And none comes.'

'Waiting is always hard.'

Linda reached out a hand and touched her daughter lightly on the shoulder.

'They'll find him, you'll see.'

There were noises in the street. More police arriving. More searchers. Someone knocked on the door. It put an end to their agonising struggle. As Julie got up to answer the door Linda dabbed at her eyes quickly with a tissue.

Linda Richards was wrong. Nash was wrong. Emma was wrong. Shane was not found. Not a trace of him. Police dogs had been given his unwashed clothes to sniff and identify but their noses led nowhere. After four days the hunt was scaled down. In seven days it was called off. Mark had further meetings with Nash and then with a psychologist, after police insistence. He was the only straw they could clutch at.

The psychologist, Bellman, was a thin-faced little man who wore glasses attached to a string and framed sentences as if each word was a bit special. Mark had a two hour session with him down at the station, in the usual room. Its poxy bareness was familiar now. Scratchy, dirty cream walls, a strip light with dead flies stuck to it, a table and two chairs. The dumb electric clock.

Julie was worried, thinking that Mark would be officially branded a nutter. She had wanted to contact Maule, but he didn't want anyone there. They had never charged him and he knew they never would. Not now. And another tosser like Maule being present would piss him off even more.

He found the session with Bellman more interesting than annoying. A change from Nash. And he found that knowing what he had to say was true gave him an inner strength. He did not have to support any lies with others.

Bellman was Nash's last chance to root something out, to get himself off the hook for not finding Shane. The papers had been screaming for his safe discovery, working themselves up into a lather over the estate. A 'wasteland' one of them called it. Cheap bastards. Cheaper than anyone on the estate. He would have been a neat, easy score for Nash. The Psycho Eyes who couldn't stand his baby brother. Who was jealous, eaten up by it until he cracked. But they hadn't a shred of evidence. They were powerless.

Bellman was a sly bastard. Always coming back to his childhood. If he remembered his father, crap like that. He ranged back and forth through his life as if he was personally fucking acquainted with it. Building up a 'profile'. Pen working overtime as he jotted notes. Stopping to take his glasses off and let them dangle on their cord, and pressing his eye sockets with the palms of his hands. As if *he* was the one under pressure.

They were on their own in the room. The usual tosser rooted by the door had been dismissed. Trying to get my confidence, Mark thought. Be my pal. At one point, tired and bored by repeated questions he had stood up and towered over Bellman, and wondered if the git would give it all up, his job, money, everything, if he could be six inches taller. As tall as he was. Yeah, course he would. His fancy words had no power. He was a wimp in a suit, trying to talk his life bigger than it was. Probably needed counselling himself.

Bellman was none the wiser after the interview, Mark was sure of it. He would present Nash with a report, which would be shoved in a drawer somewhere. Nash did not bother with him again. They were left alone, with dwindling sympathy for Julie and a lasting suspicion of Mark. Left on their own again, as they always had been.

Time passed slowly for the Richards family after Shane, each day drifting reluctantly into the next. Lengthened by their thoughts. The thoughts of the whole estate. The disappearance of her son was a daily torment to Julie that no pill could lessen. It was the ultimate mystery which could be shaped by whatever bleak thought pattern rolled through her mind. And Mark was closer to her mood than anyone thought. He simmered with her. He ached the same flesh and blood ache, but he had to dam it up, unable to allow himself the slightest public show.

Initial shock hardened into bitterness for Julie, as weeks went by and Shane wasn't found. As she realised he'd never be found. Not alive. She became a twitching, distrustful mess, unable to see good in anything. Not wanting to. She seemed to have a slight but perceptible shake, perhaps in preparation for the dread news that might one day come. She had been of even temperament, had to be with Mark. It had sustained her through her succession of poor men, allowing her to look ahead, to the next time, the better next time. And despite his life so far she had always believed Mark would get somewhere other than prison. Believed that his thieving, though she hated it, was part of his growing up, almost normal for the place. Before Shane went her hopes had always been shot through with gold. Present shit, future gold. Now this had all been blown away and her life laced with poison.

Julie became confused with Mark. Going from one extreme to another. Pulling him to her, needing him, needing his strength and support, other times pushing him away. Her eyes asking why. Why had he left Shane. And, in her blackest moments, asking if he *had* done something to him. It was a question she did not dare ask out loud, for fear of what it might lead to. It struck at her every day, a stab of horror, and once the police were removed from the scene she could not draw so heavily on loyalty to her first born.

Nicking was put on hold. The Man had contacted Mark. His voice different. Harder.

'Thing is, kid, you're too hot right now. I dunno who might be watching you. Leave it a bit and I'll be back in touch.'

'When?'

'In a bit. Chill out for a while. Oh, that's not a cool thing to say, right? Sorry about the little boy. I'll be in touch.'

Nigger bastard was pulling the plug. But he didn't need him. He'd start up again anyway. If only to take his mind off Shane. I'll be giving away motors like The Man's one day, he thought. Then he wondered who to.

Shane did nothing for his sleep. It had been patchy since he was fourteen. Especially after jobs. It was hard to come down from the rush they gave him. But this was much worse. Julie'd shut her bedroom door and he'd shut his. But the problem could not be shut out. Ever. He'd often hear her crying through the night. He almost got used to it. As if his mother's tears were a new form of wind, like when it hit the house in mid-winter and sighed round the windows. It became a ritual, sitting through the night. Tracing cloud formations over the forestry. Rolling black bastards came in early autumn, racing over the trees. Limbering up for winter. When his bed did finally call him he tossed around in it, wrestling with the old nightmare about Daniels and the hole. Now Shane was there too. Looking up from the hole, face lit against the blackness. Then he was with them up top, looking on as he shoved Daniels down. Baby eyes starting out of his head. Big, alive baby eyes, only just starting out in life. Wondering if he'd be next. Waking up with the sheets tangled. And Julie still crying in the next room, but quieter now. Exhausted quiet. Each in their own private hell, and distant as ever

Mark slipped out early after a particularly shit night. Very early. The milkman at the roundabout scowled at him as he passed. Mark looked through him. He stopped to light up by the statue, striking a match against its white stone, leaving a smear of pink on the mother and child.

It had been a dry summer and walkers had trodden out dusty patches. Flies hugged the dust, taking in the early sunshine before they died. He walked quickly, almost breaking into a jog. A manic, pumping walk. He wanted to knock himself out. Wanted tiredness to beat all the other feelings. He already had the dreamy sick feeling that came with lack of sleep. Now he wanted a knackered body to match it. He covered five miles, cutting through the forestry and passing his stash point with just a glance. He stopped when his heart wanted to fight out of his chest and the backs of his legs hurt from the constant push upwards.

Mark rested on the hillside near the house of books. Small and shining in the morning light. He'd had power there, and he might go back again. Do it a third time.

Beyond the house the valley was waking up. Cars and trucks starting out on their day. He watched them multiply until a solid chain of moving metal wound its way down the valley, the road looking stupidly small for them. He still couldn't drive but it no longer seemed important.

His head swam from the first hike but he started out again. At the same pace. Skirting the perimeter of the trees and heading back down. The going easier now. It was no use. Though he had succeeded in punishing his body it did not free him of his thoughts. They stuck like glue to his mind. Maggots burrowing. He kicked at the trunk of a tree, jarring his leg and shaking down half-dead leaves. What could he do? Dope? Booze? Emma? Where the fuck was Shane?

Julie had watched Mark go. He'd thought her asleep, finally, as he eased out of the house. But she had forgotten how to sleep. At least the kind that renewed and made problems go away for a while. She dreaded sleep now: she had to face her life all over again when she woke. The disbelief, rage, pain, all those words which meant little until they struck at you. Began to own you. And she had the full set.

Mark and his bloody hillside. They suited each other. Those trees all the same shape and dull colour that she had hated as a kid. Dark, miserable forestry that had nothing natural about it. She should have done something about Mark years ago. Or at least tried harder. Before it was too late and he was too big. But it had been easier to let him go his loner ways. She'd thought it might help keep him out of trouble. Away from the gangs anyway.

It hadn't been so bad at first. The estate was new and everyone was in the same boat, and she had gotten away from her parents. Mark had been all hers. And he had lots about him in the early days. A cute kid, standing out from the others. Especially Bat's overweight brood. He'd been her touch of class, in the middle of a place that crapped up worse each year. And Shane had brought all this back. Another beautiful kid from a relationship with a tosser. Now one was gone and one almost lost to her.

Humphries had phoned the other day, having kept clear. His whining, instant-apology voice in her ear. A voice that summed up her history with men. She told him she didn't want to discuss Shane with him, and didn't want him coming around. Ever. But when she slammed down the phone she thought that Shane had been fathered by this man and even Humphries must feel something. But she didn't phone back. She didn't need another complication. Another confrontation.

She followed Mark's track up the hillside, using the binoculars he'd left on his bedroom windowsill. He was walking like a fool, loping over the ground like some kind of long-legged animal. Was he looking for signs of Shane? Or for something that matched the strange world he kept inside him? Those shadowy trees seemed more a part of him than she ever had. She kept him in sight until he merged with the cover and his black-jeaned, black T-shirted figure turned green. She put the binoculars back on their exact spot and went to the bathroom. To prepare for another day. It was seven o'clock.

Autumn faded into winter and the estate turned ever bleaker. Matched Mark's thoughts. Dull concrete took on the colour of old snow. Houses clustered together in shapes that were a long-standing joke to him. A joke without a punchline. And the winter getting meaner by the day as it whipped its way through the holes of busted up, boarded up houses, and the broken windows of the others.

Shane's disappearance became old news. Forgotten off the estate, and fading on it. Given the occasional kiss of life by a drunk down the club, or an accusing bingo-playing woman. Mark and Julie kept on with a kind of life and Emma attempted to comfort each of them. As best she could. It was difficult, for often Julie was strange, unresponsive and moody, going deeper into herself. She did not encourage further visits by her mother. Shane's going had prised open a door that had been closed for a long time. But it was a forced entry. For her, thinking about the future was bad enough, without having old, bitter ground raked over again. Beds had been made too long ago.

In September, Emma had begun work in a salon in Pontypridd,

but what should have been a hopeful start was clouded. She rowed constantly with her mother over Mark, and wanted to get away. To move in with Mark and then to move away with him. But she knew how he'd react if she suggested it. As if they could anyway. A job was nowhere in Mark's thoughts even if anyone would give him one, and she earned sixty pounds a week, with tips. And if Mark had made any money from his stupid nicking she had not seen much of it. They had done very little together since Shane. Mark had barely touched her. He had even forgotten her eighteenth birthday. Before the baby went she had planned a party down the club, to show off her cool bloke and her new job. Hoping it would set them on the way somewhere. But Mark had gone right back into his shell. He had begun to peek out of it earlier in the year. His tantrums had lessened and he hadn't repeated what had happened in the alley, when she'd thought he might kill her. She'd never forgotten the crazy energy coming from him.

Mark counted out the notes. He hadn't for weeks. He was trying to hold onto the one constant thing in his life. He had three grand in tens and twenties, and one fifty pound note The Man had slipped him. A pretty orange colour he'd decided to keep forever. At seventeen he'd thought his stash significant. Now it seemed peanuts. Pitiful bastard peanuts. The price of a crap motor or a bimbo holiday with Emma and Julie. Three hundred CDs, three thousand cans. Three thousand dreams that lead nowhere.

Past jobs filtered though his mind. His thoughts stopping on shit memories. That fucking dog, the bearded man rolling over on him. The dark treks over the hillside, chest pounding. It had been a lot of hassle for three thousand quid. He thought of gambling. Sticking it all on a horse or something. Going down to Cardiff and slapping the lot on some greasy counter. Giving the old geezers there a shock. A long shot. Nah, that was for tossers. He'd seen Humphries pore over his racing paper, licking at his pen like a kid and putting his crosses by the side of nags. Betting a few lousy quid at a time. Living in Wankerville. No, he'd have to bite the bullet and start nicking again. Do it without The Man. And if each job was cold bloody turkey he'd have to put up with it. At least the heat wouldn't be on him. Not for houses. The pigs expected him to nick kids now.

He began scouting again. Quietly getting fit, relearning old ways almost been crushed out of him. Almost. It was early November when he got going. A good dark time. Julie said nothing. He wasn't sure she'd noticed his preparations. He wasn't sure what her eyes saw anymore. Whether they focused on anything outside her head at all. Sometimes, when he saw her sitting in the kitchen, smoking a fag she barely managed to hold, her hands shaking so much the smoke zig-zagged, he wished he could think of something good to say, but all she wanted to hear was 'here's Shane'.

When Mark slipped out of the house the first Friday of November he imagined getting caught again. What would they say about him then? He turned up the collar of his black denim jacket and walked quickly off the estate. He had selected a targeted a few days ago. Not the house of books, that could wait. This one was on its own, with its own patch of hillside, just beyond the golf course. A tosser's palace that needed doing.

It was a bitter, clear night. Frost already gleaming on the ground. No cloud cover. Too light, he would have thought in the old days. The careful old days. Now he wasn't concerned. He'd try to do a good, professional job but consequences weren't important. It came to him as he walked. He didn't care anymore. What the fuck if he got caught again? What the fuck?

The thought took hold as he made his way to the house. Self-pity pumped through him. Everything around him had turned to shit. Daniels, Shane and in a slower way, Julie. Was *he* the problem? The jinx? Was it his fault that his father hadn't wanted him, his grandparents hadn't wanted him? Was this why he didn't want anyone now? Didn't need anyone? Told himself he didn't?

The questions came relentlessly, screaming like the wind though the forestry trees. He was unable to shut them out. They fed on his adrenaline and spurred him on, propelling him over the dark hillside. He walked dangerously quickly, testing the sureness of his feet but he stumbled a few times, then fell heavily, gouging his shoulder on the freezing ground, and skinning his outstretched hand. 'Aw, for fucksake, you stupid wanker!' He gasped in the still quiet. It sounded strange and died quickly.

He lay on his back and looked up at the sky. At the hard white nails of the stars. Twinkling zits in a blue-black face. At the moon which had risen. He felt like baying at it, like a crazy loon. Which perhaps he was. Definitely he was. His eyes were wet. He rubbed at them with the back of a hand and felt the salt tickle his cuts.

He couldn't believe he was crying. Couldn't believe the fat tears which dammed up then trickled down his cheek. He didn't want any of this. He wanted to be normal but he didn't know what the fuck it was.

He stayed like this for some time, until the frost started to eat into him. Until the tears stopped. They dried up suddenly. This strange, involuntary action came from a part of his brain he had no hold over. A soft part he had hardly ever glimpsed before. Perhaps next to the bit that made him pop. Or perhaps the same bit, playing a different set of tricks.

He stood up and shook himself. Stamping his feet on the ground until they became part of him again. Carry on. Shake off this shit and concentrate on the work in hand. It was all he had at the moment. All he could fall back on, that meant something in his short life. His short life, which tonight felt as though it had gone on forever. He felt that he was every nicker in every thieving land. Every nicker who had ever lived. Every soul that was not so much lost as fucked before it had got started. By the blackness of life, and how little say people like him had in it. Black like the sky that sat above him now, its tiny pieces of light the twinkling come-ons, the tempting bits dangled in front of you. The bits he wanted so much to reach. 'Don't do this to me, Shane,' he muttered, 'don't fuck with my head. Make yourself appear again. Like you disappeared. Like magic.'

Get on, you soft bastard. Get to it. Stop now and you're fucked. For good. Christ, he could do with a can. Or six. His shoulder hurt from the fall but he walked on. He skirted the golf course, its smooth greens shining frost-spattered white in the moonlight. Like another world forced into his. A neat, controlled world where things worked out.

The house was one of the largest he had done. Double bay-fronted in sizeable grounds. Old but kept in good nick by someone who liked old. Someone with lots of dosh to blow on it. There was a lamp-post in the garden, a private fucker. Cast iron. Old. With a pool of light that was from the old days. No powerful orange glare here. Just a soft yellow that died within feet of its source. For a second he thought of the knackered twisted lights of the estate.

The rear of the house was in darkness, and conveniently hedged. From his scouting he'd noticed the people here went to the golf club on Friday nights. There was an alarm on the rear wall, pretty high up, but a ladder was parked alongside a garden shed, padlocked to a concrete post. It took him twenty seconds to pick the lock and use this gift to get at the alarm. It was a new type but he quickly sussed it. Old knowledge came flowing back. Resting on the ladder, his arse numbed by the cold, he punched out a hole in the window. He'd enter and get out the same way: there would surely be deadlocks on the doors. And he wasn't looking for videos now. Just jewellery, and money if he could find any.

There was a lot of jewellery. He tipped it all into a bag and checked though every drawer in the house. No money, but he was satisfied. He reckoned he had at least a grand's worth, if he could find a fence. The Man would have offered him a hundred. Fuck that. He'd go it alone now. Maybe sniff around the boys on the estate. Dangerous messing with dopeheads but that was the way to find out stuff.

He found the bathroom, one of them, and took a leisurely slash. It was a large bathroom, with a separate place for the shower. It was hard to imagine living in so much space, but he wanted to. Not to have things on top of him all the time, to be able to prance around to his records without destroying his bedroom. And not to have to live with the sounds of everyone else. But space had to be bought.

He swilled his face, cupping his hands in water that quickly got too hot, his head etched by the moonlight that pushed strongly through the opaque window. It put a yellow cast to his face, making it look weird, and his eyes hard and small. Making him look like what he was. He shook off any repeat of the hillside thoughts, dried himself in the soft, pink towel and was out and down the ladder in a minute. He was going to leave the ladder against the wall, his calling card, but changed his mind. He replaced it, and re-padlocked it. Let the pigs think it out. Maybe Beefy. Coming up the next morning, fat red face bleary from a night on the piss, trying to look interested for the rich people.

Going back was even colder, walking into the raw edge of the wind. He'd have to start working out. Firming up what had become slack. His body had begun to match his gobsmacked mind. At least he could control muscle. He walked up to the old hideout, sat by it for a while, back against the trunk of a conifer, trying to blend in with the tree so that the wind missed him.

Cupping a smoke in his hands and looking through a gap in the trees down the valley. Those people would be coming home from the golf club soon. They would not realise they'd been done immediately. Probably think there was something wrong with the alarm. But the woman would notice when she went to put her beads away. And her old man would charge in from the bog when she shouted, and realise that the piss he saw in the unflushed pan was not his. He flicked the butt of his cigarette away, allowed himself a thin smile and made his way home.

He got back to the estate in time to mingle with the drunks. Older men shuffling home after a night on the piss. It was close to midnight and most of the kids of his own age had gone earlier, heading for nightclubs further down the valley, or maybe Cardiff for the few with motors. Blowing their giros in one go on tits and lager. Going places where they could get rat-arsed and live their dreams for a few more hours.

A huddle of stumbling men left the club, moving as one in the middle of the road, men tailing off from the main herd when they reached their houses. Instinct told him to stay in the shadows and skirt the drunks but he ignored it. Someone recognised him.

'Oi, you. Richards, innit? Here boys, it's that kid. Psycho Eyes. You know, the one who was looking after his little brother, but wasn't, like. Looking after him, be buggered.'

The drunks lurched to a halt, some holding onto others. The talker had detached himself to face Mark. A geezer about forty, two-bellied, unshaven, bullet-headed. Fists like ham and up for it. Mark walked on.

'Oi, don' you fuckin' walk away from me, pal. What happened, then? What you do to the kid?'

He pulled at Mark's shoulder.

'You're a fuckin' weirdo. Everyone knows that.'

Mark hit him. A good shot in the middle of his face. He felt the nose give under his fist. The man's legs buckled and he sagged forward with a glazed look of surprise. This was an instinct Mark didn't ignore: best to hit them first, and quickly, because a scene like this never went anywhere else.

Then the others were on him. Kicks and blows rained in on him but they were misdirected. Only a punch to the side of his head caught him squarely. He easily evaded grasping hands and put another man down with a kick to his balls. Doors of nearby houses were opening, inquisitive light probed the street and women called out for their men. He realised more might come. Rucks were a magnet on the estate, attracting every punchy toss-er. And some of them would be sober, and half fit. The drunks were wary now, as they regarded the blood-gushing nose and busted balls of their friends. He took his chance and made off, walking quickly but not running. Never running. No-one followed.

'We'll have you, Richards,' a voice called after him. 'And have you off this estate.'

Make my day, you wankers, he thought. When this lot started up on the booze again, from midday Saturday, they'd have changed the details of the fight. Distorted it, added to it, perhaps even given him a gang. Something to fit their vision of him and cover their pathetic performance. His reputation soaring.

He felt something trickle down the side of his cheek and put a hand to it. Blood. That lucky punch sod must have caught him with a ring. There was no pain but he was bleeding freely from the side of his head, somewhere near the hairline. Because of this he let himself in the back way very quietly, covered by the sound of Bat's telly going full tilt. She had it on louder as she got older. And later into the night. It was her nightclub, fella, best friend, all rolled into one. Like it had used to be with Julie. Now she didn't bother. She couldn't take the stories about all the crap the world dealt out, the reports of kids going missing and ending up dead. Before, they had been someone else's.

He knew Julie would still be up. Sat in the living room, now dimly lit with the new table lamp. She'd come back with it one day. Liked its soft light, she said. It was more dull than soft, allowing her face to rest in shadow if she sat in her usual chair. A lamp for hiding.

He didn't go in to her straight away. He needed to clean up, and he did it in the kitchen. If he went upstairs to the bathroom she'd hear him and call out. Soaking a tea towel he used it to sponge off his face. The cut was obscured by his hair. He hoped it would scab up quickly. His jacket collar was stained but it was black anyway. Satisfied with his appearance in the small square of mirror he took a can from the fridge and joined Julie.

She was staring at a blank spot on the tatty wall, drifting on the edge of sleep, but when she glanced up at him and fully opened her eyes he could not return her look.

'Oh, it's you. Emma phoned for you earlier,' Julie said.

142

'I told her I'd be out.'

'Oh.'

'Do you want a can?'

'No.'

He sat down opposite her, circling his can with his hands. This doesn't get easier, he thought.

There were two cigarettes left in her packet, and he took one.

'You had your tablets?'

'Hm?'

'Your tablets?'

'Yeah, I think. It don' matter. Where've you been?'

'Just out.'

She lit up the last cigarette and looked him over. He turned the wounded side of his head away from her and was glad of the poor light.

'You've started up again, haven't you?'

He shrugged.

'Don' bother about that. It's not important.'

'No, it's not. Nothing is. Now.'

Silence. The atmosphere heavy enough to slice. What could he suggest? Julie had never had a close friend. Perhaps because of him. He pulled at his fag and wondered if he had more upstairs. Photos of Shane were strewn around the small table. His short life in pictures. Most of the ones Julie had taken with her crap camera were fuzzy because Shane had never stopped moving. His short life had been a blur of movement. Two years of action then gone. Missing or taken. The lager started to hit him. It was lethal stuff he was buying now. Nine per cent instant charge which seemed to shoot up from the back of his throat to his brain. And assault it. He nodded to the photos.

'Been looking at those again?'

'They're all I have of him now.'

He reached for a few photos. Shane in the sand. Spoon and all. Shane nestling in his mother's arms. Safe. This one was furred at the edges from Julie's handling. A crease turning white cut across the centre, splitting Shane's face. He tidied the rest of the photos into a pile and put the ones he had picked out on top.

What the fuck could he say? Hope had been abandoned months ago. And Julie's imagination knew no bounds. Why should it? His was no different. He finished the can but the lager was sour. The old feeling of triumph after a job had been blown away. He still had the rush alright but what pumped through his veins was filled with Shane. He'd always be waiting for him. Wherever he went. More silence. Their thoughts swirling like their cigarette smoke.

Mark increased his workload after his breaking of ice, and kept to his plan of taking small valuables. Mainly jewellery and money, if he got lucky. Just before Christmas he found a wallet in one house, with four hundred pounds in it. His present.

All the stuff was in the forestry. Lying in the hole. If the pigs ever came across it they'd have a perfect record of his work, each haul was neatly bagged and bound. A nicker's life on display. He hadn't found a fence. After the hassle with the drunks he thought it better not to put out feelers on the estate. It was finished with him. So the stuff mounted up and only the money was added to the tins.

Julie didn't change as winter took hold. He didn't see or hear her crying so much, but she moved around the house like a ghost, if she moved at all. Mostly she sat by the lamp, with photos and cigarettes. In another world, letting the shortening days pass her by. Shane's photos became so worn he had to find the negatives and get more done. He put them in a folder, so that Julie could look at them under their plastic cover. But she soon had them out. So that she could handle them and keep them about her.

Emma did most of the shopping. Mark had no patience for it, so he told Emma to do it, and she was glad to help. A professional helper. Something most people would think nice, but which only increased his guilt. Which in turn fed his anger. That was still there. He had corked it up tight but it simmered inside. It had more reason to than ever but he didn't know when it would come out.

He was surprised Emma stayed around. There wasn't much in it for her. She didn't know about his tins, and he had hardly touched her since Shane had gone. It was love, she said. She loved him, but he wasn't sure what that was. No, not wasn't sure. Didn't know. Didn't know if he would ever have it to give. Didn't know where to get it from. But it was close to pain, he knew that much. Julie proved it every day. So did Emma, when she had that wounded, hurt look on her face after he turned on her. And she kept coming back for more. She wanted to fill the gap Shane left. To say, 'I'm here with you to make it better. To make you happy.' But she didn't. Happy was not something he could think about or expect. He was looking for a third piece of shit to drop on him. Daniels, Shane and what? He'd always thought in threes. His first three jobs that had gone so well, the three girls he'd had before Emma, the three 'fathers' he could remember, each one a bit more frightening. What was coming next? Emma wanted it to be happy. An escape to the land of happy. But she had no game-plan. Just as long as they were together. That had been Julie's way of thinking. Used all through her life, applied to each tosser that came along. Failing each time. Now Emma wanted a stab at it. She was just past eighteen: that was the time for it on the estate. No-one ever learns up here, he thought. Couples that stayed together for long were rare. Extinct almost. Yet every year a new batch tried it, thinking it would be different for them. And Emma was the same. 'It'll be different for us', as if the more she said it the more chance it would come true. Where the fuck did she get her hope from, wanting to take a chance with Psycho Eyes? Where could he get some for himself?

A counsellor began to see Julie. The social services arranged it on her doctor's advice. The man with the pills. Someone Mark didn't like. He was another who came to the house with distrust on his face. As if he, Mark, number one son, might sick up Shane at any time.

The counsellor was a woman, a smart piece in a smart car. A black Jap sportscar with a fancy number plate. Must be a good racket, he thought. But it was a bit late. Why did they always want to help *after* something happened? Julie didn't need counselling, she needed Shane back. And she had always needed a better life.

She came once a week, on Monday mornings, like a regular dose of pills. Julie was particularly fazed then, strung out from the weekends, when her depression peaked. She was at her loneliest then, thinking of the times she mixed with people with a sem-blance of happiness. Mark tried to stick around for her more on Saturdays.

Mark answered the door to Mary Black. She was in her mid thirties, dressed like they always were. Stylish but not shouting money at you. That wouldn't be a good idea on the estate. A blonde with a face that looked younger than some of the girls he knew half her age. He swept back his hair involuntarily, and wiped his sticky hand on the back of his jeans. This one could look him in the eye. She returned his best stare without flinching.

He showed her into the living room and she brought her smell with her. Pricey perfume which made his chest tighten as it invaded the house. He'd expected someone older, greyer. On the way to being beaten. Not someone like this. She didn't have the usual sour, superior look of people in authority. But what the hell would Julie have in common with her? He left them to it, and joined Emma in the kitchen.

'She's very attractive,' Emma whispered.

'Alright, if you like that sort of thing.'

'What sort of thing?'

He shrugged.

'Feeding off the likes of us,' he murmured.

Mark sat down heavily, making Emma nervous. He caught her look.

'What?'

'Nothing.'

'You're looking at me like you wanna say something.'

'It's just, you're so full of... stuff. What makes you so angry with everyone? All the time.'

Mark got up from the table quickly and Emma shrank away from him. Surely he wasn't going to make a scene, with that woman in the next room. Mark breathed in deeply. She saw the veins on his temples stand out, and his rapid breathing under his black T-shirt. But there was no explosion. He relaxed, turning away from her to get a can from the fridge.

'Wan' one?' he muttered.

'Course I don't. It's not even afternoon yet. You shouldn't, either, at this time.'

'Time don't mean much to me. Not exactly your regular type, am I?'

'No.'

Emma wanted to hold him. She always wanted to hold him. To have the type of relationship her friends had. Plenty of good times, and normal rows, about normal things. But normal wasn't the word for Mark. No way. He was staring out of the window, at the garden. That sand was still there: the council had run out of money again, and had shelved the new fences.

What did Mark's eyes see? Did they see Shane, out playing? Did they see where Shane was now? She hated herself for it, but there was a small part of her which doubted. That could never be sure what had happened that day. And she knew it was the same with Julie. A feeling never spoken about – each would deny it to the other – but it was there. Sometimes it came on her in the salon, as she worked on one of the girls who came in. They droned on about their boyfriends and she thought about Psycho Eyes. She wanted to enjoy her first job but it was hard, the way things were. Perhaps Mark sensed her doubt. Perhaps he was sensing it now. If she ever said it out loud... the thought frightened her. She did not want to be afraid of him. Excitement in his presence had been a compensation for his crazy ways but now it wasn't quite enough. She needed something to happen between them. Something to move them on, away from the black mood which gripped the house. But Mark hardly ever went out in the day now. He was becoming even more nocturnal. Moving further away from her. She doubted if he knew where he was going himself.

Julie was hardly aware of Mary Black entering the room that first Monday. She heard Mark mutter something and slightly inclined her head to see a woman standing in front of her, smiling. But she did not focus on her very clearly. Not at first. The doctor had given her different tablets. Stronger ones. They made everything seem flat, but took the sharp edges away. They allowed her to enter another world, a place where she could think about Shane without breaking up. Without going bitter crazy. And she thought about his happy two years, the time he was with her. When her thoughts moved to the recent past it was time for more pills.

A hand was being offered. She took it limply and felt the wedding ring. She recognised the perfume, one of many she had once tried but couldn't afford in a store in Cardiff. Dabbing each one on her forearm under the disapproving gaze of an assistant, who called her 'Madam' as if it was a joke. She had smelt her arm and dreamed all the way home.

'I'm Mary Black. You did know I was coming?'

'Yes.'

'Can I sit down?'

And so her therapy started. Mary never said much. Just encouraged Julie to talk. About anything at all. She had expected questions about Shane straight away. Being interviewed in the way of the police. Another trial. Another test. But it wasn't like that. She began to look forward to Mary's visits and to take more interest in them, to appreciate her gentle guiding. Mary lived in another world, she could tell her things that could never have been spoken to any woman on the estate. And whatever she said, she didn't have to worry that her children would be taken from her if she came across as an unfit mother. One already had been, the other was too old.

Initially her confiding centred on 'what if' and 'what might have been'. Regret at her risk taking. Regret that she had not taken more. And how she didn't understand how time, which had always passed so frighteningly quickly, now seemed to have stopped. Hanging her up in lousy nightmare spot she couldn't escape from.

'You're still young,' Mary said, in the last session before Christmas. 'Younger than me.'

Julie looked at her incredulously, at her unlined face and clear eyes. She put a self-conscious hand to her own face, and felt the skin turning hard and leathery, like the old women she had seen on the bus.

'Don't look it though, do I?' she muttered. 'Christ, you don't look much older than Mark's girlfriend. What do they say, "you're as old as you feel"? I know that's right, now.'

She pulled on her cigarette, which she knew Mary hated. She almost winced every time Julie lit up. Mary twirled the rings on her third finger. Julie had began to notice little things again. There were two rings, wedding and an older one. She didn't know much about Mary but was sure she'd have it all. The right man, the right kids, the right place to live. What must she think of this place? What must she really think? Shame welled up in her, no longer balanced with anger or defiance. If her parents had stood by her when she was carrying Mark things might have worked out differently. Given her a bit of support. Like other people had. What might have been if any man had stayed. Just one.

Mary reached out a hand. Julie felt it fit over hers, felt the exchange of warmth with this woman who had made so much more of her life. She wanted to be a child again, with a caring, close mother, not the distant figure she had known. And she wanted to cry but had gone beyond tears. Her eyes were running on empty.

'It's the not knowing that creases me,' she murmured, 'if I could be certain that Shane was truly gone, and at rest, maybe I could come to terms with it. Maybe.'

'It must be a nightmare. But you do have another son. Mark's got all his life ahead of him. Isn't that something to live for? To be a part of? I'm sure you'll have grandchildren one day.'

Julie squeezed her hand, then fumbled for another cigarette, but the packet was empty.

'Damn, I'm always running out,' she said.

'That's because you're always smoking.'

'Mark,' Julie said, 'don't ask me about him. He moved away from me years ago. Into his own world, and I've no idea what that is. He's like his father was, secretive, never says what's on his mind, and angry, all the time. I used to sense it, almost feel it sometimes, churning away in him. Telling me what a useless mother I was. And where's he going? He's done nothing in school and has done nothing out of it. And he's been in trouble. You know what they call him around here?'

Mary knew, but shook her head.

'Psycho Eyes. I'm not the only one who knows about his turns. He's famous for popping. Another Richards success story.'

'He seems quite calm.'

'Aye, well, maybe that's because of Shane.'

'Have you talked about it?'

'Not really. It's hard to reach him. A shrug and a glare is his main language. As I said, he's deep, and I haven't got the energy anymore.'

'I know it's really difficult but I think you should try. It might help you. Both of you.'

Mary consulted her diary, which was almost the size of her handbag.

'Christmas is almost on us again. We'll have to leave it until the new year now.'

Mary allowed her eyes to stray around the room as Julie subsided into silence, holding herself as though hugging an invisible person. An invisible partner. She thought of her own partner and her two children. They had given her a Christmas list more than two weeks ago. The most expensive wants underlined in scrawly crayon. The writings of a five- and seven-year-old. She wondered how she'd cope in Julie's place. Shane looked at her from his place on the television. He was quite beautiful. Blond, with an angelic smile. Shining out from this shabby, tiny room with its worn furnishings and garish wallpaper. Julie Richards was her most difficult case. Ever. Before each visit she tried to formulate a mental game-plan. Trying to build on what had gone before.

But what could she possibly say, one mother to another, that could address a loss so huge and permanent? There had been clients who had lost children to illness or accident. That was bad enough, but this was of another dimension, a woman's ultimate nightmare. No amount of training could prepare for it. Mary felt her eyes fill up as the image of Shane held her.

Julie did not notice.

'Aye, Christmas,' she muttered. 'Mark used to like it, once.'

Mary managed to control herself and looked away from the photograph.

'Why don't you make an effort to get out,' she said. 'You could go shopping in Cardiff. And Christmas might be a good time to talk with Mark. Perhaps he's not quite like you think. His girl-friend seems very fond of him.'

Julie borrowed one of Mark's shrugs.

'Mark handles all the shopping now. Pays the bills, gets my money. I can't be bothered.'

'You can't stay at home forever. The house will become a prison.'

'Maybe I deserve to be in one.'

'No. You don't. You've got to stop blaming yourself. What happened to Shane could have happened to any woman. It could have been one of my children.'

Julie gave a short, nervous laugh, and gnawed at her nails. They took the place of a cigarette.

'No, I don't think so,' she said. 'Not one of yours.'

'Why not?'

'Cos it always happens to the likes of us. I'm not stupid. It's always on the telly - when I used to watch it. Whenever a kid goes missing it's always off an estate like this one. We don't have to attract arseholes. They live here already. And one of them has had my Shane away.'

'I'll make an appointment for the first Monday of the new year,' Mary said.

Julie was sinking back into a semi-comatose state, letting the medication take her, envelope her in its vague, blunt nothing. Sank into the orange sofa, like a lost child.

Mark saw Mary out, walking down to the car with her.

'Anyone tried to nick this?' he muttered, tapping the low roof of the sports car.

'No, not yet. It's alarmed and I can disable the engine.'

She regretted he answer. It sounded like an insult. Mark offered her a thin smile.

'I can't drive,' he said.

He stood awkwardly before her, hands in pockets. Impervious to the cutting December wind.

His tall figure looked very fit, out of keeping with his run-down environment. She sensed menace in him but also a certain magnetism. A close-to-the-edge burn which would have attracted her in her student days. It still did, if she was honest. Coming to the Richards' house highlighted the safeness of her own life. Perhaps it had become too far removed from the people she tried to help. In an hour she'd be shopping in Cardiff. For those expensive, crayoned requests.

'Will she get better, then?' Mark asked.

'You could try talking to her. Julie needs all the help she can get. In time –'

'Nah, forget about "in time". She won't come out of this. Never. Unless you can bring Shane back.'

He turned abruptly and went back to the house. Leaving Mary to point her key at the car and disengage the alarm. She looked up to the abandoned house opposite. The words 'Peace to all People' were still fresh against their grey background. Had someone painted them for a joke or had they really meant it. She shivered in the wind and was glad to be gone.

Julie heard Mark shut the front door and called to him. Her voice was shaky, but could not stop it. Christmas, Mary had talked about. How the hell could she get through that?

'Do you want anything?' Mark said.

'No. Well, fags, if you got any.'

He brought her in half a pack from the kitchen.

'Couldn't even stop you smoking,' she murmured.

'Uh?'

'Nothing. It don't matter.'

They shared a match. She saw herself in Mark's eyes as he struck it. She was locked in them. A small face trapped by one son, destroyed by another. She remembered the pride she'd felt when she'd held Mark in hospital. Just minutes old. Pride despite his useless father, the nurses who treated her like shit, her absent parents and the hopeless future looming ahead of her. She had something of her own. To love without fear of having it thrown back in her face. No-one had come to see her that night but it didn't seem to matter. She hadn't wanted a man around, spoiling things, stealing the mood away from her. Mark's eyes had stared up at her. 'I'm yours,' they said, 'and you're mine.' She could not believe she had made something so perfect.

And he had been enough in those early years, before sex got in the way again. Always sex. Never love. Trying to build a future on a hopeless fuck, with Mark asleep only a few feet away. Seeing it collapse quickly. Tossers had marked her life, right through to Humphries. But when Shane came she'd felt free. Humphries leaving had been like lancing a boil. The panic that had always been in her reached a peak then but Shane blew it away from her. For good, she thought. When Shane came. When Shane came.

Julie started to nod and Mark took the cigarette from her before it burned her hand. He put a blanket over her legs. Perhaps she could sleep after a visit by the counsellor. That would be something.

Christmas loomed like a challenge for Mark. He decided to meet it head-on by doing as many jobs as he could. It had been a good time for him before. People got careless. Drank more. Went out more. Injected themselves with a bit of seasonal happiness. Other nickers would do a place and take all the presents. One geezer off the estate had even taken a Christmas tree, complete with lights. Lit it up in his own window like the stupid fucker he was. Mark'd stick to his usual stuff.

Three targets were scouted. The third would be the house of books. He doubted if there would be much in it for him but he wanted to confront it again, to tell the geezer his defences hadn't worked. Hadn't frightened anyone. And he planned a daytime raid. A first for him. Increasing the risks, but increasing the satisfaction too. He had to soak himself in action again, do what he knew, what he was good at. Keep busy. Stop shit from clogging up his head. In the new year he'd try to find a fence again. Failing that he'd go up to London and hawk the stuff around. Take Emma and make sure she looked sweet. Even dress like a ponce himself. From what The Man had paid him he reckoned he had about a grand's worth of stuff already. Maybe more if he sold it legit.

The daytime hit was a small private development farther up the valley, where it ended blind. Half a dozen detached houses nestling against the mountain, just waiting for him. A smaller version of the place where he'd been caught. Same type of houses. Same distance apart. Just as rigid in their way as the lines of old terracing. People must like being the same, he thought.

He'd put the glasses on the houses a few times before. Once in early morning, when he'd noticed them emptying. Women working was good for business. He decided on the end house. It was the easiest to skirt round and there was more cover near it. He thought of using the balaclava again but dismissed it. That was kid's stuff. Black gear. Hiding. Slithering around in the dark. He'd go as he was now. Mark fucking Richards. If he was done again he was done. After Shane there was nothing they could threaten him with.

Monday morning. A greasy, cold start. Bursts of rain then clouds breaking, letting through the odd bit of sun. A few teasing shafts, then gone again. As if the valley was on strict rations. He took the bus up. Only two other people on it. Muffled-up old geezers, who wheezed at him as he sat down. They looked as if they could snuff it at any time. One looked as if he already had. Red veiny chops and eyes that seemed to be swimming in a lake. Both men held the stumps of roll-ups in their hands. He thought of the old black and white photos in that nicked book and wondered if anything had changed. Really changed.

A woman was getting into a car as he reached the back of the houses. Probably she was the last to leave. He'd seen no kids or babies. As he flanked the rear fence he couldn't believe the change in his routine. Cool head, Mark, cool head, he kept telling himself, but it had no effect. There was no alarm on the house. It had not long been built and maybe no-one had thought of it. Or they thought this place was too far out for the attentions of the likes of him. But nowhere was too far. Or safe. He noticed the patio doors and checked through his bag with his right hand. He had a range of tools. It really would be Christmas for Beefy if he was caught carrying this lot in broad daylight, and going to work on a bus, for Christsake. But he didn't search for meaning in his actions. Just get it done.

He went to the front of the house and rang the bell. If someone answered he'd say he was looking for gardening work. Wear his best smile. His only smile. More a twist of the mouth and a glimpse of his top teeth. No-one answered. He glanced round casually. The other houses did not have a clear sight of him. He went to the rear, picked up half a building brick, one of a pile in the garden, wrapped it in the cloth he carried and quickly smashed the glass top panel of the kitchen door. The noise was sharp for a second but died quickly in the wind. It was strong here, whipping off the mountain as it prepared to work down the valley.

Yes there were presents. Yes there was a tree. A silver, tinselly thing on a dark red carpet. Next to a telly the size of a cave. And two piles of wrapped presents under it. One for him and one for her, he thought. He was in no hurry. He could see everything clearly without having to worry about stray flashlights. This place could have been done out by Julie. It had the same crap colours and shop-window furnishings, but expensive, new stuff. No kids yet, it seemed. He found the usual mug shot on a shelf. Woman about twenty five, bloke quite a bit older. Grey poking around his ears. Looked like the types who'd want to sell you something.

Upstairs he found a jewellery box and put it in his bag without opening it. He looked out the window but nothing stirred. He was not sure if he was disappointed or not. Part of him wanted to meet a geezer coming up the drive. They had a good view here. He could see two-thirds of the way down the valley, following the main road and the river. There was a glimpse of the estate, rooftops trapping the sun.

He thought of making himself a cup of coffee in the large kitchen and sat at the table for a few minutes, surrounded by white. Then went. There was still this much caution in him. Yet he knew he was changing. The Man had been right to drop him. He was getting slack.

He was back on the estate before midday. Without bothering to stash the box. He couldn't be bothered. He couldn't be bothered to see what was in it either. It was slung under the bed, where it lay in the white dust among unwashed socks and a few loose cassettes.

Julie was hardly aware of his activity. If she worried about it she didn't show it. It would be a small worry, lost in the vastness of her grief. She had been a fixture in the living room for three months, and Mark always expected to see her in there now. Julie, sofa, fags and the photos of Shane. Maybe the container of pills and a glass of lager, if she could be bothered to get it. She ate sometimes, slept sometimes. Went through the motions of life, but whatever energy she burned it was not physical. He did not like to think too much about what might be going on in her head. It sparked off his own nightmares.

He thought of taking Mary Black's advice. But how could he talk? It had always been hard before. For so long it had been just the two of them, with words too often used as weapons. Each taking out their frustration on the other, without anyone else to deflect them. Now it seemed impossible to communicate. She cut down his mumbling, late night attempts with her hazy lack of response. They ended up smoking and drinking, listening to the odd, echoing footstep in the street, which was quieter now that the estate had settled into winter. The fog was back. As impenetrable as Julie's silences. Rolling down the hillside like clouds that had been shot down. Deadening the estate, bringing icy rain.

'We gotta do something for Christmas,' Emma said.

They were in the kitchen, Mark mellow after his third can of skull attack. His second target had been accomplished no problem. Only the house of books was left, and he was saving that for Christmas Eve.

'What do you think?' Emma asked.

'Uh?'

'About Christmas. Are you listening?'

'What you on about?'

'Julie isn't getting no better, is she? Perhaps we could... well, you know, get closer to her, somehow.'

'Oh aye. "We", is it?'

He drained his can, slurping loudly and licking away his froth moustache.

'You're gonna be pissed,' Emma said.

'Hope so.'

'I've saved a bit since I been down the salon.'

'How much?'

'About a hundred quid.'

He smiled.

'Thought you'd be pleased,' she said, a little shyly.

For a moment he thought of telling her about the tins. Dashing upstairs and bringing them down, tipping out the notes onto the plastic table. Then watching her face as money showered her. His secret work. His success story. Part of him wanted applause for it. Adulation. But he already had it from Emma. It had been easily come by and constant ever since. So constant he didn't respect it. He loved and hated himself in equal measure and was the same way with Emma. Not wanting her around but glad of her help since the summer. When his restlessness and guilt threatened to boil over he could only wonder at the depth of her calm. She had only turned on him once, the time by the statue. He had thought her stupid for a long time, an easy bimbo shag, but was not so sure now. Her life had been as shit as his, almost, but she seemed able to rise above it.

'We could trim up,' Emma said timidly. 'It's not too late, though there's only three days left. We haven't got nothing yet.'

She was getting fond of 'we'. Shopping. He'd never given it a thought. Julie had always handled stuff like that. And now Emma. He saw the look on her face and knew she expected one of his outbursts. But he controlled himself. He knew he had to, with Julie the way she was. Put all his anger into nicking.

'If you want,' he mumbled.

She was surprised, and encouraged.

'How much money have you got?' she asked.

'I got a few quid in my wallet. From the money they give Julie.'

'I never seen you with a wallet,' Emma said.

'I keep it upstairs.'

He went up to his bedroom and took a hundred pounds from a tin. As an afterthought he added another fifty. He fanned it out on the kitchen table.

'God knows how you got this,' Emma murmured.

'An' He won't tell.'

'It wasn't from saving your mother's money, I know that. Two hundred and fifty quid!' Emma cried, 'I can hardly believe it.'

She threw herself around his neck.

'Make sure you get plenty of booze,' he said, fending off her pecking mouth.

'Are you coming?'

'Don't be funny.'

'How am I gonna carry it all?'

'Get a taxi back. You got enough there.'

This deflated her somewhat and she sat back down. Taking one of his cigarettes.

'Shouldn't you check on Julie?' she murmured.

'What for? She's not going anywhere. Not doing anything. Just sitting there. Like a cabbage.'

'Don't talk like that about her, Mark.'

'Okay, leave it.'

He opened another can. She was right, he was almost pissed. That comfortable, dizzy feeling, when the ceiling started to shift, just very slightly. Emma took the last can, and he didn't object. She pulled at her cigarette and blew the smoke at him.

'I want to spend Christmas here,' she said, 'Mam'll be slobbering over her new fella and I can't stand him.'

'He give you any hassle?'

'No, I just can't stand him. Like you felt with Humphries – and everyone bloody else.'

'Where's your old man these days?'

'Down Newport somewhere.'

'Don' you never see him?'

'Not much. I saw him just before my last birthday. He gave me ten quid.'

'Generous bastard.'

'Look, I don' wanna talk about *him*.'

He could understand this and for once did not push it. Their lives shared a lot of missing people. Parents, grandparents. Missing in thought and deed.

When Emma went home he thought about a present for her and found one in the jewellery box. A string of pearls. Real pearls, but Emma wouldn't know that. She'd think them twenty quids' worth of paste and they were probably worth a grand. There was no way he would have considered something so risky a few months ago. But that was then.

Emma would have liked to stay. Move in with him. She dropped bigger and bigger hints but didn't dare ask straight out. He couldn't get his head round it. Sharing. It was what other people did, and a lot of them failed at it. He could give things – money – but share, he'd never thought of doing it. As he sat on the bed, examining the rest of the jewellery, he tried to think of a present for Julie. But there was only one thing she wanted and he could not provide it.

He fingered a few necklaces, old brooches, and assorted earrings. All good stuff. Letting the light catch them. Pretty things, but useless. It was strange to think that Shane had disappeared only feet away, and Daniels had gone down a few yards further on. Maybe they were watching him now, if the religious lot were right. He reached for a diamond-clustered ring, held it up to the window and made it shine out at the blackness. Shining towards heaven with the fruits of his labours.

Emma got trimmings. And a miniature Christmas tree she put in the corner of the living room, then changed her mind and placed it on top of Julie's teak-effect unit. Where it shone out its glittering silver tinsel finish. They hadn't had one since Mark was ten. And then one of the tossers had trashed it in a drunken performance.

Mark helped Emma put up the decorations, and had never felt so weird. Doing this stuff. What other people did. What wankers did. He was going along with it, and didn't know why. There were parts of him that he knew his mind kept hidden. Just the odd flash when he was in temper, or in action. Feelings he wanted to plunge into, and let them take him with them all the way. And now he was putting up fluffy Christmas things.

Julie sat watching them with a hint of a smile on her otherwise blank face. Rocking slightly with a cardigan draped over her shoulders. Zonked out of her head on pills, like someone's mad grandmother. But wherever she was now it had to be better than the nights of crying. And her eyes no longer drilled him with accusation.

'S'nice,' Julie murmured, as Emma showed her a large paper bell. Father Christmas in a balloon, waving.

'It's really cute,' Emma said, 'innit, Mark?'

'Oh aye. Cute.'

He was not sure which life he was living anymore. Psycho Eyes the thief, the brother loser, or the reformed character with a steady girlfriend, looking after his wasted Mam.

'What you thinking?' Emma asked, as she held one end of a trimming whilst he pinned up the other.

'Nothing much, but I'll be going out later.'

He was sure of one thing, that he wanted to finish his last job of the year. Give that bearded bastard a Christmas treat.

'Okay, love,' Emma said.

She was amazed that he was helping. Maybe he *could* change. Was changing. His eyes didn't flash like they used to. Maybe he wouldn't be Psycho Eyes anymore.

So, it was Brynhyfryd again. The house of books. He wondered what the name meant, like he wondered what the words on the statue meant. It was typical of the poxy valley. Lots of stuff around in a language no-one understood or wanted. No-one he knew, anyway.

It was a shock going out into the night. Leaving the house at its baking best. Julie really pumped up the heating now, and sat still in it for hours, like she was some kind of lizard. She had forgotten how to worry about paying bills. Anything real passed her by now. He had responsibility for everything. For her. Sometimes it brought on blind panic. How could he go now? Follow his dreams? He wanted to be strong enough to go, to leave her to it. But there was a something in him that kept him here, tied to her problems, and he hated this knowledge, that he was not quite the heartless bastard he wanted to be. He kicked a loose stone in the road and cursed himself for a stupid fucker. Stop thinking useless stuff and get on with it, you cloth-headed sod. Stop now and where will you be? Sinking into soft shit like a ponce. Like Humphries and Daniels, and everyone else he'd known.

He struck out over the hillside and rain welcomed him. Squally bursts sprayed over the valley by a vicious wind. He kept his hooded head down but it found his face just the same. As if it was looking for him personally. Wanted to single him out, knowing he belonged in the wild, black night.

He reached the house by ten. The man was out, as expected. He got in the same way as before. The place hadn't been alarmed. He'd expected this too. In the main living room he flicked his torch around. Small yellow circles picked out the books, in cases standing taller than a man. He found the ones that had interested him before. This geezer had them in a section. The old valley days. He took out an armful. The curtains were heavy and drawn so he risked the table lamp and sat down in the armchair next to it. As if the place was his own. Fingering books. He flicked open the pages of the first one, looking for photographs. Words were no use to him. He didn't have the patience for them.

Some photos were black and white, the oldest a brown colour. He'd never had much sense of the past and tried to forget his own but there was something about these old images that had hooked him the first time. Like a secret, forgotten world, opening up just for him. Working men in black suits, often in large groups. Very large groups. As if they were machines themselves. Hawkish, hard faces, sometimes hostile. Outside pits and other workplaces. As if proud to be there, even if they were piss-poor. And they were that. Piss-poor like the people he knew now. He saw the same faces, every day on the estate. Whether there was work or not, that hadn't changed. Maybe the valley was designed for crap. Maybe it was all the people deserved, if they had put up with it for so long.

He noticed a glass cabinet in the corner. It had a good range of booze in it. He poured himself three fingers of whisky, something he rarely drank but which seemed right for the house. Old and smoky. It hit him like a hammer, combining with the cans he'd drunk before setting out. What the fuck was he doing here? He couldn't even be bothered to search the rest of the house.

He looked through other books. Tracing picture headlines with his finger. Not attempting to read the words? Endless rows of the fuckers. He glanced at the books surrounding him. If he swivelled his round the room they were still there. This geezer couldn't have read them. Not more than a few. No-one could be that sad.

Another large tumbler was half-filled. The house was warm and the drink relaxed his body. He rested his head back against the leather chair. Lord of the fucking manor.

He was with Shane again. And Daniels. And the black hole. Only bigger this time. A chasm in the ground, inviting them all to jump into it. Into its lovely, peaceful, evil dark. Shane and Daniels did. He saw them fall, spiralling down into the blackness without a sound. Shane turning to look up at him. Wanting him to join them. How were his eyes lit like that? So that he could see them no matter how far Shane dropped. Dwindling specks of brother-light.

He tottered on the edge of the hole, its cruel updraught raising the hairs on the back of his neck. Knowing there was such a thing as cold sweat. Wanting to follow them. To end all the shit. To get it over with. But not being able to work his legs. They were lead, rooted to the spot. Not letting him go. Not letting him get away this easy.

Someone was calling him. From the hole? From inside his head? His eyes began to focus. He tasted stale whisky in his mouth, saw the room, saw the books. Saw the bearded man standing over him. He tried to get up but was pushed back into the chair.

'Not this time, mate,' the man shouted. 'The police'll be here any minute.'

He was awake now. His senses screaming at him. He'd fallen asleep. A-fucking-sleep. Unbelievable. His first instinct was to get up and try to charge out. Get away like last time. But this geezer was standing over him, with a cricket bat in his hand. Fifteen stone of the fucker.

'It is you, isn't it?' the man said. 'Without your balaclava. What the hell are you doing? Reading my books. Drinking my whisky. What kind of burglar are you? And on Christmas bloody Eve.'

He made a move to get up.

'Stay where you are. I'll use this, if I have to.'

The man didn't want to do anything. Even with the bat, he could probably have got away from the sod. He could see him shaking as he clutched his weapon. Charge him in the balls with his head and he'd be down. But something stopped him. A tiredness gripped him and wouldn't go. He'd been dreaming something. It had gone from him, but left him with a feeling of being unable to move. Of not wanting to. And he was more than a bit pissed.

Winking blue lights again. Stopping outside. Stopping for him.

'Come in,' the man shouted, 'the door's open. He's in here.'

It was happening again, and this time he had made it happen. Same pigs. Same questions. But calmer. Tossers didn't surround him. No dogs barked. And the pigs were baffled and suspicious. They were not used to this.

'And you say nothing is missing, sir,' Pig One said.

'No, I don't think so. There's a broken window out the back but nothing else has been damaged. He's taken a few books from the shelves and drunk my scotch.'

He was handcuffed to Pig Two, a geezer built like a derelict shithouse. He felt his own height and weight diminish. Pig Two took him into the hall, whilst the householder was questioned.

'Don't you have a life?' Pig Two said, 'any life at all? Doing a house on Christmas Eve, for Christsake.'

He shrugged and did not reply. They had already cautioned him. Pig One came out with the Beard, who was minus cricket bat. He'd probably stowed it when the police knocked.

'I can't understand what he was playing at,' the Beard said, 'but I'm sure it's the same boy as before.'

'All that will be gone into at the station, sir. We have your statement. That'll be all for now. Hope this hasn't spoilt your Christmas.'

161

And they were gone. Mark jammed into the back with Pig Two. The Hulk.

'How big are you?' Mark muttered.

'Aye, aye,' Pig One said, as he drove, 'we have lift-off. It talks.'

'Six six,' Pig Two answered, with a touch of pride, 'and about eighteen stone.'

'He's a fat git,' Pig One said.

They were in the station in minutes, so empty were the roads. Everyone was inside: in pubs, clubs or houses. Getting rat-arsed. Getting ready. Beefy was on the desk.

'Brought you a present,' Pig Two said, uncuffing Mark.

'Jesus Christ. It's SAS Man. Not at it again, are you?'

Mark raised his eyes and half smiled. He expected a mouthful but Beefy seemed puzzled when he heard the story. Not triumphant at all. He took him to the interview room.

'You stupid young sod,' he said. 'Why didn't you learn? This is going to be great for your old girl, isn't it? After all that trouble with your brother.' He pushed him into a chair. 'It'll be Crown Court this time. They're getting tough on house jobs now, and on repeat young offenders. You're going down for sure.'

Mark had never doubted it. Beefy stood over him for a few moments, hands on hips, red face trying to work him out. He thought he might get a slap but the man just waved a fat hand at him. Waving him away, to someone else. Letting him become someone else's responsibility.

The procedure was the same as before and passed in a blur. A new guy interrogated him. Thin-faced. Tight-lipped. Sour. Looked like he had a permanent guts ache.

He'd been caught red-handed again. Redder-handed. But there was no buzz this time. No searching his mind for defences. No attitude. Just a calm, grey blur through which questions came. The sergeant mistook his mood for sullenness and started to get angry. He wanted to be home with his wife and kids. With his family.

It was a sudden decision. Mark began to blab. To reel off his old jobs. Places, times. The sergeant almost had a turn. His mood changed and his mean face started to glow as he realised he was getting his Christmas present early. He double-checked the recorder and winked at the guy by the door.

'Attaboy, Mark. Now you're making sense. Hang on, you're going too fast. Jesus Christ, are you for real?'

He reeled them all off. A photographic memory of each job. At one point the sergeant stopped him while he changed the tape.

Mark wasn't sure why he was doing it. He was surprised, too. But he liked the release. The long outpouring of confession. Each job declared eased him, even though he knew he'd go down. Emma had said they had to do something for Christmas. Well he was doing that alright. She'd be getting worried by now, wondering whether to say anything to Julie. Wondering if his mother could take anything in. Had the pigs phoned the house yet? He realised he hadn't even asked for a solicitor. No wonder Gutsache looked over the moon.

'You're a one-man crime wave,' the man said, not without admiration.

Mark reached the last job and the sergeant ended the formal interview by switching off the tape. He put his hands behind his head and stretched.

'Well, that's a job well done,' he said. 'If you're bullshitting us, mind....'

'You know I'm not. What happens now?'

'It's serious, but you've helped yourself by coming clean. House burglary is being given priority now in the courts. People like you are being targeted. There'll be a special Magistrates' in the morning, Christmas or no Christmas. Your solicitor can apply for bail. We'll oppose that, with the amount of work you've done. It'll go to Crown Court, before a Beak.'

The sergeant went on. Wanted to know how he got rid of the stuff, but the bloke seemed to know he'd never grass, and didn't push it too much. He was too high on the confession. Busting a gut to phone his guvnor, to risk a bollocking for interrupting his Christmas with the good news: We can wrap up fifty jobs at least, sir.

He was taken to a cell and banged up. It might have been the same one as before but it had been painted. Not much stuff had been written on the walls yet. Someone had drawn a prick, that was about it. There didn't seem to be anyone else home. Just silence and a faint murmur of voices somewhere else.

He sank onto the thin mattress of the bunk – usual piss and fags smell – and closed his eyes. It was half a year since Shane had gone. He'd handed Julie that nightmare and now he was about to hand her another one. She'd already been zonking herself up for Christmas, taking more of her pills. She'd need another shed-load when she found out about this. If she could take it in. He should have felt yet more guilt but maybe he had reached the limit for that. The world fucking record. Instead he was able to feel relief. In this stinking poxy cell facing a prison sentence. That something was over. A part of him was over. He had talked it out of himself in half an hour. And he didn't know where it had come from. Something made him do it, like when he popped or lost it. He thought about the tins. He hadn't confessed them. Oh no. And they wouldn't be found. The pigs would go through the house, but without ripping it apart. They knew the stuff was long gone and would think any money he'd made he'd have spent instantly. Why should he be any different? No-one saved. Other nickers couldn't even spell the word. The law would be too pleased with his confession. They thought in nice straight lines and liked neat endings. That sergeant had thought him stupid for falling asleep in the house of books. End of story.

The Man would sweat for a while though, if niggers could. He thought about him in that silver motor, listening in disbelief as some other nicker told him how Mark Richards had grassed himself up. Fingering his gold chains with those huge soft killer hands. That was a good image to sleep on.

Beefy phoned Julie late on Christmas Eve. It wasn't his job but he felt he should. Emma answered. Mark didn't like her to stay in the house overnight but she had decided to wait for him. At first, when he didn't show, she thought he was just being a sod. Making her wait, maybe even wanting to spoil their Christmas, if his mind was on the twist again. He had it in him. Whenever things looked more hopeful, and they'd gone a few days together without rowing, he'd draw away, as if anything remotely approaching happiness was a slap in the face. A personal insult. As it grew late she began to worry. Surely he couldn't be out nicking. Not tonight of all nights.

But he was. Had been. And had been caught. The voice on the phone told her so, after she said it wasn't possible to speak to Julie. She was out of it, having had a can with her pills. The policeman told her he knew Mark from before. Told her there was no point in anyone coming down the station now. He was banged up for the night and would appear in a special court in the morning. Emma couldn't believe they'd have a court on

Christmas morning. She was told the name of Mark's solicitor but she knew it anyway. His number was in the book Julie kept by the phone. One of the few in it.

Her hand trembled as she looked for Maule's number. There were two. She phoned the one for emergencies which she guessed must be his home. It was. Laughter and music in the background when Maule answered. She was shaking all over now, and concentrated on keeping her voice steady as she explained the situation to Maule. She heard the distaste in his sharp intake of breath as he recognised Mark's name.

'The police are right,' Maule said. 'There's nothing I can do now, but I'll be there in the morning.' A woman's voice called him. ·

'Will he have to stay inside?' Emma asked.

'I can't say anything now.'

That means yes, she thought, biting her lip.

'Thank you,' she said quietly, letting Maule get back to his normal world with normal people in it.

She turned out the lights downstairs and went up. Julie was sleeping when she looked in on her. The sheets pulled tightly around her with only her head showing. She was snoring, a struggling snorting sound, as though sleep was more an effort than relief. Her container of pills was inches from her face, waiting on the bedside table for her in the morning.

Mark would go mad if he knew she was sleeping in his room but she banished this thought from her mind. He did not deserve her fear of him. Even after Shane he could do this, and with such perfect timing. It was impossible to understand. *He* was impossible to understand.

Emma lay in Mark's thin bed. Christ, this might put his mother over the edge, when it sank in. Could Julie's life get any worse? But Emma hung on to hope. If it could all end here. If Mark could be changed by going down. She allowed herself to think this for a few minutes. Mark coming back a changed man. All the anger removed. Ready to get a job. Then she got real. All the boys she'd known who'd gone to young offender places came back worse. Every one. As if their minds had been tooled up for more crime. Bigger stuff. Training by other nickers and nutters. God knows how it would affect Mark. And just a couple days ago he'd helped with the trimmings. It made no sense. No sense at all.

She found herself crying without realising it, so slyly had the

165

tears come. Rain was beginning to fall. She heard it brush against the window, then drum steadily on the roof. It came on strongly and she heard someone running home down the street. Mark's house was more exposed than her own. A chunk of brick jutting out from the hillside.

Her future seemed as bleak as the weather if she stuck with Mark. How would they ever get off the estate now? The faces of girls she'd known in school flashed through her mind. So many of them had kids already. Some were pregnant again. It seemed crazy to her, but no crazier than getting involved with Mark.

As she finally drifted into sleep she thought she saw Mark standing in front of her, face reddening, a savage put-down on his lips as he was about to pop. If he disappeared now this would be how she remembered him.

Court time again. After a long night of snatched sleep. Woken by a drunk shouting. Kept awake by his own thoughts. They were doing time themselves, inside his head. Permanently on parade. Stubborn little bastards that liked to get stuck in. Even so, the relief stayed with him. It hung on by its fingernails, and now that he had a taste of it, he was fucked if he'd let it go.

Everyone was pissed off that the court had been called. Apart from the law. A good catch was a good catch. Anytime. Maule met him half an hour before he was due to appear.

'Do you want to retract your statement?' he asked.

Mark could smell last night on him. Maule's eyes were bleary and shot with red.

'What for?' he answered.

'We could say it was down to duress.'

'To what?'

'Stress. You really shouldn't have said anything before contacting me. It'll be difficult now. Very difficult.'

Maule was going through the motions. The man didn't want difficult. Mark didn't mind. He knew Maule would be thinking about how he'd conned him the first time. Owning up to only one job. He was surprised that Maule had even shown up. He must need the work.

'It won't be difficult at all,' Mark muttered. 'I've come clean with the lot. That's it.'

Maule got closer in to him and whispered.

'Did you really do all those houses? This is not something

166

you've made up?'

He glared at him.

'Leave it out. I may be crazy but I'm not mad.'

Maule looked unconvinced.

'Bail will be difficult,' he sniffed.

Maule thought of Mark's disappeared brother. It was a card he might play. Family trauma and all that but he hesitated to bring it up. It was another can of worms altogether and that case was still unsolved. He could have done without being in court on Christmas Day but thought of the thirty thousand pound extension just finished on the house.

Mark didn't take a lot of interest in the proceedings. He'd made a decision and knew where he was going. *Really* knew. For the first time. He did notice Emma sitting at the back but kept his eyes from her. He was glad Julie hadn't made it. Christ, it seemed a lifetime ago they'd both walked out of this court the first time. Together then. Allies. Pals. Mother and first-born.

Bail was denied. He was remanded. Maule said he'd try again, after Christmas. Emma was crying as they led him down. He heard her but did not look round. It would make her worse. She'd been at it all night, probably, and he wasn't worth it.

He was back in his freshly painted cell again. And would be in Cardiff nick for Christmas dinner.

There were no other prisoners in the van. Just Mark and a guard. Bits of the valley flashed by through the grill in the back door. He could have charted his journey down it by the jobs he'd done. He'd nicked the arse off this area, bled it dry like the good pro he'd been. Been. Was it over?

They reached Cardiff by midday. Early rain had petered out and a weak sun tried to show itself. He tried to stretch a bit as he got out of the van. Walking tall. Thinking of the movies he'd seen when the guy was delivered to the hole. Wondering whether he'd be shagged by the other inmates or fucked in a hundred different ways by the system. He laughed to himself. At himself. That was in the real world. The big wide world. Not here. Not in poxy little Wales. Losers' country. Wales, England.

The part of the prison where they put young offenders was full. Chock-a-block with bent kids. So they put him in with the older guys. Which suited him. He wanted the test straight away. With kids he could easily be top dog.

He was with remanders, and would share a cell with two others, a screw told him. There was no interview with the governor, nothing like that. Nothing like in the films. And remand prisoners were not banged up all day. They were allowed out most of the time.

He didn't think much of his cell-mates, Scouse and Duane. Scouse was a car nicker since the age of twelve, and a smackhead by the look of him. A short, shifty little geezer with a yellowish permanently sweating face and darting eyes. A bit like Daniels. Same hang-dog expression. Scouse was afraid of him as soon as they met, but then he'd be afraid of everybody. His life hung on fear. His mate Duane was different. A big bastard. Muscles turning to flab but still impressive and crap tattoos all over him.

'What you in for?' Duane asked.

He told him.

'That all? No violence?'

Duane snorted with derision and flexed his muscles, his eyes appraising Mark's physique.

'Looks like he keeps in shape, just like you Duane,' Scouse said.

'Ain't like me, man. No-one like me here.'

Mark saw the challenge in his eyes but ignored it. These twats probably thought him years older than he was. Let them think it.

The prisoners had food on their mind. He joined the queue for Christmas dinner. It was the closest he'd ever got to a group activity. Even on Community Service he'd gone his own way. But the speed of change in his life did not faze him. It would be day to day stuff from now on. Had to be. No more dreams. If he had a future, if there was a future, it would have to wait. And the tins could wait with it.

'Oi, Psycho Eyes!'

He flinched, but did not acknowledge the call. But the voice did not give up. He turned to see an estate tosser on another table, one of the older druggies.

'Got you at last have they, butty?' the man said.

He nudged someone next to him.

'That's Mark, that is. Psycho Eyes we calls him.'

A screw shouted for them to keep the noise down.

Duane had heard the name. He sat next to Mark, with Scouse close by. They seemed to have adopted him but he didn't like it. Duane wolfed his food, a human mechanical digger. Scouse picked at his without much interest. Mark knew what he'd rather have.

The food wasn't bad. He'd expected swill but it was alright. Julie had never been much of a cook. Egg and chips was her speciality. And Emma was worse. What would they be doing now? Eating dinner together? Nah, Julie would never be up for it. Not if last night had sunk in. And Emma would be hating him. Blaming him.

As he ate the prison food he wondered what it would be like to go straight. If he ever could. Work, pay tax, have a wife and a few kids, and a house that wasn't a run down piece of shit. What most people wanted, and did. The thought of all that had always turned his mind to puke. Turned his whole body sick until it brought on a mood. Even thinking about it was a defeat. A failure. But being different was fucking hard. It made other people mean. Almost as mean as himself.

Duane bumped his elbow. They were on the Christmas pudding.

'Fucking lovely jubbly this, innit?' Duane said. He pointed a spoon at Scouse. 'Look at that sad wanker. Eats like a fucking bird. Like a fucking sparrow. Ain't got a body like you and me, Marky.' He took Scouse's pudding. 'Want some?' he asked Mark, scooping half into his bowl without waiting for an answer.

Duane was the instant buddy type. Wanting to latch onto someone straight away. Someone like himself. He would be a dangerous bastard, if crossed. And there was something else about him. Maybe queer. A big arse bandit who was taking a shine to him. He'd have to watch himself. Scouse grinned at him, as if he was a new addition to the family.

Emma stayed with Julie over Christmas. Her mother was relieved, there'd be less tension in the house, less chance of a row with her new man. More chance she'd hang onto him. Word was soon around the estate about Mark. It started tongues wagging again with the old stories from the summer.

'They're on about little Shane again,' Bat said, as she sat smoking in Julie's kitchen. Sucking on her cigarette with purple-painted lips, which made her wrinkled, rouged face even more of a joke. She was going down the club for the Boxing Night 'do'. Emma imagined her bulk drunk and wobbling to the music, knocking wimpy men flying.

'They say he must have done something,' Bat said. 'I don', mind. No way. Mark is a funny one but he wouldn't do nothing like that.'

But her eyes said she thought he might have. Even wanted him to have. She would overdose on the biggest nastiest piece of news ever and have enough gossip to last the rest of her life. Emma didn't want her around and didn't want her talking to Julie but she kept quiet.

'How is she now?' Bat asked, nodding her head at the ceiling.

'Bout the same. Getting some sleep.'

'Poor kid. She's had it bad. Bastard men'

Emma still wanted to defend Mark, but what could she say? He hadn't cared about her or Julie when he'd been out nicking. And it was big stuff, doing houses. Not like cars or the bits of shoplifting she'd done in school. Bat went after she'd finished her smoke, eager to get legless for Christmas.

Emma went upstairs and looked in on Julie. She stood in the doorway and watched her breathe steadily under the sheets.

'I'm not asleep,' Julie murmured as Emma was about to close the door. 'Come back in.'

Julie sat up and patted the side of the bed.

'Was that her next door?' she asked.

'Yes. She came round for a chat with you. I told her you were in bed.'

'Aye, sniffing round, more like. Watch what you say to her.'

'I do.'

'Good.'

Julie seemed more alert, as if shaking off a long sleep.

'I haven't taken the tablets today,' she said, 'you never noticed.'

'You feel okay?'

'Things aren't so hazy. I wasn't sure what was happening yesterday, with Mark, but it's sunk in now. I didn't think it could get much worse. They'll bring it all up about my Shane again. I know how people think round here.'

'No they won't. I haven't heard nothing.'

Julie sniffed out a short laugh.

'You're a good girl, love, but you'll never lie like a Richards.'

Julie sank back down in the bed.

'I been watching the moon through a gap in the curtains,' she said. 'I used to love looking at it when I was a kid. My grandad told me it was a torch, a huge yellow torch which a giant shone when he was looking for something. And the stars were the torches of other giants, but much farther away. All out there looking for something. Something lost in all that blackness. I was always amazed at how bright the moon could get. On a clear night. They've put men on the bugger, haven't they? God knows why. God knows why men do anything. Aye, they can do that, but they can't find my Shane.'

'No,' Emma said quietly.

'Don' worry, girl. I'm not going to start.'

She rested a hand on Emma's arm.

'I should be asking you how you are. Going to the court on your own.'

'I thought it was working out with me and Mark. He seemed to be getting better.'

'Go and get me a fag. I've run out.'

Emma went downstairs to get her packet.

'Don't worry,' Julie said as she lit up, 'I won't burn the bloody house down. Look, the moon's going down now. The giant's off.'

She pulled back more curtain. It was a clear, blue-black night, frost edging the garden as it grew colder.

'Do you think there's anything in it?' Julie asked.

'In what?'

'God, Heaven, and all that.'

'Never really thought about it.'

'Nor me, 'til lately. It would be nice though, wouldn' it? To have something better to look forward to. That no bugger could take away. Don' laugh, but I used to love going to Sunday school. I did. Went until I was nine. My mother was keen.'

They sat quietly for a few minutes. Julie's cigarette glowing to the last of the moon. Each woman lost and locked up in thought.

'Nah, there can't be nothing up there,' Julie muttered. 'Why would He let things like Shane happen? Why should we have it so shitty down here? It don' make sense at all.'

'I haven't really thought about it,' Emma repeated.

Each minute clung to Mark. Being on remand told him all he wanted to know about the real thing. He was alert when they were banged up in the night. Prepared for anything. Looking for a wrong move from Duane. None came.

As he heard each man fall asleep, a heavy sigh from Duane, and a thin, raspy rattle from Scouse, he realised there would be a few years of this. Living on the edge, inches from fuckers like these. Low-life. Which was what people thought he was. Maybe he was. Perhaps this was his true level.

Prison echoed. Clanking when something was shut, screws walking outside, a chorus of coughs and cries. Every noise was a public one. Nothing was private in here. That would be the real punishment. There was a tiny barred window, but big enough for him to tell there was a moon out tonight. Strong enough to cut through the city lights. He'd walked back from a job many times with one over his shoulder. Now he was cut off from it, from all those free wild nights.

He stayed awake as long as he could. Knowing that the nightmare would flourish here. He was in a black hole so he was bound to dream about his own. And Shane's face would be waiting for him.

The rumble with Duane came two days later. In the showers. Duane came up behind him and tried it on. Making out it was a joke at first. He slipped out of Duane's soapy grasp, spun round and dug a fist hard into his stomach. Knowing that his face would be granite. It hurt him but he didn't go down. He came back at him. Beating the crap out of someone was probably just as good as sex for Duane. Maybe better. Mark knew he had to stay out of range to have a chance. He caught sight of Scouse. The little sod's smile just visible through the steam. Everyone else had fucked off. Left them to it. He shouldn't have let himself be distracted. Duane punched him to the side of the head and slammed him against the wall. His head cracked against it but he got a knee between them. It took all his strength to keep him off, but it was only a matter of time. He bit at his ear as their heads closed. Crunched right through it. Duane screamed as the blood poured down the side of his face. He lost it completely.

'Fucking bastard shit. You're dead, man.'

He tried to get away from the wall but Duane forced him back. Though he blocked some punches, more got through. He felt his nose go and his head crack a second time against the wall. His legs were tiring but he held on desperately. 'Come on, you bastard,' he screamed inside, *'you're supposed to be the Psycho.'* He caught Duane with an elbow to the face but it was no use, the man was too strong.

Then there was a lot of shouting that wasn't theirs. He heard

Scouse's warning voice, then Duane was held by two screws. Then by two more. He knocked one off but the others wrestled him down to the floor, where he was quietened with truncheons. No-one bothered with Mark for a few minutes, they all were too eager to give Duane a kicking. Which was justice he understood. An inert Duane was dragged away.

'Tried to have you, did he?' a screw asked him. 'Come on, move yourself, and don't bleed over me.'

It was all pain as he walked, but it was the involuntary tears from his busted nose that he hated. They took him to the first-aid room where he waited a long time with tissues up his nose. His ribs hurt and the back of his head told him all about the wall. The medical officer finally turned up.

'I've been attending to your dancing partner in the next room,' the doctor said. 'You did quite a bit of damage.'

He checked his head, and told him his nose would heal on its own. The doctor gave him pain killers and he was taken to a new cell, with just one other occupant, old geezer who told him through toothless gums that he'd been in and out of prisons all his life. In more than out by the look of him.

Mark was out himself before the new year. Maule had gone back to court and been successful in his bid for bail. Allying Mark's confession to the state of his mother, and the fact that she had no-one to look after her. Maule drove him back to the estate himself but Mark did not feel grateful. He didn't know what he felt and wasn't sure if he wanted to be back. Caught between Emma and Julie and killing time until he went down. Nah, course he was glad to be back. Even the wasted estate was a welcome sight.

Maule didn't stop. Mark managed to utter thanks but the word almost stuck to his lips, so little had he used it. Emma was back in work after her short holiday which made things easier. He had only Julie to deal with, and expected her to be still out of it. More so, after what he'd done.

He was wrong. He saw the change in her straight away. She was not back to what he'd always known, that woman had been blown away for ever. But she was no longer pilled-up, and her eyes didn't look like they belonged to someone else.

'Maule told me he'd got you out,' Julie muttered. She held the door open for him but did not touch him. He went through the kitchen to the fridge. There were no cans in it.

173

'Where's the lager?' he asked.

'I'm not keeping it in the house any more. Make yourself tea if you want.'

He couldn't remember a time when the fridge hadn't been well-stocked, no matter how short money was. But now wasn't the time to say anything. Julie was obviously trying to break out of the downer she'd been on since summer. Despite him. They sat at the plastic table, each cigarette burn on it familiar to him.

'I think I'll buy us a wooden table,' he said. 'I'm fed up of this crap.'

'I'm fed up of *your* crap,' Julie said. 'Couldn't you have let it go? At least over Christmas. And how the hell did you get caught like that? That fat Pig said you were sleeping in the bloke's house. What were you playing at?'

'I dunno,' he answered. 'I drank some whisky and felt tired. Next thing I knew the geezer was there.'

Julie looked at him carefully. Was her son really more than strange? Mad? Psycho? She'd always dismissed his reputation, but they said mothers were blind. And those on the estate didn't seem to have eyes at all. Mark's face was paler than usual and his nose had been rearranged. A bruise was darkening. Yet he had never looked more attractive. Not just his looks. More than that. A kind of power below the surface that would have made her jump through hoops if he'd been an early boyfriend. Just like Emma did now. Yet he'd done nothing good or even useful in his life.

Mark caught her look but was not angry. He felt that the grey-green eyes, calmer than he had ever seen them, looked right into him, into all his dark, secret passages.

'Don' look at me like that, Mam.'

'Like what?'

'I dunno. Look, I'm...'

His words tailed off.

'What?' Julie asked.

'I'm... I'm sorry, for ruining Christmas. For getting myself done.'

It was his first ever apology. He was almost shaking with the effort it had taken.

'It was ruined six months ago,' Julie said.

'Aye, it's been a fucker of a year.'

'Don't swear.'

174

Mark smiled.

'You haven't said that to me in years.'

'No. I phoned Emma's salon. Told her you were getting out.'

'Oh, right.'

'Want to tell me about the nose?'

'It's nothing. Just a bit of messing about in the nick.'

'Was it bad there?'

'Nah. Piece of piss. And the food was good.'

There were long silences, cigarettes and more tea. It rained heavily and dried up again during the time they sat in the kitchen. A bit of sun even came out. A touch of gold on the hillside, shining on what was left of the mound of sand.

Julie felt close to Mark for the first time since Shane had disappeared. She wished she could hug him, that they could hug each other, to help each other come to terms with his absence. She wished she could mother him all over again, and not leave a trail of waster men in front of him.

'You've never said sorry before,' Julie murmured, an hour after his apology.

'Haven't I?'

Tentatively, she put a hand over his. She felt it tense, about to recoil, as it had done so many times before, but it stayed beneath hers. Hard, knotted, powerful. Not a youngster's hand at all.

'Look love,' she said, 'it's nearly the end of an awful year. We can't go on like this. Can't you change a bit? Can't *we* change?'

'No-one else seems to round here.'

'No-one else has had a kid go missing, and stay missing. Anyway, you've always wanted to go places. And you could. You've got something between your ears that isn't shit.'

'Don't swear, Mam.'

They laughed. Mark laughing was a rarity. Together with his apology she took this as a sign. Her eyes brimmed with tears but none fell.

'You know I'm going down, don't you?' Mark said quietly. 'There's no escape this time.'

'Maule told me to prepare for it. He's been good to you. He didn't have to try for bail again.'

'Aye. I said thanks.'

'You never! Jesus, perhaps you *can* change. They can train you in those offenders' places. You can learn a trade.'

'I'll have plenty of time.'

175

She could no longer hold back the tears. They started to flow, and her bitten-down nails dug into his hand as she tried to control herself.

'I'm sorry, love. I just can't help it.'

'It's alright.'

He was starting to go himself but a knock on the door saved him. He got up quickly to answer it, dabbing his eyes as he went. Emma flung herself into his arms as he opened the door. Another crying woman.

'I got away early,' she gasped, 'when Julie told me you were getting out. I can't believe it. I hadn't even got used to you being in there.'

She clung to his neck.

'Alright, alright. Better come through to the kitchen.'

More tea, cigarettes, tears. And talk. Talk he was able to join in with, to some extent. As if his apology had prised open a door that had never worked before. It was only a crack but he didn't want it to close. Maybe Julie was right. Maybe he could start off fresh, get to a point where he didn't think everyone was a useless tosser.

Mark lay on uneven turf. A green gash in the forestry. The estate like toy houses below him. His heart pumped, lungs worked overtime and sweat soaked through his tracksuit. He'd taken just twenty minutes to jog up the hillside. His fastest yet. Part of the fitness regime he'd imposed upon himself since Christmas. It had him in its grip. Whenever shit thoughts hovered he worked out. Sweated the bastards out of him. Jogging around the forestry in all weathers, in a black tracksuit he'd bought early in the new year. He wanted to be the fittest young offender ever before they banged him up.

It was mid-March, two weeks before he was due in court. A time of waiting, of reports being prepared as the system moved against him. And he wasn't allowed out after six o'clock. Part of his bail conditions. But this was cool because he had expected it. For the first time in his life he knew where he was going. He had a secure future, ha ha. Portland Bill, Dorset, wherever Dorset was. The young offenders' doss for Wales and the west of England. Where all the cowboy car nickers, junkies and mental punchers went. Some of the boys there would be a combination of all three. But there'd be no-one there like Duane. No-one as powerful. He'd noticed that most of the kids the police pulled were the opposite. Weedy little runts who looked as if they'd break in the wind.

Mark spent two hours every other day on his weights, two hours jogging. In all weathers. If a winter rain pissed in his face he still went. On New Year's Day he had stopped smoking and had cut down on the booze since. He was filling out, fourteen stone now but he wanted more. More power, and greater escape from his thoughts.

It was a fine day, shaving the edge of spring. The land settling itself down, ready for the new stuff. He put his hands behind his head and studied the sky. He would have liked a fag. Smoking had always helped him focus his thoughts on essentials, but he hadn't broken his pledge and the worst of the craving had gone. The yellow stains on his fingers were also fading.

It was warm, with air currents hugging the hillside, wafting up off it like big fans. Buzzards were about. There were plenty around at this time of year, he'd seen them increase steadily in number. Good predators. High above him five or six pairs wheeled around. Females in tight circles, the blokes prancing around them, showing off. One broke away upwards, then tucked in his wings and plummeted down. A feathery arrow in flight, screaming past its target at seventy miles an hour, pulling up and away when it looked certain to hit the deck. The flyer pulled: an impressed female paired off with him. Everyone, everything, wants to get together, he thought.

Gradually all the birds paired off. A nice even number. He was glad one didn't miss out, but there was no room for the likes of Daniels in nature. Runts and losers never got past first base. Maybe that was how it should be with people. Nature worked up here on the hillside, things had a pattern that was always stuck to, unless some arsehole blew it apart. He let himself slip into sleep with this thought, resting up before he jogged back down again. He had committed no crime since Christmas and was getting used to it.

Emma had moved in with Mark a few weeks after Christmas. He was not sure if he wanted it, but if he was really going to change he couldn't do more to prove it than this. Having Emma share his box-bedroom was the biggest change he could think of. Someone else sleeping inches from the tins.

The very first night Emma stayed the nightmare came back. Perhaps it was the strangeness of her beside him, a new warmth in the bed, new sounds and smells. The way she muttered and wheezed lightly in her sleep. Sleep that came easily to her. So easily he was envious and taunted by his own pathetic attempts. Not that sleep was always welcome.

The hole again. Only blacker. Deeper. Going right into the guts of the earth. And Shane was there. Lying cold and broken, his face stripped of colour and life, a white death mask though his eyes still burned their accusation. He could feel and touch them but couldn't escape. He was shouting and screaming his innocence, and shaking with a fear he'd never known awake.

'Mark! Wake up!'

Emma was shaking him.

'You'll wake the whole street. Stop shouting.'

He came out of it. Tried to take in the room. Didn't know who Emma was for a moment. He could still smell the cold damp of the hole.

'I'm alright,' he said, 'just a bad dream, that's all.'

He had been shouting 'Shane, Shane', but Emma didn't tell him this.

'You're soaking wet,' she said.

He lay back and breathed deeply, felt the fire leaving him. Replaced by a sick emptiness.

'Fucking hell,' he muttered.

Emma stroked his head, running fingers through his spiky, cropped hair.

'Okay now, love?' she whispered.

'Aye.'

He still frightened her, and she could only deal with Shane's vanishing by blocking it out. Yet she felt stronger when Mark was troubled, thinking he might need her then.

Mark got used to Emma being around. Gradually. She was the one who went out to work and came back every evening. A rarity on the estate. Julie seemed glad Emma was there too, so when he felt pressured and the house too small, he thought of this. A tiny payback for losing Shane.

Julie had a few more visits from the counsellor but stopped them before January ended.

'Mary can't do any more for me,' Julie told Mark. 'I'm off the pills. She says she's proud of me for that, didn't expect it so soon, she said. But I had to, or I'd never come off the buggers, like lots round here. Lots of women.'

She looked at Mark across the kitchen table, which he hadn't replaced. He hadn't even checked the tins lately. Hadn't felt the need to.

'I'm going to go it alone now,' Julie said. 'No-one else is going to deal with my thoughts.'

She tapped her head. He knew he was expected to say something. Before Christmas he'd have ignored it but now he managed a few words of support.

'I'll be here for a while yet,' he said. 'Can't go out at night anyway, can I, with this curfew thing. I'm off for a run.'

Julie smiled and watched as Mark jogged off. Over the bank where his friend had died. That funny little Daniels. Another one who'd gone before he had a chance. She wondered if Mark was really trying to change, or whether it was another of his mind games. If it was, she'd surely lose it altogether. 'Don't lose hope,' Mary said. And there had to be some, no matter how tattered. Something to enable her to go on. It was all on Mark now.

His tall figure was soon away, long-legged strides taking him past the shrine and onto the hillside. The statue stood out white in the weak sunshine, making his figure even blacker as he passed it. She saw him glance up at the woman and child without stopping. It seemed just days since she pushed him in his buggy to that spot.

Court Time Three was approaching. Coming up in the fast lane like a speeding truck. Emma fretted and Julie braced herself, drawing on new-found strength. Mark was the calmest, the one it was going to happen to. He jogged and worked out even on his last weekend.

Maule visited on Friday afternoon. He fidgeted with his papers and fingered his tie, making its knot tighter around his pink neck. I still make him nervous, Mark thought. He looks around the living room like he expects Shane to appear, and he looks at me as if I might pop any minute.

'They have good facilities at Portland,' Maule said. 'There's a full-size soccer pitch there too. Big clubs go down to train on it, in the summer.'

'Sounds like a regular holiday camp.'

179

Maule told him to expect two years.

'But you might be able to get out on probation after a year,' he said, 'if you keep your nose clean. We don't want a repeat of that Cardiff incident.'

Julie would be used as a character witness in court. Something that Mark didn't like but Maule thought necessary.

'It's essential that we build up a good profile of you,' Maule explained, 'to go with your confession. Convince them you're going to change.'

'Why? I'm going down anyway.'

They exchanged looks. Two ways of life colliding in a glance.

'People have been given up to four years recently, for less than you've done.'

'I don't want Shane brought up. Julie couldn't handle it. And I don't want you to talk about it.'

'I don't intend to.'

Maule was glad that Mark had confessed. If not, playing on the sympathies of the court by stressing the traumatic loss of Shane might have been useful but fraught with danger. Cans of worms were best left unopened. And a barrister would not have to plead the innocence of a client they knew to be very guilty. It would be a rare day, relatively free of legal bullshit.

Maule took in the living room. It was the first time he'd visited while the sun was shining. It cut through the front window and mocked the tired, lurid colour scheme, the exhausted furniture and the scattered tat that was beneath any sort of taste. Like a poor working class sit-com. No, not working class, under class. Typical of most of his clients. He should be used to it but still wasn't. It was too ugly. Too hopeless. And too bloody hot. Despite the pleasant day the house was pumping with heat. It pushed against the painted-shut windows, and condensed into pools on the windowsills. A human pressure cooker, with a large, disturbed youth enclosed. His tie felt even tighter. He had another twenty years of this, until the kids finished college at least. He wondered if he'd look back on cases like Mark Richards and be proud of his work. He was glad to leave, to cool the sweat under his arms in the car's air conditioning.

'See you Monday, at nine,' he said to Mark.

'Aye, see you.'

Julie kept off the pills, but as the trial approached she felt the need to take them grow. Her first son about to be taken from her. She was glad Emma was around. In the last three months she'd been able to rely on her for support and understanding beyond her years. Often when they talked she thought back to the times with her mother, and realised how little she'd been involved in her own growing up. Everything had been channelled to Dad, who took it all. And still did. That was an unnatural kind of mother. One she found hard to forgive. But Emma did not make her feel like a failure. The warmth which came from her did not want anything in return. She'd forgotten there were people like that. Mark was lucky, or would be if he thought straight. And Emma unlucky if he didn't. She'd be chained to him and his useless situation, a carbon copy of herself. She should tell Emma to get out. Get away. Do the hair of rich people in Cardiff, get into their world. But she didn't say anything. And wasn't sure if that was selfish or kind. It would only make Emma stubborn anyway. Determined to open the wrong door, go down the wrong road. People seemed infected with it on the estate. Women especially.

She must think positive, like Mary said. That Mark would come out changed, with his dirty slate wiped clean. And that he'd have a chance with Emma. They'd have a chance to get somewhere, even if she was left alone, with thoughts of Shane.

'I'll wait for you,' Emma said, 'you know that.'

She sat on Mark's bed. He stood at the window, looking at the hillside one last time. It was seven o'clock on Monday morning. By the time he got out the view would be changed. They were due to cut down a section of trees. Whenever they did this he realised he was looking at a piece of land that hadn't been clearly seen for thirty years. For a while it was easier to judge how things looked before, until new growth sprang up again, three foot tall before you had time to spit. Thousands of bits of green pushing through brown waste, all looking for their place in the sun.

'You never answer,' Emma muttered.

But he had answered. Many times. Told her she was nuts to bother with him and more nuts to stay. It always upset her and she always stayed. He turned to face her.

'A few years away is a long time,' he said.

'No it's not. It only seems like yesterday I was doing my GCSEs.'

He sat down beside her and looked up at the jacket and trousers hanging up on the door. His only jacket and trousers, bought by Emma with money he'd given her. For court. For the system.

Emma snuggled against him.

'Do you love me?' she said.

He sighed, and lay back.

'Can't you just say it? Just once? Even if you don't mean it.'

No, he couldn't. It was only a word, always had been for Julie's tossers, but it gagged in his mouth, it didn't belong there. Saying it would be an admission of something, something he didn't understand. Yet. He played with Emma's hair for a minute. She still wore it long and now it fell over his chest.

'I like you a lot,' he managed to say. 'Come on. We better start getting ready. I've got to pack a case, Maule says.'

Mark took in the Crown Court. It was bigger, and grander than the other place. Lots of wood and posh stone, built to impress. And it came complete with judge, a geezer in a red robe and wig. He had a face like a ripped trainer and looked old enough to be dead.

The trial was quick and uncomplicated. Maule did his bit, and Julie did hers, without crying. Making him out to be a Jesus who had taken the odd wrong turn. Eighty-two to be precise.

He got two years at Portland. As predicted. As expected. It was March the first. Saint David's Day, whoever he was. He was getting off the estate at last, but not as he'd expected.

It was a long trip in the prison van. He was alone with a sour-faced screw who read a paper and talked a lot of crap about sport. About his rugby team. Talking about it like it was a woman. Sad bastard.

'There's a lot of sport down Portland,' the screw said. 'Should be alright for a big lump like you. Make a good flanker, you would.'

He didn't know what the man was talking about. Had never taken an interest in any sport. Couldn't stand the close involvement with other boys. The pretence that it meant anything. In school they'd let him alone with that as well.

'We can take the championship if we win the last few matches,' the screw said. 'For the first time.'

Mark managed to doze, and woke up at Weymouth. It was almost dark but he could sense a town. They stopped at traffic lights and he heard people his own age laughing at the door of a pub. And smelt burger and chips. What he always associated with the seaside. The few times Julie had managed to get him down to Barry when he was small. He'd never liked it then, either. Too many snotty kids. He'd always pissed Julie off with his moods. 'Why don' you ever join in with nothing?' she'd say. 'Play with the other boys. Go on the rides. Don' you wanna even go on the rides?'

'Be there in a few minutes,' the screw muttered. His rugby talk had long-since ended. He was as bored as Mark. 'Good spot for a nick, down here,' he continued. 'Two of 'em side by side almost. The Verne is for when you get older.'

The van drove down a gradient, slowing to a stop. The driver got out, came round the back and opened the door.

'Alright, Bill,' he said. 'Long bloody drive, innit?'

'Too right.'

The screw got out with Mark.

'Stretch your legs a bit, sonny. And don't even think about it.'

It must have been a nice day down here. There was a lot of red fighting black in the sky. The van was parked at the top of a narrow road, which was the causeway, the screw said. Only way in. Only way out. He could see the island. Portland Bill. It loomed out of the half-light at him, a big chunk of rock smack in the middle of nowhere. There were no trees on it. It was naked to the wind. Mark saw the causeway thing could be easily blocked by a single police car. The screw was right, it was a good spot to bang people up.

He looked out at a darkening sea, heard its dominating sounds. A light shone from somewhere on the island, a powerful bugger coming to life in the dark, and the sea was thumping and sucking a few feet from him. He imagined it coming over the causeway and taking the van. Like a big fish taking a fly. The screws had stopped for a fag before handing him over, but hadn't offered him one. Just as well or his resolution might have been blown away. For a moment he craved a shot of nicotine, something to cup in his hands. He thought about what might lie out there in the darkness, over this thin strip of road. He was about to start paying his dues.

The van passed through the iron gates of the prison. They were fancy buggers, like those stately homes he'd seen on the telly.

Places he'd always imagined doing when he was older. Mark the master nicker. Put that out of your mind, he told himself. That's yesterday. He was delivered to a tracksuited man at the main entrance. The tracksuit surprised him. He was expecting tin soldiers, medals even.

'Richards, Mark,' the man said. 'I'm Mullen.'

He appraised Mark.

'You look fit. Got some size too. Weights?'

Mark nodded.

'Steroids? Pills?'

Mark shook his head.

'You must have worked hard, then. Right, hang on and we'll get you kitted up and sorted.'

Tracksuit talked to the van boys and signed a few papers. And the van was gone, back over the causeway, to where life was. They'd stop off for a few pints in the town, before heading back to Wales. Lucky bastards. That he was going to be banged up hit him hard now. He thought of the hillside and the rows of forestry trees all the same which were beautiful. A beautiful green family. Then he thought of Duane and Cardiff nick.

Tracksuit tapped him.

'Come on, then. There's a nice warm cell waiting for you. Well, warmish.'

The bloke seemed unconcerned that he might try to make a break for it. Why should he be concerned, when they were surrounded by sea with only a narrow strip of road that any clown could police?

Day three. Saturday. He'd been kitted out. Blue trousers and tracksuit top. Like the cheap tracksuits of his local market. Stuff the kids on the estate wore. But not him. Not since he'd started nicking, anyway. Then he bought better stuff, knowing that it set him apart. Said that he was going places. Well he had. Portland. In all its glory.

He hadn't seen anything of the island yet. Hadn't even seen much of the prison. First night they put him in a cell with one empty bed, and a kid who blubbed all night in another. A kid with an accent that said he shouldn't be in here. He ignored him for a long time but had to give him a slap in the end. To quieten him down. Not a good start, but he was stressed out himself, knowing he had to learn quickly. What the score was. Who had the power. Who were the crazies, the druggies, the trainee rent boys, the ones who couldn't hack it, like the kid he'd slapped.

Next day he was in a dormitory. Raleigh it was called. They had names for the 'houses'. Just like school. Raleigh, Benbow, Drake. All famous sailors, Tracksuit said. Great Englishmen, the man called them. Tracksuit was about forty, maybe a few years more. A fit, strong git, but with a gut getting tired. Wanting to be bigger. And he was a ginger bugger, what was left of his hair was like red fuzz close to his head. Tracksuit was the link between the white collars and the screws. Number one screw.

Raleigh was like a long stone barn, holding maybe twenty kids. He couldn't be bothered to count them. They were all under twenty, most of them younger than him. There didn't seem to be a Duane amongst them, in Raleigh he was easily the biggest.

Sharing would be the real punishment for him. Being around so many others. A school you couldn't bunk off from. Yet he soon learned things were not that tight here. There was not that much to do in the day. He'd expected stuff like in the films, making useless shit like mailbags. But there didn't seem much shape to the place. It seemed like it had been around too long and was fed up with itself. Knackered for ideas. Like the estate. The staff as much rejects as the kids.

The food was crap, too. Not like Cardiff nick. Or perhaps that had been a bit special for Christmas. He was hungry most of the time. Maybe it was the weather, always in your face. A keen salt wind blowing endlessly off the sea. They were at the short side of the island, with piddling twenty foot cliffs. Someone told him they had five hundred foot buggers at the north end. Where the lighthouse was. Its beam winked at him in the night, cutting through the bars of the dormitory windows. Like a searchlight waiting for him to escape. Daring him to.

Once he'd settled in and knew his way about the days would be long. And all the fucking same. But at least there was a gym, if the room full of old gear could be called that. He'd keep working out. Tracksuit would like that and he wanted to keep on the right side of him. Get a good report and get out quick.

Visits were allowed every twenty eight days and he was glad they were not more often. Regular doses of Julie and Emma here would not be good. And they couldn't afford it anyway. Unless one of them came across the stash. He thought of the house being done up. Workmen finding the tins. He thought of this a lot. Dreamt it. Sometimes it made him shiver, other times he thought so what. He was no longer sure what the money meant to him. Maybe it had been controlling him. Making him add to it all the time. His drug for two years. It had been all he wanted. All that drove him forward. Now he'd have plenty of time to work things over in his mind. To think where he was going when he got out.

He got a letter from Emma the first weekend. She must have written it after she got back from court. He could sense her tears in the words and almost expected the paper to be damp. She had big writing, with big loops as if she was ten years old. His own was small and scrawly and hard even for him to read. Not that he had ever written much. In school or out. Emma talked about 'fresh starts' and the like. She had been as influenced by Maule as Julie had with her counsellor.

He lay on his bunk and read the four pages. It was free time and they were allowed to smoke. He was the only one there who didn't. Clouds of blue wafted around him. There was a card table of blokes from Bristol, druggies and car nickers. Small–time tossers. Skin-headed, tattooed, skinny bastards. Others ponced around, going through the motions of being hard or funny or stupid. Whatever it took to get them through the day.

No-one had tried it on. Not in any way. He was glad about Cardiff nick now. It had prepared him. He'd made a point of stripping off the second morning and going through a few exercises. Making muscles jump to attention and catching the eyes of his room-mates. It had the right effect. They came up to him quietly in ones and twos to ask where he was from and what he was in for. No-one made any sheep-shagging jokes. There were no Welsh kids in Raleigh, but he knew at least half-a-dozen tossers from his area were in Portland. It wouldn't be long before 'Psycho Eyes' got around. Good.

'We're both down,' Emma wrote. 'I think about you all the time.'

Tracksuit watched him in the gym. Mark knew he was standing in the doorway but didn't acknowledge him, not on his back, pumping iron. He got up to thirty press-ups from the bench. And he had steadily increased the poundage in the three weeks he'd been inside. When he stopped Tracksuit approached him.

'Been watching you, Richards. Pretty impressive.'

He towelled down and gave no sign he'd heard.

'Ever thought of the army?' Tracksuit said. 'You could get in, if you keep your nose clean here. The army'll wipe the slate clean. Very forgiving place, it can be.'

Aye, I've thought about it, Mark said to himself, thought what a crock of shit it all is.

'Well?'

'No sir.'

The 'sir' was becoming easier. It was just a word.

'You're the fittest kid in the place,' Tracksuit said. 'You've seen what they're like. Weeds. Runts. Queers. Not many bother with the gym. You're in here all your free time. I like that, a man who takes a pride in his body.' He tapped his spreading gut. 'Wasn't always like this you know. Not when I was in the army.'

This was a guy who couldn't let go. Holding on to something that didn't want him. Holding on to a past because he had no present and couldn't even think of a future. A loser.

'Think about it,' Tracksuit said. 'You got plenty of time. I could set it up for you. Right, carry on.'

It would be cool to string Tracksuit along. To get him off his back. Yet he knew he wouldn't even try.

Beezer was eighteen, jelly-fat, pink-face, greasy hair. He slept next to Mark in Raleigh. A middle class git. One of only two who were banged up here. The other was the one he had slapped the first night. Beezer had burnt part of his posh school down, and his parents hadn't been able to get him off. He was in his third month and had three more to go. It if had been an estate boy he'd have been looking at three years. Beezer read books. He had them sent to him, and got some from the collection in the broom cupboard they called a library. It caused him even more hassle. He was treated like shit as it was, but the sight of the fat ponce reading inflamed some of them. Especially the Bristol boys who had been joined by a Rasta from St Paul's. A big dreadlocked bastard, called Winston. As big as Mark. And heavier. Winston almost licked his lips when he first saw Beezer. As if he was something he might barbecue. He was known by the card players. He was one of them. And they got cockier after his arrival. They had more muscle on their side.

Mark had taken no notice when Beezer was sometimes slapped and kicked and made to run errands for the card table. But when

Winston came things got nastier. This guy was another Duane. Mark knew it straight away. They checked each other out but nothing much was said or done. Winston had to find his feet, just like he had.

Beezer must have sensed something different in his bunk mate. Mark did not take any interest in him but he didn't fuck around with him either. The night before Emma was due to visit he dared to ask if Mark wanted something to read.

'You what?' Mark said.

Beezer talked through his nose, like he had a permanent cold.

'I've got plenty of stuff here,' Beezer said.

He pointed at the piles of book under his bunk. Sometimes they were flung around Raleigh, or cut up into chunks. Mark thought back to his arrest. The house of books. Beezer mistook his silence for interest. He offered him a large book.

'This is good,' Beezer said, 'UFO's, unexplained phenomena. I've always been interested in stuff like that.'

He held out the book.

'Lots of good photos,' Beezer said hesitantly.

Mark noticed Winston taking an interest, from the other side of the room.

'Fuck off, you stupid wanker,' he said to Beezer, 'don't hassle me or you'll be eating one of your books.'

Beezer recoiled as if slapped, while Mark glanced over to Winston, who flashed him the pearly gates of his teeth.

Emma sat opposite him. At a table in the reception room. One of many prepared for the monthly visitors. She looked good. New hairstyle and clothes he hadn't seen before. Lots of the boys eyed her up. Their visitors were nearly all parents. Strung-out mothers mainly. He noticed there were not many men, apart from Beezer's old man, an even fatter and pinker git, who looked nervous. Tracksuit stood by the doorway. Other screws prowled around looking for anything that might pass between visitor and inmate, despite the checks that had already been made. Dope often came in this way. It was there if you wanted it. And could pay.

'You look nice,' he mumbled.

'This place must be good for you,' Emma said. 'You never give me a compliment before.'

He shrugged and saw the way she worked her hands. As if they were fighting each other. Nerves. She wanted to touch him. Hold him. She wanted it bad but wanted to keep it from him so he wouldn't feel down.

'This dump is really hard to get to,' Emma murmured. 'It took ages.'

'Best not to come down again.'

The hands worked overtime and her teeth gnawed at her lower lip.

'Don't you want to see me?'

'It's too far to come for just a few minutes.'

'It's not.'

'How's Julie?'

'Not bad. Better than I thought she'd be. She wants to come down next time.'

He winced inside. His mother here. He felt a wave of shame wash over him and his skin start to burn. Emma noticed it.

'You alright?'

'Aye. It's hot in here, that's all. Look, try to put her off. It's too far and there's no point. I don' want her getting upset.'

He realised how stupid this sounded. After doing eighty houses in the last few years. After Shane. Emma's hand reached for his. Tracksuit clocked it immediately but didn't come over. Emma's eyes filled up with the exchange of warmth. Her blue eye make-up started to smudge.

'Don' start,' he whispered, 'not here, for Christsake.'

Tracksuit walked over to their table.

'No touching, love,' he murmured. He winked at Mark and showed Emma his best military walk.

'This place looked awful when I saw it outside. Even in the sunshine.'

'Aye, they picked the right spot for it. But it's not so bad. No-one messes with me. And I'm working out.' He flexed an arm. She wanted to reach for him again but Tracksuit was watching.

'What's he like?' Emma asked.

'Don't laugh, but I think he rates me. Wants to get me in the forces.'

Emma's interest was pricked.

'Maybe that's a good idea,' she said.

'Get real will you. Me? It's another type of prison.'

'Well, what are you gonna do? Please, Mark, I couldn't stand it if you kept on nicking. Went to real prison.'

'Most do, who come here.'

He realised she still saw them as an item. A couple. And always would, if he didn't put an end to it. Did he want to? Sometimes he thought he wanted to put an end to everything. Dive off those big cliffs at the far end of the island. Down like a stone into the deep. Like the buzzards over the forestry. Free like them. Wonderful, falling, floating free. Quick and green. Nothing like that place he dreamt Shane was. That bastard hole. Nah, that was tossers' talk. He'd tough it out, as he always had. Ask for nothing off no-one.

Emma saw the turmoil in him. She could only guess at his thoughts, and dread them. They were quiet for a moment but when it was time to go she could not prevent the tears. They coincided with the leaving bell. She obeyed it quickly, dabbing at her eyes as she went. Not noticing the bye-bye smile of Tracksuit. Mark's glimpse of freedom gliding through the exit door, her arse fed on by many pairs of starving eyes.

Shane's nightmare came that night. Maybe Emma's visit brought it on. Same shit. Same cold sweat and shakes. Waking with a start and looking to see if anyone had noticed. Seeing Beezer's eyes on him. Not worrying, because Beezer was no-one. Hearing the sea bashing the fuck out of the island as a storm got up. The suck of it off the beach, like a sheet the size of a cloud tearing.

Mark was outside the prison for the first time. One of eight in a working party to mend a wall. Cementing back stones that the sea had prised out over the years. Tracksuit had picked the biggest and fittest. He'd been first on the list, then Winston. The job was considered a perk. It was a warm June day. A clear-sky sun competing with the breeze.

Once out of the fancy gates space smacked him in the face. Portland seemed like Paradise for a minute. All its sky. Its air. Its beautiful ugly, stony flatness, pockmarked by quarries. He wanted to walk all over it, then walk home.

'Stop dreaming, Richards,' a screw said, 'and get down to it.'

They had two screws with them. They did everything in twos.

He piled up stones, ready to be cemented into place. But his eyes were on the coastline, and the big sky and the big sea. And he knew if he was ever banged up for a long time he'd lose it big time.

He missed Julie. And Emma. He realised he missed the estate.

With all its hopeless crap. The place he'd spent the last few years planning to get away from. Did this make him a sad bastard? Maybe. It was as though he was only just getting to know himself.

They took a break at midday. Eating sandwiches as hard as the wall stones.

'I got three months left, man,' Winston said.

It was the first time he'd spoken, but he acted as if they'd always talked.

'How about you?' Winston asked.

'Doing two years.'

'They calls you Psycho Eyes, don' they, where you come from?'

'They call me nothing in here.'

'They say you crazy man. I like that. I like crazy.'

He shrugged and sank another bite into the sandwich. Its thin strip of shiny ham tasted salty.

Winston was checking him out. Mark had changed his mind, the Rasta was no queer. There'd be signs of it by now. But he liked to be in control. Had been, probably, of the tossers on his Bristol patch. And was in Raleigh, apart from one big Welsh guy. That would worry him. He was the type to be bothered about crap like that.

Now that they were up close, in sunlight, he saw how old Winston looked. A few pencil scars already, black cuts on brown and a forehead marked up with lines and furrows. Winston would have had it just as tough, on an estate like his. But surrounded by city concrete. They should be together, but never would be. They were rivals, set up for it by their size. And Winston's colour. He was only the second black he'd known, but he'd been brought up to piss on them. On their difference. And the fact they were in his country. But not many on the estate had even met one. Niggers were the unknown who lived down in Cardiff.

As he lay back and tried to digest the iron food he realised the estate hated just about everything. Especially what it didn't know. Niggers, foreigners, rich gits. He'd been part of it. A willing part. Still was. But as he looked back now something about this troubled him. It got them nowhere, yet it was hard not to go along with it. Difference was pounced on. Trampled. He'd only got away with it himself because he was so big. And weird. And not to be fooled with. But it had never made any of them feel better.

Just seemed to turn the anger. So they kept angry. Then started to hate themselves. And blame every other fucker. Until they were hung up on a vicious circle. He could see this much now, but did not know how to break from it.

'Why you bother with that Beezer?' Winston murmured, his soft voice going easy with the sun.

'Huh?'

'I seen you talking to the sad cunt.'

'Nah, you seen him talking to me.'

'Give him a slap. I do.'

'I noticed.'

'Got something to say about it, man?'

He leant on an elbow. Their faces just inches apart. Each smelling the remnants of the crap sandwiches on the other. Winston's eyes were a mottled green-brown. Cat's eyes.

'Come on, move yourselves,' a screw shouted. 'We're only half finished.'

Mark felt Winston watching him all afternoon. If he was going to change he'd have to ignore the fucker. But he knew they shared the same type of anger and the same need to let it flow out.

He made sure Winston saw him talking to Beezer that evening, still felt the need to go down the wrong road, open the wrong door. Crap up and feed off the anger. He couldn't change overnight – it was all he had ever known. But identifying the need was a giant step. It might take him to a place he had no experience of.

Beezer was chuffed that someone had actually spoken to him. Especially Mark Richards.

'Why do they call you Beezer?' he asked.

'My name's Breeze. Bernard Breeze.'

'Jesus Christ. You poor sod.'

Beezer smiled, reminding him of Daniels, his hang-dog expression when someone was taking the piss. He added him to the list of people he missed. Beezer had more books. A parcel had come for him. Beezer opened it, touching each book as if it was alive. They'd be flying around the room before long. He noticed the one on top. A bit bigger, with a picture of a whale on it. Beezer caught his glance.

'Want a look?' he asked.

He brought the book to him.

'I've always been interested in the sea,' Beezer said, 'I want to be a marine biologist one day.'

He did not know what the git was talking about but he took the book, sensing the eagerness in Beezer for him to have it. To share a bit of the crap of his present life. With someone who didn't fuck around with him. Didn't punish him for what he was. Different.

The back end of a whale. In mid plunge. About to sink down into a dark blue sea. He didn't know much about them except that they were big and not really fish. He remembered hearing that somewhere. And men had always killed them. They had that in common with everything else. He turned the pages of the book. Lots of good photos. Lots of whales. He saw a chart of where they roamed. Everywhere. The whole fucking watery world. He liked that. They were totally free. If they could stay alive. He checked out some of the writing. Lots of words he couldn't get. He traced some with a finger, as if by highlighting them their meaning would become clear. It didn't. Beezer watched him, desperate to explain, but he warned him off with a glare. He lay on his bunk and took in the photos, like he had with that book about the valley. He did not need words. What the eyes saw was enough for him.

Whales came in all shapes and sizes, as long as it was large. He saw them under the water, on top of it. Pygmy guys swimming alongside. Great humps of flesh that seemed to glide and hang and move as if they were weightless. Power had impressed him and what these guys had leapt off the page. He quickly got used to their fat, perfect shape. It *was* perfect. The spread of their rear fins, flukes, the book called them. Like giant rudders on a boat. He stopped on one double page photo of a humpback and calf, the young 'un with a flipper on its mother. Sun was pushing through the top of the sea, whitening the blue. He felt like he had at times in the forestry, watching the buzzards. Taking a bit of their freedom and control for himself, getting lost in it, until it was time to be Mark Richards again. When he'd wonder how a world that could make stuff like that could be so crappy for people like him. But this was just a book. Pictures on a page. The time to lights out went quickly. When they were killed he was hooked on whales.

He was hard on Beezer in the morning, but only with his tongue.

Otherwise he'd try to attach himself, use the book as a link. Look to him for protection. But he kept the book, and accepted another – *Creatures of the Deep*. This was meant for young kids and had been sent to Beezer by mistake. Its words were easier. Winston saw everything. Checking it out with a grin that wasn't funny.

In a few days even the screws knew he was looking at books. Tracksuit took note.

'Books about the sea, eh,' he said as he made his routine inspection. 'Never could stand the sea, or bloody sailors – limp-wristed ponces. Here, you're not thinking of joining the navy, are you?'

'No sir.'

'Good. You stick to the army. Keep your feet on land.'

Tracksuit looked through the book, just in case it was a front for something else. Mark almost expected him to sniff it.

'All about whales, eh? Where you come from. Get it. Wales? Christ, can you read this, Richards? Some of these words are a bit long.'

Tracksuit traced them with his finger, just like he had, and for a moment he saw him as he might have been thirty years ago. A scruffy, lanky, piss-poor kid walking through a piss-poor part of London.

'Whales have lots of parasites, it says here. Just like prison warders.' Tracksuit gave him back the book, and looked round suspiciously. 'Right, carry on.'

Word soon got round, but no-one said anything. No-one took the piss. And Beezer lived in hope. After a week Mark could identify nearly all the whales in the book. Humpbacks became his favourite. They were not the biggest, but he liked their style. Humpbacks were the best roamers, going anywhere they wanted. And they were the ones that passed closest to land, and had been fucked the worst by hunters. They had the longest flippers and they fooled around a lot on top of the water. There were photos of forty tons flopping out of the sea, like huge divers going into reverse. The same colour as the sea but more alive. Tons of blood pumping, brains the size of small cars. And Humpbacks could be seen up north, off Scotland, the book said. Some of those island channels there were on the world cruising route. On their tour. He couldn't believe these creatures came so close to the poxy collection of islands that was his own. But they did, and he'd like to see it one day.

Julie was a little jealous that Emma was seeing Mark, not her. But it was probably right. She didn't know how she'd be in that place. Leaving him there. Another son lost. Mark going down sharpened her thoughts of Shane. Their edge came back. To cut into her in the mornings, when she woke up and knew once more it was not a bad dream.

When Emma was in work the house was so empty. All the usual sounds, the kids in the street, Bat shouting next door, someone pumping up the hi-fi, jarred on her. Before they were a normal part of her life. Now she had no normal life. No way. Not even by the standards of the estate. She'd been marked out by her loss. When she started going out again people either avoided her or treated her with kid gloves. As if her tragedy was contagious. Not that she ever went out much. Just a bit of shopping. Nothing social. But, when Mark went down, she knew she'd have to make an effort to get out of the house. Or take root in it forever.

Emma helped her. A lot. A young girl who didn't know much about anything yet, comforting *her*. Doing more than anyone in her own family. Her mother didn't get in touch about Mark. And she didn't phone her. They'd each made their last stab at family.

'How was he?' Julie had asked when Emma had returned from Portland. They were in the kitchen, looking out at the garden. Where it all went wrong. The mound of sand had almost been weathered into memory. Shadows worked patterns on it as the sun was obscured by clouds.

'He never says a lot,' Emma answered, 'you know that. But he seemed okay. I was much worse than he was.'

'Aye, that figures. Mark the control freak. What was the place like?'

'It was on an island. I didn't see much of that. But the prison was old. And big. Much bigger than I thought. And the wind was blowing all the time.'

'Usually does by the sea. No hills. No forestry. He won't like that.'

'But he's not supposed to, is he? They don't get out, anyway. He said he was just banged up most of the time. With lots of other lads.'

'Time will go slow for him,' Julie murmured. 'Maybe he'll learn something.'

'He was starting to change before,' Emma said. 'I know he was.'

'Maybe. I hope so. It's the only thing I've got to look forward to.'

Emma poured the tea, wishing she could say something more to help Julie. Magic words that would pick her up and make her pain vanish. People had stopped saying anything hopeful about Shane. They'd stopped saying anything at all. It had been too long. He'd not been found safe. Or dead. And they'd heard nothing from the police in months.

Mark lay on his back and flicked the sweat from his eyes. Forty eight. Nine. Fifty. His best yet. The last ten press-ups were tough. The chalk welding his hands to the bar. His shoulders and arms punished. His back screaming, as if each push would rip out his spine. But he'd done it, and it felt good.

He got up and went to the bike. Ten miles to do. As he pedalled he tested himself on the whales. Recognising shapes in his head. Humpbacks, Sperms, Blues, the smaller Brydes and Minkes. Why the Right whale was so called. He'd got used to reading maps, and knew the shape of the world now. And the whales' movement in it. The big red arrow in the kids' book which pointed the route of the Humpbacks from East Africa to Scotland. He always worked back to the Humpbacks. The question mark of flesh on their backs was familiar now. Maybe it was a question mark for him. But asking what? Why the fuck was he so interested in whales. Coming from the estate, that place of sea experts. It was a question he couldn't answer.

He flashed the books' photos through his head, making the big animals move. Plough through the sea with a white 'V'. And added to this the scraps of memory from old tv programmes. Not that he'd ever watched much. Telly was for indoors and he'd spent his time on the hills, and in other people's houses. So he had to imagine. Make his own film out of the contents of two books, and put himself in it. Beezer had offered to get more stuff for him, and he'd told him to go ahead.

Winston was lounging against the open door, and might have been there for a while, so wrapped up was Mark in his thoughts. The Rasta was in vest and shorts, his legs powerful and long. 'You doing good,' Winston said. 'Thought I'd join you, man. Get on the screws' right side, like you have.'

He reached ten miles.

'I've finished here,' he said.

'Going back to your books?' Winston said, flashing him a grin. He shrugged, and left the gym without answering.

Beezer was sitting on his bunk, trying to stifle a sniffle. Everyone was ignoring him. Even more than usual. A trickle of blood sneaked from his mouth, which he smeared on his chin. Mark would have ignored him too, until he saw the books. What was left of them. They'd been cut up. Bits of whales scattered around the room. The covers stomped and well smashed. Beezer's look was wanker-pitiful.

'I tried to stop him,' Beezer mumbled.

He didn't have to ask who. Looking around Raleigh he knew that no-one else would have the bottle, not even if they ganged up together. The card table was watching closely. He walked over to them, picked a kid up and threw him across the room. He landed heavily on his back. The rest sprang up to scatter but he caught one by the neck. A small ginger tosser. He squeezed the neck and slapped him a few times as he tried to kick out.

'Go and tell that bastard coon I'm waiting for him,' he whispered. The screws wouldn't be in for ten minutes. Time enough.

There wasn't much time to think. Or keep the anger at bay. But he knew that a rumble was not the way to get out early. The boys in Raleigh had gathered at the other end of the room when Winston came in.

'What your problem, man?' Winston asked.

It was his smile that did it. But he did not lose control. It was more a sense of the inevitable. That Winston was old ways challenging. Trying to keep him where he'd always been. Down. When Winston trashed the whales he was pissing on any future Mark might have. That was the way he saw it. And he had to answer him.

He was on the bastard, grabbing for his throat. But Winston was ready. And good. The Rasta chopped his hands away and landed a few strong jabs to the side of his head and face. He felt his nose go – again. This guy had been in a lot of situations like this. He tried to corner him a few times but was kicked and punched back without getting in a clean shot himself. One eye was shutting and the other was filling up as he snorted blood.

'You outa your class, honky,' Winston said. 'Way out. I'm gonna fuck you up good.'

His bloody face encouraged Winston in too close. The Rasta

197

tried to kick him to the floor, putting on a show for Raleigh, announcing his authority with boots and fists. It was a mistake. Mark pushed hard into his gut and got a hold on him. Took a lot of punishment in doing it but didn't let go. Put his faith in the strength he'd been building up for years, and it didn't fail him. They fell to the floor, Winston twisting desperately to get on top. Biting at his ears, spitting into his eyes. But Mark kept him under and worked a forearm repeatedly into his face. He felt some of the fight leaving his opponent and risked pushing off him to land his heaviest punch. Square in the jaw. Winston's eyes rolled like shutters. Your jaw's never been shot at before, he thought. It's all glass. He followed up with his head, and repaid the compliment to his own nose. Winston was gone. This was a different fight. This was calmer. As if he was losing his appetite. Losing the rush that came with action. If it hadn't been the books he doubted if he'd have tangled with Winston. Christ, fighting over books.

'Screws!' someone shouted.

There was a scramble for bunks. He slapped some alertness into Winston and dragged him to his place, then went to his own. There was blood everywhere. Tracksuit came in.

'Ah, girls have been falling out, eh?'

Tracksuit sussed it straight away. It couldn't have been easier. Everyone's eyes drilling the floor and two bloody tossers lying on their backs. One still not quite conscious. Tracksuit went to Winston first, and checked over the damage.

'What you been doing, beauty?'

Winston was coming around. Suspicion, defence, arrogance reasserted themselves. Finding the victor with his eyes, and not looking at Tracksuit.

'Nothing, sir,' he answered.

'I can see that. Nothing at all, I'd say.'

Tracksuit kicked some of the pieces of book with his black polished boot. He barely glanced Mark's way. He could see he was alright, and that he'd won.

'Right, get this mess cleared up. Get yourselves cleaned up. Lights out in twenty minutes.'

Mark was surprised. He'd expected a lot more. Up before the governor, all that crap. Loss of good behaviour time. Being done for assault, perhaps. Tracksuit didn't seem interested. Not even in the busted noses.

He found his favourite photo intact on the floor. The mother

Humpback with her calf a flipper's length away, drifting through sea the colour of Emma's eye make-up. He stuck it on the side of his bunk. His warning to the others. Not that anyone would need it after this.

'I'll send for some more books,' Beezer murmured quietly in the dark. 'My father sends me whatever I want.'

He expected more trouble from Winston, but none came. The guy almost became friendly. He'd seen it before, on the estate. Beat someone and they became your pal. As if you had bought a piece of them with your fists. Within a few days they were even sharing the gym together. Winston's nose a bit flatter, his own still sore and bent. He was wary of Winston at first, very wary until he was sure the guy wasn't acting, and waiting for revenge. Then he relaxed enough to talk.

'Why'd you do it?' he asked, after a punishing session on the weights. He could outlift Winston easily. The city boy had no patience. He wanted to conquer instantly.

'Had to, man,' Winston answered.

'Why?'

'Because you were there. And big as me, almost. I knew trashing them books would get you going. I seen the way you looks at 'em.'

'Beezer's getting me some more books,' he said, looking into Winston's face.

'They won't be touched. I'm done. You proved yourself to me. It's cool, man.'

Winston wasn't bothered by little things. And to him the fight was a little thing. Part of his routine, his hustle. But Winston was still The Man, amongst his own and Mark Richards didn't threaten that. He was something else. Beyond Raleigh.

'I saw dolphins once,' Winston said. 'The old folks went back to Barbados a few years ago, and took me with 'em. I went out on a boat with my cousin, and they played about with us. But maybe I imagined it, I was so wasted on ganja. Hey, want some dope? We got plenty stashed.'

'Maybe.'

He was envious, not having been past Cardiff, voluntarily. Dolphins were like miniature whales, but they didn't do it for him. Not enough power, and too willing to mix it with humans. When he got back to the dorm Beezer had two books for him. One a copy of the first book on whales, the other thicker, with less photos but more graphs and diagrams. Lots of stuff over his head but he was beginning to understand. Fitting the visuals together in his head. He couldn't explain it but he could see it. Track the whales round the world. He knew he was getting close to asking Beezer to help him. And he could sense the kid's eagerness. It would be his guarantee of safety.

He got through the summer this way. Working out and whales, with Beezer explaining all the big words. And another day outside. Another repair job, further away from the prison this time. Towards the other end of the island, where he could see the lighthouse and check out the height of the cliffs. There wasn't much else to see but he sucked in the air and space. Knew it had to be saved and eked out over the coming winter.

Emma came a few more times. She was doing well in the salon. Saving her tips. She didn't bother much with her own family now. The Richards had been adopted and she couldn't wait for him to get out. There were regular letters from her and Julie added a few lines sometimes. Like him, she wasn't much for writing.

Winter arrived. There was ice in the wind, and regular storms. Lashing the island. Lashing the prison. Lashing the minds of the inmates. As if they were all being banged up again. More books came via Beezer. His old man was spending lots of dosh on his son. Tracksuit called Mark the 'Whaleman of Portland' now, just like in the old film, he said. Whatever that was.

In November he was sent for by the governor. Walked to his office by Tracksuit. It was only the second time he'd seen the geezer. At first he thought it might be about the fight. Some sort of delayed action. But it wasn't. He stood in front of the desk, hands behind his back. More polished wood, like the courthouse. It must go with power, he thought, or bullshit.

'I've had good reports, Richards,' the governor said. The boss was small and round. Four-eyed, hair spread out thinly over his pink head. Each strand working overtime. 'You like to work out in the gym. Mr James here says you are really fit.'

Tracksuit nodded. He stood easy, by the door.

'If you keep it up through the winter, there might be a chance of an early release. With your second year outside, under a probation order.'

'Back home, sir?'

'Yes, if you keep it up.'

'Thank you, sir.'

The governor rattled papers as a way of dismissing him. Just a few minutes in a poxy office, but enough to put a charge through his head like a million fucking volts. Out. By March. Winston had left a month ago. Beezer was going home for Christmas.

'You could be in the army before you're twenty,' Tracksuit said, as he took him back to Raleigh. 'Make sergeant before you're thirty. I seen the way the others take note of you in here.'

But he wasn't listening. His thoughts were on the shitty, clapped-out, wonderful estate. Every square foot of it he'd ever walked. And the tins. Fuck it. He'd spend all the money.

He was out. It was the first Monday of March. A heavy lead-coloured sea bashing the causeway. Spray in his face. A dark sky. All for him. Just for him. No-one else was getting out today. Feeling strange in his own clothes. The T-shirt tight against his chest. The denim jacket stretched against his larger shoulders. Jeans cramping his balls. Rain starting to spit at him. Each cold spot on his face a welcome.

Tracksuit went with him to the station, where he handed him a folder of army stuff with his travel warrant.

'The best thing you could ever do,' Tracksuit said.

They shook hands and Tracksuit left him on the platform. With his small case, the books Beezer had given him nestling in his clothes. His mobile whale library. Six of them now. All known by heart. The big words explained and learnt. Mastered.

He had two quick pints waiting for his train, another at the Bristol connection, wondering how far away Winston was. A few more at Cardiff. He'd have to learn to drink all over again but was nicely spaced out when he got up to the estate.

It was late afternoon and the rain had travelled with him. But the edges of the sky had lightened, promising a better day tomorrow. Everything stood out wet-sharp. The wedges of forestry looked as if they had been washed, brushed up, and painted. The sheep-dotted fields lower down shining, and the golf club clinging to its patch. The white statue caught all the dying light and flashed it at him. Even the housing had a special glow. Showing off all its shit. No wonder strangers took just one look. He loved it.

He hadn't told them what time he would arrive and had beaten Emma back from work. As he inserted it, he half expected his key not to turn in the lock. As if his year away had excluded him.

201

But it turned, and the door opened. Bat saw him from behind her curtain. He nodded to her ducking head. Even smiled. Then Julie was in his arms, blubbing before he could stop her. Her excited words rushing at him in a jumble. She took him into the kitchen, where she managed to stand off him, and collected herself.

'Well, you haven't starved, anyhow,' she said, working a tissue around her eyes.

'Over fifteen stone now.'

'Oh Mark. I can't believe it. It's only been a year, but it seems such a long time.'

'I'm out.'

She started towards him again so he sat down quickly.

'Get us a cuppa, then,' he said.

He kept his eyes away from the garden, but it was there. All of it was still there.

When Emma got back it was the same scene. Each woman's emotion supported the other. With him in the middle. But not running or brushing it away any more. Wanting to but not doing it. With Emma's tear-puckered, mascara-running face close to his he thought of all the times he'd turned on her. Abused her with tongue and fist.

They sat around the kitchen table. Emma picking at its frayed edge. Both women smoking. Julie smiling at his refusal to join them.

'Someone tried to burn down the club,' Emma murmured.

'Best thing for it.'

'Bat got a fella,' Julie added.

'You're joking.'

'She 'as, 'an she, Em? Bigger than her. From down the valley.'

'He'd have to be.'

'He comes and goes, stays on the weekends. She's like a big kid round him.'

'What happens with this probation stuff, then?' Emma asked.

'I have to see someone regular. Guy called Regan, they said. If I show him I can be a good boy for a year that's it. Off the books.'

'Aye, but you gotta stay off this time,' Julie said. 'For all our sakes.'

Emma's hand reached for his and squeezed. He felt her desperate hope in her fingers, matched by Julie's pleading eyes. There were bags under them. Twin sacks of worry he'd put there.

'Alright,' he mumbled.

'I got beer in the fridge,' Julie said. 'I got a bloody fridge full for you.'

He was up and out early the next day. Past the statue by eight. The previous evening hadn't been fooling. It was a clear-bright March day, with a firm sun cutting through the moist air, making the dewy, green turf steam. He headed for the top of the ridge where the first layer of forestry swathed the hillside. He wanted to be in its heart within the hour.

At first he went fast, as fast as he could. Despite his fitness regime in the nick, long walks had not been an option there. The backs of his legs soon complained. They had a lot more weight to carry now. Why was he rushing? This land was not going anywhere. There was nothing to stash. No-one to hide from. He slowed his pace.

A strip of trees had been felled while he'd been inside. He picked his way over the debris. Then he was in the dank, dark brown-green, stepping on years of decaying pine needles. He kept to the edge, so he could see the two valleys twist and collide below. All the familiar lines were appearing out of the haze as the sun burned it off. He saw the estate. Perched on its hilltop like a big stone bird. Just waking up. Ant figures emerging. Going down the social, to court, or hanging about 'til the club opened. A few even going to work. Unimportant insects. That's what the outside thought of them. Of us. He sat down and took a blow. He was heading for the old church between two sections of forestry, and the pub alongside it. He'd get a beer and a sandwich there.

He was at a cross-roads. And it seemed the crap road Tracksuit had suggested was the only one open to him. He couldn't see anything else ahead. What lay below was much sharper. But there was no vision or worthwhile life there. He could work this out, when Daniels, Humphries and a thousand others couldn't. Or maybe he was underestimating them. The fact that they were dopehead wasters or drunken arseholes might be the result of what they realised. The nothing they saw ahead.

It had seemed simple. Get good at nicking. Do a lot of it. Get the money and ship out. Getting caught hadn't come into it. That was for others. But he'd been wrong. It was for him too, cutting into his life like a big, bloody knife. Right on the back of Shane. And he still wasn't sure what he'd been up to in the house of books. Whether he wanted to be caught. To fuck up. He'd read in one of Beezer's mags that stupid sods who tried to top themselves were crying out for help. Maybe that was it.

He got to the church. Three miles from the estate. But feeling much longer over the mountain. Its boneyard had been built on a slope, and landslip had fucked up the graves. Capsized and tumbled them, tweaked the stones until they fell or split. No-one seemed to do anything about it. Perhaps anyone who might have cared was long gone. He found a flat spot on the lush grass and parked himself. Until the pub opened.

Most of the older stones had Welsh on them. That language again. That dead language. He smiled at that. Some were almost smooth, their words worn off by two hundred years of weather. Just lichen-covered grooves left. There were lots of young uns sunk here, too. Kids of two and four and ten. Death that soon didn't happen much now, unless it was an accident. Or what had happened to Shane. Nothing could describe that. No word. No book of words. His thoughts started to turn darker but he fought them off. They did no good, and he did not want them to call up Psycho Eyes. He wanted that fucker to lay low, until he might vanish forever. Just like Shane had.

Regan was a short-arse, put together like a bull. Bull neck, barrel chest, a stocky thirteen stones. His people were from Ireland but he was a valley boy from Porth. Which was why they assigned Mark Richards to him.

Regan was giving him a lift to the estate. After their third meeting. Rules had been established. Mark knew what he had to do to stay on the right side of the system. How often he had to check into the office. The report Regan would write on him.

He had one thing in common with Regan, at least. They both liked their music strong. Regan had the cassette on so loud it blanked out any noise outside. He saw other cars ploughing through the heavy rain, saw the effect of the wind ripping off the hillside and driving down the squalls but inside there was just the music. Classical stuff he knew nothing about. Mahler, Regan said ...Maahler... it sounded like a noise a sheep might make. But he had to admit it was powerful.

Regan drifted his Mini over the central line as they tackled the long hill. An oncoming car swerved and flashed them. Two fingers sped by. Regan changed down from third which was just enough power.

'Why you got such a small car?' he asked.

'It's cheap. I couldn't afford anything else after my divorce. Anyway, I always wanted a Mini – twenty years ago.'

Regan glanced at his client and smiled. Mark was a challenge. But then they all were. Case histories that seemed to stretch into oblivion. For a few minutes he'd lost himself in the music, dying with Aschenbach in Venice, chasing shadows with him, wallowing in his nostalgia and dreams. Letting the aching melody swamp the car. Letting his thoughts flee light years away from the estate. Clouds hung low, dumping their load on 'fortress hopeless', as he liked to call it. To himself. He turned Mahler off as they turned into Mark's street. Alien culture erased at a stroke. It seemed very still for a moment. A crushing silence. Until the rain replaced the symphony.

'Quite a storm,' Regan muttered.

His eyes scanned the houses, and almost recoiled. The estate symbolised the tail-end of the sixties, when fresh ideas had got it so wrong. Leaving people like him to pick up the pieces a generation later. He saw crumbling, wasted, modern housing. All he'd known since coming into probation work.

Regan tried to fix up with work for Mark, but no-one was biting. Shane and Portland were a powerful combination. It got to a point where Mark didn't mind Regan. The guy had something about him. He didn't spout bullshit like a park fountain and he knew the score. Dropped plenty of hints that he'd been around, had left school with nothing and worked his way to where he now was. That made it possible to talk. Just a little at first, then loosening up when his thing with whales came up.

'I've been wondering when you'd notice that,' Regan said.

It was Friday afternoon. Mark was the last to be seen. Regan's cubby-hole office looking as tired as the arse end of the wet week. Mark had seen a book about oceans on one of Regan's shelves and had gone towards it instinctively. Attracted by the Humpback leaping off its cover.

'I got a file about you from Portland. The 'Whaleman', eh?'

Mark shrugged, and felt his shoulder muscles flex.

'Go on, take it out. You can borrow it if you like. I've never got round to looking at it.'

He did. It was smaller than the ones he had, more wordy, but he found the pictures quickly.

'Fascinating creatures, aren't they?'

He nodded, wanting to keep his cool but also wanting to share his new knowledge. To share. It came as a shock.

'Know much about them?' Regan asked.

'A bit.'

And he talked. Let himself go. Showing off what he knew. Ten minutes went by without Regan saying much. He just listened, hands behind his head, tie at half mast, coffee stains on his shirt cuff. The interview ended.

'I won't see you for a fortnight, now,' Regan said. 'Easter holidays coming up. Keep your nose clean, and don't forget to join the library. You'll find lots of stuff there.'

But he didn't need a library. He'd gone to Cardiff a few days after getting back and bought everything on whales he could find. Using some of the tin money. There were books all over his bedroom. Confusing Emma and Julie, but not worrying them. This interest was at home and safe.

Regan watched him from the window, whistling to himself and tapping a pencil to Mahler's Fifth. Mark might have possibilities. He took a file from a drawer in his desk. Outward bound courses for young offenders. What the slut press was going nuts over. He found the one he wanted. An outfit in the Shetlands. He checked on the fees. Bloody pricey, but Mark had possibilities. Maybe.

There had been no trouble waiting for him on the estate. Thoughts about Shane were fading. Someone had strangled and stabbed his wife since he'd been inside. That was number one in the tongue chart now. And that he'd gone down had helped. Doing time was something the estate boys could identify with.

The weather was good. Dry from May, steaming by the end of June. Other places like the estate turned nasty in the heat, but this one just went to sleep. Like a lizard in the sun. By July he'd read all his whale collection. Some of the books twice over. Reading was never easy but at least his eyes didn't recoil from the words, now.

During this time Julie functioned, after a fashion. And the edge between them was gone. Shane was mentioned less and less, for there was little more to say. But he saw the way she was whenever something came on the telly. How her face twitched when a kid went missing. And how bitter-glad she was if he turned up unharmed. He found himself thinking less about Shane.

It was into summer before Regan told him about the Shetlands. And Mark knew where they were now. Off the north of Scotland. A long way off. Before going down he wouldn't have had a clue. It amused him. Most boys banged up learnt more about thieving, and any other way to fuck the system and themselves. He'd come back with knowledge. Rarer than a leopard on the estate.

'I'm recommending you for this,' Regan said, pushing a folder across his desk.

It was some sort of camping Centre. Where middle class tossers went. He saw a few in the photos, wandering about in green wellies, and jumpers like sacks.

'What is it?' he asked.

'An Outward Bound Centre. Where people commune with nature and all that.' Regan lit up a cigarette. He chain smoked. 'A healthy place,' he coughed, 'where you can do hearty things, like fiddle about in kayaks, go fishing, hike around the landscape.'

Mark looked at him blankly.

'Is this a wind-up?'

'Nope. It's part of our new master-plan. Send young offenders on stuff like this, in the hope that something might rub off on them.'

'Aye, something might rub off their boots.'

His voice was full of scorn but his mind was working overtime. Shetland. Whale country. Or sea. An area Humpbacks passed through on their world tour. And sometimes Pilot whales. Doing a spot of trawling in all them inlets and channels he'd read about. Excitement punched his guts like a fist.

'Lemme get this straight,' he said. 'Someone pays for people like me to go to places like this. Leave it out.'

Regan smiled.

'I couldn't believe it either, when I first heard about it. But it's happening and I'm recommending you for this place. Grab it with both hands, Mark, because it's not going to last long. Now that the press have sniffed it out. The good tax payers are apoplectic.'

'When will you know?'

'If you're going it'll be in September. When those highland midges are really biting.'

He was almost whistling when he left. For weeks he'd been planning to use the tin money on some sort of expedition, once his probation was over. Get to somewhere where there was plenty of ocean, where he might have a chance of seeing whales. Now

207

the system might deliver a chance to him. Nah, leave it out, he told himself. Luck like that don't happen to people like you. If you go you won't see nothing except toffee-nosed ponces. Even so, he almost whistled.

He'd never been anywhere much. Had never used any of the money to get away. It had been all saving, for a future that had been attractive because it would be an escape into the unknown. All this was blown away now. And in its place came a holiday from the state. It was weird. Regan had gone on about character building, but he didn't seem to believe it either. Yet it was happening. It was late August and he was days away from Scotland. Regan had fixed it all.

Julie and Emma were puzzled. Emma had been wary of his new interest from the start. For her, bringing books into the house was almost as strange as nicking. Whales were something else she couldn't share in. He'd tried to explain what he felt about them a few times. Wishing he had a better way with words. His just dribbled away about size, and power, and beauty. He felt a prat, but at least he got it over to her that they weren't fish. And he tried to tell her that his own needs were somehow summed up by them. It was hard going but it pleased her, even if she couldn't understand it. She liked the fact that whales were mammals, and had babies.

'But what about us?' Emma asked. 'What are we gonna do after your probation?'

'I dunno yet.'

'Well, getting interested in whales isn't going to help us, is it?'

They were in the bedroom, his whale books taking their place amongst the Clash and Pistols, and his other out-of-date music, all the anger and spit stuff. Which he hadn't played much since he'd got out. He'd even allowed some of Emma's soft modern shit on the hi-fi.

He lay on the bed, Emma stood by the window picking at her nails in the nervous way she had. Worrying the varnish off it as soon as it was dry. He looked beyond her shoulders to the denuded forestry slopes, in which he could see the outline of a Humpback. There was even a wedge of trees that looked like a fin. Christ, he was seeing whales everywhere now.

'What you thinking?' Emma asked. 'Bet it's not about us.'

He made an instant decision. Going for it before he had time

208

to change his mind.

'Lift that mat up, by your feet. Now that loose board. That's
right, just prise it up. Don' worry about your nails. You've
destroyed them already. Take them tins out.'

'Mark?'

'Go on, open 'em. Here on the bed.'

She sprang back when the notes tumbled out.

'Oh my God,' Emma gasped, 'now what you done? You
haven't killed nobody?'

'Leave it out, it's the money from the jobs. I saved most of it.'

He smiled and put his hands behind his head. Savouring the
relief and danger of her knowing. This sharing thing again.

'There's three grand,' he said, 'just about.'

Emma looked around fearfully, as if eyes were peering through
the window.

'Jesus, all this time, and you never told me.'

'I've told you now. And I'm telling you I won't be nicking no
more.'

'Do you really mean it?'

'Aye – maybe.'

He laughed at the look on her face.

'Nah, I mean it.'

And he did. It came on him as quickly as showing her the tins.
That there must be something else. Even for the likes of him.

He let her wrap herself round him as she fell onto the bed, scattering the notes.

Regan had given him all the instructions he needed to get to his
destination, and a bunch of tickets. And no-one was going with
him, thank Christ. They 'trusted' him, but he knew he was being
tested. Portland could welcome him back anytime. The system
had even thrown in money for some gear – anorak and boots. He
recoiled when he first saw the green anorak with its blue hood. As
if it was another kind of uniform. And the heavy army-style hik-
ing boots. Size twelve. Tracksuit would have been proud of him.

He had to get to Aberdeen by train, then ferry to Lerwick,
Shetland. One hundred and eighty miles across a sea that he knew
would be stormy. Had to be for him. Emma saw him off at
Cardiff station. Looking cool in a yellow mini skirt and shoes that
put three inches on her. Dressing for him and attracting all the
starving old men's eyes on the platform. Julie had said her good-

byes in the house. A brief brush of her lips on his cheek as she
gave him thirty quid she'd put by. He gave it back to Emma as
soon as they were out the house.

'Put it back in her purse,' he said. 'And don' ever tell her about
the money. It would be one more thing for her to worry over.
Christ, she might even turn it in.'

Emma went straight back on the valley train. She didn't want to
look round the shops. She'd done that too many times on her own
before. When Mark was inside, her old friends made themselves
scarce. This time he'd be gone three weeks. Nothing compared to
Portland, and it might help him. And add to the change she saw
in him but hardly dared believe. Maybe the anger was being hidden. Stored up until it came rushing out. At her probably. But
maybe it wasn't. She'd seen what losing Shane had done to Julie,
and wondered if some good could come of it for Mark. Somehow
that tragedy might take away some of his strangeness. That would
be fair, after such an awful thing. The Richards deserved something.

Julie was waiting for her.

'He got off okay, then,' Julie said.

'Aye, right on time. He's got to change a few times before he
gets to Aberdeen, and he's got a night there then another day on
the ferry. I don't think he fancies that.'

'Don' blame him. I'd be as sick as a pig.'

Julie whisked around her tea-bag.

'Whales,' she muttered. 'I remember watching *Moby Dick* once,
with my father, 'bout the only thing I can remember doing with
him. But I was too young and it frightened me.'

She reached for a new pack of cigarettes, unwrapped them and
took one out in one smooth movement. Emma lit it for her.

'I can remember the thing's eye, though,' Julie said, 'even now.
What gets into Mark's head, eh? Goes down and comes back with
stuff like this in it.'

'It's better than him doing houses,' Emma said.

'Aye, I know. Maybe he'll become a fisherman.'

Emma laughed, but Julie did not know if it was funny. Not
knowing which way her son would turn out. After Emma had
gone to work she took some of Mark's books from his bedroom
and looked through them. Some of the photos were nice but she
didn't get it. What did he see in this? Stuff a million miles away

from the estate. Shane watched her from his place on the telly. It had been a few weeks since she'd looked through his album. Nearly a month since she cried for him. Cried openly. There were always tears inside. She'd had two years of hell, and not much of a life before that. Her fault, she'd always been told. What the papers told her. What the telly told her. Her own parents. Everyone ready to point the finger. That single parent crap. That they did it to get a house. Social money. To live the wonderful lifestyle that was the estate, and hundreds like it round the country. Never much said about the men who left. Or that there was no-one to mind the kids if they tried to get work. Finger-pointing was easier. If she could believe in a god she'd pray for Mark now, pray that he'd turn out alright. Whether it took whales or anything bloody else.

He stood on the quay at Lerwick, taking it in. The place smelt salty, and the people looked salty. Lots of chunky sweaters and wellies. Accents he couldn't quite understand. And a surprising number of foreigners wandering about. He heard German, which he recognised from the war films he'd watched, and other stuff he'd never heard. His stomach was still moving to the sway of the ferry. What sort of stupid bastard actually wanted to bother with the sea? It didn't make sense at all. Yet it fascinated him. A bit different up here to the stuff he'd always seen off Barry or Porthcawl, sluggish, oily and full of shit. Here it was all green, like an endless, wet version of the forestry, but one you couldn't roam around in without a poxy boat. To get tossed about until your guts felt like cardboard. It had been as he'd expected on the ferry. A choppy gun-metal sea, wind-whipped into white, the boat pitching and lurching, and his guts joining in. He'd been heaving within an hour. Fourteen hours had seemed two lifetimes.

A man called McGinley met him personally at the quay. Looked a bit like Tracksuit. But from a different world, with a different voice. He'd expected that thick Scots stuff he'd heard before but this geezer had an accents that could have come from anywhere. Rootless, but saying its owner had done alright. He was fit and almost Mark's size. Blond and blue-eyed, his face weather-creased, he looked older than he probably was. Which was forty-five, Mark guessed. He took the hand that was offered and matched it for firmness.

'Alright,' he muttered, wondering how much McGinley was

getting for him, and wondering if he needed the money.

He carried his gear to a green Range Rover. It had to be green. 'We're still quite busy,' McGinley told him, 'but things will tail off, now that schools have started up again.'

The guy seemed okay, for what he was, but Mark stayed wary, his senses alert. Until he found out what the set-up was. He thought of Portland. Winston would never believe it. That went double for Beezer.

McGinley drove along a road that kept close to the coast. Any road would keep close to the coast here. He'd looked up Shetland in the library. His first ever visit there. It was a thin snake of land with a bulge at the side. Like an old axe-head. He took it in.

Green. Lots of shades. An open land. A big, flat wide-open that welcomed the wind. No native tree had ever thought of growing here. No tree would dare. It was nothing like the hillsides of his valley but all grassy, low-lying stuff, and nowhere very far from the grey-green sea. It would be often stormy, and always dangerous. Untidy, stony beaches, and tiny sandy bays guarded by cliffs. Towering bastards, some of them, jutting out from the coastline, and on top a solid olive coating that looked like green fur from a distance, it was so thick and unbroken. Near McGinley's place four of them pushed out at the sea, probing it like giant stone fingers, making it foam with anger. Only the thumb was missing. He had never seen anywhere so naked, so without cover. A nicker's nightmare, if there were any here.

McGinley's centre was a collection of wooden huts, near Scalloway, six miles across the island from Lerwick. From the hut that served as an office a wooden walkway led down to a small quay, where the rowing boats and kayaks were kept. A small inlet swept up against the huts and there was a shingle beach running off to one side of the quay. He would be with another bunch of young guys here, but this time he was the odd-one-out. The Beezer.

Mark had blisters on his feet the size of coins from breaking in the new boots. Blisters on his hands from rowing. A sore arse from the hard seat of the boat. He'd sought to conquer it with brute force and was soon knackered. He had been at the centre a week. One of twelve young men. Eleven middle class blokes and him. Beezer's revenge. They didn't know anything about him. And no-one asked him much. But even a blind man could see where he'd come from. Wankersville. Craptown. The rough edge of any place. The others were all English, a group from one area. Somewhere in the Midlands. On a course before they went off to college. At first he felt like he was amongst Martians. And they didn't know what to make of him either, but they accepted his presence after a few days. No way this could have happened if they'd been on the estate and the situation reversed. That was confidence, he reckoned, which came with knowing you were going somewhere, and had support to get there.

It was amusing to see them recoil from his language on his first day, and their attempts to decipher his accent. Theirs was easy because, like McGinley's, it came from nowhere. They were mainly sizeable guys, a few like him. Nothing like the estate runts. These were well-fed and well-bred. Good teeth, good skin. Lots of good food from way back. And all with two parents. That he could tolerate them at all was another breakthrough. A year ago it would have been all over quickly. Broken by his fists or psycho-tongue or both.

All of them knew about rowing and kayaking and map-reading, the boy scout stuff, and most were keen to help him. Which made him cringe. One guy, Latimer, a sort of a fit Beezer, seemed to think it was his duty to take him in hand. But he put up with it, knowing that McGinley would be writing a report on him for the probation service, and that he needed a crash course in boats. Needed to get out on the water. Alone. Even if this was against McGinley's rules. Seeing what he could see. Smelling out what he'd seen in his books. On the train up he checked all the known places for Humpbacks up here. There were a few not far away. But no-one at the Centre had ever seen one. No-one except McGinley.

He wanted to keep whales to himself, but he had to make his interest known. But very cautiously. Letting it out like a long fishing line and seeing where the hook would drop. McGinley made out he was surprised, but he must have known. Regan would have seen to that.

'I've made two sightings,' the man told him. 'Two in fifteen years. Not much of a record. But the local fishermen do better. You want to talk to them.'

They were sitting on the quay. He'd returned from a rowing trip with Latimer, his hands blood-salty as he learned to match his power to a regular rhythm. Not to fight the oars. He was getting better.

213

'So, how long have you been interested in whales?' McGinley asked.

'Long enough.'

'They're fascinating creatures. What's left of them. The Japs and Norwegians still take them. They call it scientific research now.'

'Aye.'

'They've got some books on Shetland marine life in the library at Scalloway. I'll take you down tomorrow, if you like.'

'Okay, ta.'

McGinley waited until Latimer had left the quay.

'So, what do you think of it?'

'What?'

'Our set-up here.'

'S'alright. Bet it costs, though.'

'Not that much. You'd be surprised.'

'I would.'

McGinley stoked up his pipe. Cupping a match in his hand and re-lighting it. It didn't seem right for him. Didn't go with his blond hair the wind was whipping across his face.

'You're the second lad, er, in your circumstances, I've had here.'

'Where was the other one from?'

'Glasgow. And he'd never been north of it. Didn't really work out though. He stole a car from the village, and wrapped it up against a sea wall.'

Mark suppressed a smile.

'Oh aye. Taking another chance with me, are you?'

'Yes. The rest of the lads are going into Lerwick tonight. Saturday night and all that. Why don't you go with them?'

'Am I supposed to?'

'You're not a prisoner here. You have the same freedom as anyone else.'

He shrugged.

'I think I'd rather stay put.'

He craved a pint but he wanted the place to himself for a while. To look around without a dozen pair of eyes on him.

'Well, see how you feel later.'

McGinley gave up on his pipe as he got up.

See you at dinner, Mark.'

'Aye. And I don't drive.'

McGinley grinned at him and stuck the upturned pipe in his shirt pocket.

He sat on his own for a while, watching the sun go down on a flat sea. The calmest he'd seen it so far. Like a grey slate. Just lying there. Nothing on it. And looking as if nothing was in it. An island showed in the distance, pushing up black against the low orange band in the sky. Whales could be gliding along right now, less than a mile from him.

His Saturday night special was to be alone. McGinley had disappeared somewhere, his staff of two were off, and the English group were in town, leaving him last man standing at the centre. Alone and trusted. He still couldn't get his head round it. That they didn't think he might burn the place down, set fire to the boats and float them out to sea. Each one a fiery torch of defiance. He knew plenty of tossers who would if they had the chance. Most of Portland for a start.

It was a cool evening, and it got dark a lot quicker up here. Not like back home, where it gave plenty of warning. On the island if there was a sun night quickly followed its setting. Mark walked out on to the beach in the last of it. Shingle scrunching under his boots.

The beach stretched around a rock to another. This one longer, and part sandy. Beyond it the cliffs started to grow and he headed for these, and found a grassy top to sit on. He'd make this place his lookout point. Where he could sweep the sea between the centre and the far island with his old nicking glasses. Looking for whales. Any signs of them. He imagined them now. Humpbacks rolling out of the water for an evening splash. His glasses fixing on them. What a buzz that would be. He had two cans Latimer had given him when he said he wasn't going out with them. Probably given in relief. He opened one, lager fizzing over his hand as he raised it to the fading light.

The dream took him that night. Wiped him out. When he thought it had left him for good. He'd come back late, picking his way carefully over the shingle, under a night sky cloudy-black and starless. Most nights here stars were like golfballs. The English were just getting back from the town, pissed up and not noticing him. Playing games like the schoolboys they'd been just a few weeks before. They were all snoring in their bunks before he thought of sleeping. He lay in the dark a long time, listening to the sea sucking off the shingle. Wondering how many thousands, millions of year it had done. And all the time whales going past. Mammals that had gone down to the sea an age ago and never came out. Most creatures did it the other way.

It was as if the dream became more powerful with time. The longer it left him alone the more of a fucker it was. Shane was talking to him this time. Asking him where he was taking him. What was down the hole. How deep it was. His voice was eerie, a fragile whisper echoing in his head. Shane wanted his mother. Wanted Julie to save him. Screamed for her. But she wasn't there. Only Psycho Eyes was there. Daniels floated up out of the blackness. His zitty face still ruined by glue, his wasted, sniffling nose running. Smiling with his rotten teeth. Beckoning to Shane.

Fuck it. He sat upright as he woke. Wondering if he'd been gabbing. If he had the others in the hut hadn't noticed. Quietly he went out onto the wooden veranda. To the seat there. Shaking in his own sweat. The night was brighter now. A few stars visible through breaks in the cloud. A light silver sheen to the sea.

Would this nightmare never leave him? An eternal punishment for losing Shane? But he didn't lose him. Shane just went. The perfect vanishing. Unless the dream was true. Something he had blanked out because his mind couldn't take it. Maybe all that 'you can change' stuff was pure crap. Maybe he was rotten. Rotten enough to think this dream. Rotten enough to maybe...

Something heavy breached the water. He heard the deep thud of it coming down. He ran down to the beach and tried to see through the gloom. Nothing. And no further sound. He stood there for some time, cold in his T-shirt. Nothing. He felt sick inside. A deep sick. A deep sense of loss. That something was being taken from him before it had chance to take shape. That whales were just a sad dream. And what was real was the nightmare. He wanted the one to cancel out the other, but it wouldn't happen. He went back inside, to the safe snores of the rich kids.

McGinley let Mark go into Scalloway on his own. The guy seemed to encourage it. Telling him he was trusted. He hitched a ride with a delivery driver. Who talked at him in an accent thick enough to cut. He made for the museum in Scalloway. His first time in one. McGinley had told him it concentrated on fishing. It did but there was not much for him in it. He hung around the town for a while, thought of approaching the fishermen he saw in the harbour, but in the end did nothing. He couldn't bring himself to ask, to be thought an anorak. But the dream was still bugging him. He found a quiet bar and had a pint and a pie there, spending the system's money and reading the letter Emma had sent. It was almost getting normal, being away and having letters.

He'd never said much to Emma about the dream. It would put ideas into her head. And from hers to Julie's. Portland had seemed part of the Richards family life, a natural part, a place everyone had expected him to end up. And he hadn't disappointed. But being on Shetland was different. A touch of the other side. A place it took money and education to get to, unless you were a young offender. Now he had an idea of what it was like not to have to worry about every penny. To be able to walk somewhere without being challenged by a pin-head tosser, or pulled by the police, just for being off the estate. To feel that he was not useless, or that his life had been mapped out for shit before he was born. As Julie's had. As his own kid's might be. All he had had was the hope the tins gave him. False hope. Other people's money. He'd like to have the strength to burn the lot, or better still, give it away. Which would really make him certifiable. Or really changed. But shrugging off the past was not so easy. Not if it was also the present and maybe the future. Now he understood why Tracksuit had gone into the army. It had been his only ticket out, for someone who'd never pass no exams. Exams be fucked. Everything came down to stuff like that. Stuff he knew he could never get his head round. Marine biology, Beezer had talked about. He'd never even be able to spell it. Nah, the only place that would take him would be the army, but it seemed a bleak answer. Another kind of prison that might hold him until he was past caring.

Emma's letter was full of hope. She even joked about him 'swimming with the whales'. And Julie was thinking about him. He felt their pressure. That they expected him to keep changing, to come up with some magic formula which would transform him, wave a wand and he's a nice guy, wave a wand and he's got a good job, wave a wand and there's the cool house, a copy of one of his targets. What he'd always thought was a crock of shit because he could never have it. Legally.

Hope. Another difficult word. Like change. Small words – even he could write, but they represented something vast. He replied to the letter. Which would amaze Emma. Painfully writing out the words in his scrawly hand.

It was Thursday, second week of September. The English group had gone off on a hike together. They did everything together, as if they had one mind. He hadn't heard any arguments. McGinley had gone into town thinking Mark had gone on the walk. But he'd slipped back telling the rest he'd felt rough. It was the only way to be alone and to go out in the boat alone. McGinley had told him it was too soon for him to do it. But he had to. Because he felt whales close ever since that noise in the night. He couldn't explain it, but they were there. Some sense told him. The same one that told him if danger was around when he was nicking. It was like something scratching his skin, rubbing it with awareness, putting an edge on the back of his neck.

He took the usual boat, the one he shared with Latimer, and rowed out quietly. The cook having a drag by the kitchen door saw him go but just waved. He nodded back, and settled into a steady rhythm. It would be a long row and he wanted to pace himself. He was heading for the channel between the Centre and the small island. McGinley had seen Humpbacks there. It took him thirty minutes to get where he wanted. Where the current would take him down the channel for a time. Conditions were good. Some breeze, some sun, some cloud. Nothing to trouble him, as long as he didn't go too far into unknown waters.

Nothing, just the bob of the boat, and a few gulls bombing him. He wished he hadn't had the bacon for breakfast. He was thirsty, his throat dry. And the sun was getting stronger. Maybe his sense was taking the piss, maybe it didn't mean sod all. Except that he was cracked. Time passed and the boat was being carried far enough. He didn't like the thought of the long row back.

That sudden breaking of water was unforgettable. The sluggish surface churned, the boat tossed and heaved, and was showered with sea. An instant island alongside. For a moment he thought he'd dozed off and was dreaming. No, for once life wasn't that cruel. It was a Humpback. Charcoal shot through with lighter grey, lumps of parasites marking the great body. Like armour. A flash of white as it turned over. Chilling out as it checked him over.

It was a family of them. One calf at least. A fifteen ton baby brushed the boat. He'd heard the saying 'heart in mouth' and now knew it was true. He could almost taste his. Chew it. This was not the old bitter copper taste of fear. It was excitement, a pure, rushing charge. Two swam ahead of the boat, rear flukes spooning the water like ladles, flicking spray into his eyes with their power. He felt the salt sting. An eye came close to his own, not more than a foot from the boat. It looked at him idly. There was another calf, so there must be two females. This one darted around him, having fun with the boat, before seeking the safety of its mother. He held onto the sides and hoped it didn't go over. But he knew he was quite safe as he locked the oars. For the first time in his life he felt this, as he was enveloped by the presence of the whales, their power and mystery. He could float with them forever. Untroubled. Safe.

Ahead, the incurious parents ploughed on, spouted water marking their progress. After a last bump the kids joined them. He tracked the group as long as he could, wanting to stretch out each second, his eyes greedy for every scrap of knowledge. As they blended into the distance one of the adults breached the water. Flopping down with a thwack. Sun turning the spray silver. He imagined it waving goodbye with a fin. Goodbye, he muttered to himself. Wondering how long tears had been streaming down his face.

He gathered his senses. Feeling like he'd run around the forestry very quickly. The boat had drifted quite a way past the island and the weather was changing in the sudden, stealthy way it could up here. Sun gone. Grey-choppy water. A swell getting up. He unlocked the oars and started to pull hard against the flow. Which was taking him farther away from the centre. He could see rocks at the foot of the promontory up ahead, marked by waves crashing against them. Though still elated, he knew he was in trouble. The current was too strong for the oars so he gave it up, turned the boat around and let it drift. Towards the rocks.

His plan was to get in close then use the oars to guide the boat into an inlet. There were a lot of them. But as he neared the rocks the sea was rougher. The boat was spun around and it was all he could do to hold on. He managed to push away from the first rocks, and the second, but a sudden wave took him against the third outcrop. Smashing the boat against the base of the cliff and keeping it there. Only now did it occur to him that he couldn't swim. Had never attempted it.

To go down would confirm all his thoughts about life being a pisser. He'd just had a glimpse of something rich, a reward for carving out an interest when everyone he knew had none. Making him feel something that might have been hope. Now minutes later it looked as if he'd be taken out. For daring too much.

The boat was breaking up. One oar was wrenched from his grasp and his shoulder took a blow from the cliff wall. He was being dragged along its base, trapped in the current in a boat starting to resemble matchwood. He thought to abandon the craft and get a hold on the rocks but that was impossible. An inlet was appearing up ahead. He might be able to reach it, if he could swim.

Another wave struck and the boat was gone. He was in the water. The cold of it shocked him. Like ice instantly pressing against him. He went down and took in some sea but struggled up again. Three times for a drowning man, they said. Fuck it. He struck out blindly on the surface, arms flailing. He went down again but was calmer this time. Numbed by the cold. If this was a film the whales would save him. Give him a ride to the shore where he would meet the girl and walk off into the sunset. It was only moments ago that he had felt so safe with them. The safest man in the world.

He broke the surface again, an angry sky wheeling above his head. Once more and he'd be gone. But he was free of the cliff and in calmer water. In the inlet. A wave took him further in, a spluttering, useless land animal bobbing on it. He could see the shore just yards off but it might have been miles for he knew he wouldn't come up a third time. His chest was on fire from the salt water, but his body frozen. Down he went. To touch the bottom with his feet. He bounced back up, brain just functioning. He was not out of his depth. He was in about five feet of water. Keep your feet, you stupid, tall bastard. Or you'll be sucked out again. Sucked out into hell for sure.

He bounced himself above the surface. Feeling each time that his feet would not touch bottom. But they did. Every time. And he gained the shore, fell onto pebbles in an exhausted lump. Not quite conscious. But alive. He must have been there for some time. The advancing tide roused him. Lapping at his legs with more ice. Christ, he was cold. He got up, sea squelching in his boots, and shook himself, rubbed himself, slapped himself, any-thing to get the circulation flowing. He was on a thin strip of beach. Ahead were cliffs. Two hundred feet straight up. What the hell. He'd got away with it and it wouldn't be dark for hours. He brought up some sea water and smelt the breakfast bacon on it. And his thirst raged.

He was on the tiny beach for two hours before McGinley came along. In the small trawler that sometimes called at the centre. He shouted and yelled from the beach and the boat turned into the inlet. McGinley seemed more relieved than angry.

'We saw the wreckage in the channel,' McGinley shouted, 'and feared the worst.'

'I'm alright. Just cold.'

'You're a lucky young bugger,' the trawler skipper said. 'Must be a bloody good swimmer.'

He didn't answer as he waded into the sea to clasp the hand offered to him. McGinley handed him a cup of coffee and draped a blanket round his shoulder. This geezer was showing him more care than any of Julie's men ever had. He felt embarrassed.

'Want to tell me what you were up to?' McGinley.

'Just wanted to get out on my own. See if I could do it.'

'Well, you've had the answer to that, and it's cost us a boat. You were out whalehunting, weren't you.'

'Aye.'

'Well, I hope it was worth it.'

He shrugged.

'Finding them is not so easy, is it? Bill here hasn't seen any at all this season.'

The skipper nodded.

'Getting scarcer all the time,' he muttered.

Mark felt triumph inside.

'So, no luck then?' McGinley asked.

'No way. I was just stupid.'

He wasn't ready to share it. Not yet. Maybe never. He had something of his own, something unique to him which hadn't been stolen or taken from anyone else. It was all his and he wanted to get back to the huts to feast on it. To go over every second and not ever let the memory fade. Keep each image fresh, smell the sea, the salty exhilaration, keep the rocketing buzz alive:it might be all he would ever get. All he would ever see of his obsession.

The trawler took them back to the centre. He looked down at the sea swirling green and rough in the wake of the boat as he shivered under his blanket. And realised his luck. Two kinds of miracle.

'How much was the boat worth?' he asked.

'Why, you can't pay for it. We're insured,' McGinley said.

Paying for it hadn't crossed his mind.

As they neared the quay the sun came out again. Sly bastard. Making the sea look quiet and welcoming. Another sly bastard. Good sly bastard teamwork. But the whales were master of it. They had no enemies. Not *in* the sea. He had more regard for them than ever.

'Better have a shower and put on some dry clothes,' McGinley said.

Mark walked over the shingle beach. The others were waiting with him on the veranda, excited to hear his story. He imagined Julie with them, her face a mixture of relief and despair. At the never-ending trouble he caused. He went inside without saying much, hoping she'd never get to know about this.

While Mark was being battered in the boat, Julie was in her garden with Emma. Sitting on the plastic kitchen chairs. The sand heap was just a scrubby tump now, a miniature slag-heap. Emma was amazed Julie could sit so close to it, that she could even be in the garden at all. If it had been her kid she'd have left, no way could she bear staying in the same house. But Julie had. She was strong deep down, like Mark was on the surface.

'I got this letter off him,' Emma said, handing it over.

Julie read it.

'Sixteen lines. Must be a record. How do you think he's doing up there, really doing?'

'Hard to say. In the letter –'

'Forget that. Don't trust words, 'specially Mark's.'

Emma was a little hurt at this. She could see the change in him, almost feel it in the words, but Julie had been moody since he'd gone to Scotland. More than when he was banged up. And she was drinking again.

'He'll be back soon,' Emma said, 'maybe he's seen them whales.'

'Whales – another game of his. How's that gonna help him? That's not real. It's not what people like us do.'

Emma looked at her hands.

Julie took another long pull from her bottle.

'Christ, this American stuff is like cat's piss.'

'Everyone's drinking it now.'

'Aye, they would round here. Most of 'em would like to be American, I reckon, if they had the chance. Anything they can't have they want.'

It was a warm day. Heavy, moist Autumn warmth. Emma had a day off from the salon and had a full week of holiday coming, which she was keeping for Mark's return. As Julie fumbled for her cigarettes Emma stole a closer look at her. At her face which had aged so much. A half-moon of bag under each eye, blotchy red skin and thin lips even thinner. Like someone had pencilled them on. And her hair gone to pieces. Despite her best efforts. Now and then Julie noticed herself and was really down. Like today. When she went right back to the early days of Shane going missing and relived a complete, perfectly-formed hell in twenty-four hours. It was hard to do anything for her when she was like this. To say anything hopeful was to cut her with a knife. Perhaps she shouldn't have shown her the letter.

Julie knew Emma was studying her. She couldn't do anything slyly. She didn't have the make up for it. Emma was a nice kid but sometimes she got in the way. At times, nice wasn't enough. And she was jealous of her, if she was truthful with herself. Jealous of what she might have with Mark. Of the children they might have. Then hating herself for it. If Mark could learn from her mistakes, and his own, that would be something. A tiny piece of success to throw at life.

Sometimes when she was on the booze she'd mix Mark and Shane up. Their faces merging. Their childhoods merging. Then she'd be getting off that bus and seeing Mark's face. A kind of staring loss in it. Knowing something bad had happened but not guessing how bad. Not even getting close.

It had been hard getting through the anniversary of her loss. Anniversary, that wasn't the word. That was a word for good things. Despite her efforts, her brave thoughts when she'd stopped the counselling had run out of steam. And Mark coming back from Portland seemed to make it worse. When she looked at him she saw Shane. And each minute of that awful day came rushing back. There was still doubt in her. About what might have happened. What could have happened. Like the head of a nail buried inside, a head which sometimes glittered and winked and pointed her thoughts to black conclusions. Then she'd have another can, or three.

223

'You alright?' Emma asked.

'Aye, I 'spose.'

She smiled at Emma. At her hopeful, pretty, young, got-it-all-to-come face.

'Let's have a look at that letter again. We'd better keep it safe. It might be a collector's item in years to come.'

Mark was flat the next morning. Trying to hold onto that feeling he had with the whales. Which he knew must be happiness. Without strings, conditions or payback. Though it had almost cost him everything. If he could get a life which gave him this on a regular basis perhaps the anger would die.

He sat on the veranda and tried to fix yesterday's happenings in his head. Weld them there permanently. It was just after six and no-one was up. Just him and pale yellow light against a lead-coloured sky. And the sea sucking insistently on the shingle. He could get used to this. Not being hemmed in by crap buildings, crap people. People like him.

If Shane hadn't gone he wouldn't be here. And he'd never have gone down. Because he would have kept on with his perfect nicking and never have been caught. Be on his way to copying The Man by now. Not knowing any better. Would have kept to the city, any city, kept his cramped, seething cesspit of a mind well filled up with crap, kept his money, kept it all for himself and shat on everyone. He doubted if he'd have seen Julie much after he left. And Emma would be old history. Traded in for something sleek and smooth and bitch-hard. Who'd give it him all back.

So he knew something better now. Big deal. They were allowing him a look through a window, that was all. There was no way he'd ever get inside the room.

He didn't hear McGinley come up. Another old skill lost.

'You're out early,' the Scot said. 'Especially after yesterday.'

'Couldn't sleep.'

McGinley sat alongside him. He could not be sure if the guy was genuinely interested in him or just earning his corn.

'Weather's breaking,' McGinley said. 'We've had the best of it.'

He wondered what the worst of it might be.

'It gets pretty grim in the winter.'

'Do you shut down?'

'Yes. We have another group coming up next week then that's it.'

They sat in silence for a while. McGinley didn't feel the need to constantly talk, which he liked. He liked McGinley, in fact, as far as he could tell.

'You saw some, didn't you?' McGinley asked.

'Uh?'

'Must have been Humpbacks. No-one's seen any Pilots this year.'

He told him. It all came tumbling out, like that time in the pig station with Beefy. Talking to strangers when he was dumb with those closest to him.

'How did you know?' he asked.

'You were obviously a man on a mission. And your face told me everything. Even after you nearly drowned. But to see a group is very rare here now. You've been lucky. I haven't managed that.'

'They came close enough to touch,' Mark said, with a touch of pride. 'I was eyeball to eyeball with one. Felt like it was looking right through me. Like it was the eye of the world.'

'Yes, size can be humbling, can't it?'

McGinley looked at him with interest.

'That was quite a talk, Mark. Why don't you tell the other lads. They'd be very interested, and a bit jealous.'

He became self-conscious, and felt naked. What he had just said was a kind of exposure.

'Nah, I don't think so,' he said. 'You won't say nothing, will you?'

'Not if you don't want me to.'

For a moment he thought McGinley might know about Shane, that Regan might have told him. It was all he could do to prevent himself from jumping up. But the man said nothing else. He left him on the veranda.

'Go for a walk before breakfast,' McGinley said, 'this is the best time of the day.'

A year ago he would have laughed at this. It wouldn't have meant nothing to an estate boy. But he'd been away from the estate. Now he understood it a little, and could experience the gulf between McGinley's life and his own. Gauge its vastness. Between all the McGinleys and all the Mark Richards. Between him and the man in the house of books. Even Regan and Beefy. But he didn't understand how the gulf had come about. Who put it there. And why.

It was quiet, with a light breath of breeze. He felt it work its way through his growing hair, rubbing his face with its salt touch. His tongue licked at his top lip for a taste. He walked along the beach stretching away from the centre. A thin band of sand that banked into deep water.

It was quieter. No gulls. Usually they pierced each dawn with their babble. Always on the lookout for stuff. Good nickers. But none today. He screwed up his eyes against the brightening sky and walked on. He knew this quiet. Had known it. The day Shane went.

He walked to the end of the beach, looking down, and not more than a few feet ahead. Rounding an outcrop into the next cove he did not see the whales until he was almost on them. Three humped bodies lying just out of the water. Their flukes lapped by it. He started, expecting them to rise up at him, but they were motionless.

Their smell was quickly on him. Nothing gut-churning yet but it was there. A hundred tons of flesh getting ready. He stood on the sand motionless for a time, his boots washed by the sea. Not daring to move. His chest was tight and his breathing shallow. These heavy, lifeless lumps were what he had seen yesterday. They had to be the same ones. He prodded the smallest with his foot, his ridiculously tiny size twelves. Tried to loosen the covering around the eye. He wanted it to spring back into life and thought it might when he dared touch it with his hand. Imagining the eye still warm with the memory of life, he wanted it to plough back into the sea like a demented monster surfer. To take control again. To be king. But it wasn't warm. It was cold. Dead cold. As cold as any fish. And the parasites on its great body living on, though their host was dead. He kicked out at a clump of barnacles, cursing as he did so. A rapid series of rhythmic oaths. Until he felt his breath catch.

They must have come ashore in the night. He sat down a few yards away from them, glad now that he couldn't get the eye covering open. The stare would have been too much. He looked round nervously, as if he was at the scene of a crime. His crime. Bitterness welled up inside him. Maybe this was his crime. And punishment. Confirming that everything he touched turned to shit. Daniels, Shane and now this. He felt sick and giddy. He shook. Like when he used to lose it, lose it completely. But this time there would be no triumphant aftermath, no high when he'd feel all the poison drained out of him. This was nothing he could shout at.

He could not get his mind round it. That trawler skipper had said how rare whales were getting. But he'd seen them, swimming in their sea. And now he was seeing them dead, on his land. A solitary gull now wheeled down, checking out the scene as it arced on the warming air. 'Aye, you're gobsmacked an' all,' he thought. A low sun came through the haze. Sprinkling the wet tails of the whales with silver-grey light. He thought of that kids' crap that used to charge through his head, Mark the Black Avenger, and wished it was real now. That he could be superhuman, breathe back life into the Humpbacks and launch them back into the water. Be God. A god. Any god.

His eyes were wet. It was getting to be a habit up here. He wiped at them with the back of a hand. Christ, Regan had talked about 'new experiences', but he couldn't have reckoned on this.

It would have been easy to run. To turn away, get back to the centre, to know nothing of this. Play dumb when the news broke, and everyone and his brother came down on the beach. He'd always been running. Chasing himself inside but wanting something better to catch him up. To make things right. Like his unknown father never had. The nicking was all about this. Each house had been a new place to run to. Another piece of piss to con himself with. Self-knowledge slapped him in the face. He was growing up in minutes. Seeing himself clearly in the presence of three dead giants. And knowing that it was all down to him.

The dream was another con. Another refuge that could keep him angry. Let him blame himself mercilessly. His way of making sense of his shit life. There was no mine shaft. Hadn't been since before he was born. And the only pit was inside his head. The perfect place to mine. Other kids had games, toys, sport. He'd had anger, and had grown to love it. But it could fuck off now. He wanted it to fuck off. He got up suddenly, as if brushing something away from him, and saw McGinley running towards him.

'God,' the Scot shouted, 'three of them. They do this, you know. One gets sick, disorientated, and heads for the shore. The rest follow. No-one really knows why.'

He didn't answer, but he didn't hate McGinley's intrusion, as he would have once. Hated it so much the man might have been in danger.

'Perhaps the family bond is too strong to lose one of them,' McGinley said.

'There's a mother and child here,' he murmured.

He should have said calf but said child.

McGinley examined the calf.

'It can't be more than two years old,' McGinley said. 'What a shame. I'd better get back and do some phoning. There'll be a small army of folks up here today. Once word gets round.'

He turned to go.

'Will you be alright staying?'

'Aye.'

'You think these are the ones you saw yesterday, don't you?'

He nodded.

'Have to be.'

'You might have been the last man to see them alive.'

'And the first to see them dead.'

'Stay up-wind of them. Looks like it's going to be a warm day, our last one probably.'

'Do you know about me?' Mark shouted suddenly. 'Did they tell you about me?'

He reached out and took McGinley by the arm. The Scot was startled, but didn't pull away. The shout broke the silence. Tore through the heavy curtain that cloaked the scene. It was too loud. Too alone.

'Did they tell you about my brother? About Shane?'

He was inches from McGinley's face now, inhaling the deep sea-earth smell of the whales. McGinley's eyes were two inches below his. But they weren't frightened. McGinley hadn't been brought up that way. To duck and dive through life, to crouch, cower, threaten and bully. He'd been brought up to look straight ahead.

'No. The social services don't divulge personal details. Do you want to let go of my arm, Mark?'

He loosened his grip.

'What about your brother?'

'He went. Disappeared. Walked out the fucking garden, or got took. While I was on the phone. Talking deals. Jesus Christ. Deals. I used to do houses for a few quid. And think I was some-one. I couldn't even look after my own brother. He's never been found.'

McGinley saw the tears but said nothing. They seemed out of

place, intruders in that hard face and powerful, muscular body. A punch away from his. He knew better than to offer up any words at all. Mark made a strange sight. Standing with tear-streaked face, hands clenched, and three mounds behind him. Silhouetted black against the early sun.

'Look,' McGinley said, 'we can talk later, if you like. I've got to report this.'

He wanted McGinley to stay. Needed him to. Now he understood why Emma hung onto him. He couldn't go it alone any more. What had happened with Shane was too big. The desire to go back to being a kid shot through him, more than a desire, a big electric charge of longing. But this time with two parents who cared something about him. He couldn't have it over. That was what cut into him. And feeling old though he was still in his teens.

McGinley made to go but Mark pulled him back. Not able to bear another desertion. The man stumbled and fell backwards onto the wet sand. His hands moving to block the expected blow. But only words came.

'I didn't do nothing,' Mark shouted. 'Don' no-one understand that? I didn't do nothing.'

His voice lightened, as he slumped down, his back against the baby whale. And the voice turned into a wail. A wail that spoke of closed-in valleys and minds, alien in this sea-swept, open place.

'Don't know what happened,' he said, quietly this time. His voice diminishing, then dying as the excited voices of people running towards them took over.